# The Diseased

S.M.Thomas

Written by:
S.M.Thomas

Published by:
A.R.Hurne Publishing

Edited by:
Lmwilkinson - Laura

Cover Art by:
Germancreative – Les

ISBN
978-1-7396769-1-9

# DEDICATION

For 'Grandad Joe'.

Love you always.

Reviews for 'The Diseased'

# CONTENTS

Chapter One.................................................... 13

Chapter Two .................................................. 25

Chapter Three ............................................... 37

Chapter Four................................................. 44

Chapter Five.................................................. 51

Chapter Six................................................... 56

Chapter Seven ............................................... 71

Chapter Eight................................................ 78

Chapter Nine................................................. 84

Chapter Ten ................................................. 91

Chapter Eleven.............................................. 104

Chapter Twelve ............................................ 114

Chapter Thirteen .......................................... 125

Chapter Fourteen .......................................... 131

Chapter Fifteen ............................................ 140

Chapter Sixteen ............................................ 145

Chapter Seventeen ........................................ 151

Chapter Eighteen........................................ 160

Chapter Nineteen ....................................... 166

Chapter Twenty ......................................... 175

Chapter Twenty-One ................................... 180

Chapter Twenty-Two................................... 185

Chapter Twenty-Three.................................. 190

Chapter Twenty-Four ................................... 194

Chapter Twenty-Five ................................... 198

Chapter Twenty-Six .................................... 200

Chapter Twenty-Seven................................. 208

Chapter Twenty-Eight ................................. 213

Chapter Twenty-Nine .................................. 216

Chapter Thirty .......................................... 223

Chapter Thirty-One .................................... 230

Chapter Thirty-Two.................................... 235

Chapter Thirty-Three................................... 240

Chapter Thirty-Four .................................... 246

Chapter Thirty-Five ........................................... 251

Chapter Thirty-Six ........................................... 254

Chapter Thirty-Seven ........................................ 257

Chapter Thirty-Eight ........................................ 262

Chapter Thirty-Nine ......................................... 266

Chapter Forty ................................................ 273

Chapter Forty-One ........................................... 279

Chapter Forty-Two ........................................... 283

Chapter Forty-Three ......................................... 288

Chapter Forty-Four .......................................... 295

Chapter Forty-Five .......................................... 302

Chapter Forty-Six ........................................... 307

Chapter Forty-Seven ......................................... 311

Chapter Forty-Eight ......................................... 316

~ The Diseased ~

"We were drowning. That's the last thing I remember."

The light was harsh in her eyes as she rubbed them, removing the crust that had embedded across the lids. How long had she been asleep?

"And do you remember what happened to your husband?" a voice loomed out from the unfocused room around her. Without her glasses, they were nothing but a blurry shadow.

*The panic in her stomach as the water poured into the car.*
*Reaching over into the backseat to unbuckle her son.*
*Exchanging one last nod as they pushed the doors open and made for the surface.*
*Legs tangled in seatbelts.*
*Losing her grip on their child.*
*A strong current dragging her down as she watched him float away in dirty water.*
*This couldn't be happening.*
*This couldn't be real.*

"No. Like I said, we were drowning. That's all I can remember." Her tongue wouldn't formulate the truth, something inside of her needed to hold back.

A soft moan came from the cot next to her bed. His small body still seemed blue as he lay beside her on a ventilator.

"He'll be okay." A kind voice now. A nurse. Someone who cared. "He's a fighter your boy."

"The vehicle you were in wasn't government-sanctioned," the voice came again, professional and clipped. Feminine.

"An anniversary present from my husband's friend. He had the permit."

"And who was driving the vehicle?" Yet another question.

Her hands on the steering wheel turning white as she gripped tightly, trying to correct their path.

"My husband."

"She needs to rest now," the kind voice said. Her only protector.

The light turned off. Darkness returned. She was drowning in it all over again.

# Chapter One

"Do you know where your husband is?" The same question was fired at me over and over. I never had any answers for them, but still they came daily to ask.

The porter asked me with every meal, the nurse asked me with every check-up and the cleaners had taken to asking me at the beginning and end of each shift. It was all anyone cared about. Everyone wanted to be the first one to hear the truth. To scoop the gossip. But I didn't have answers to give. Every time I tried to drag my mind back to my hazy memories, my blood went cold and grief began to stroke my skin, causing painful goosebumps. No, I wouldn't revisit that memory. I couldn't.

"Your neighbours heard you arguing?"

"Louder than the other times?"

"What were you so angry about?"

"Where is your husband?"

The questions came at me over and over in succession but I never remembered. I couldn't remember. I wouldn't remember.

I lay awake in my hospital bed. The room kept in the constant shadow of darkness. Occasionally, I would hear the nearby chatter of the nurses as they changed shifts near my room. I became obsessive about differentiating between their voices. Trying to pick out any clues in their chatter about my situation. But it was pointless. They never discussed the patient in room 14, and I knew without a doubt that I was in that room. I had, after all, helped to pick out the generic artwork for it. Once or twice, I'd allowed myself to call out to them, desperate for answers, but nobody ever responded to me.

To try and avoid sleep, or more importantly to try and avoid dreams, I'd taken to counting ceiling tiles in an attempt to keep my mind logical and focused. At least two of the tiles had been replaced recently, they were a slightly starker white than the others and the pattern didn't quite match. Judging by the tiny flecks of brown staining their frames, there had been some kind of leak. Highly unusual in such a pristine and well-built hospital, but not information they'd ever bother me with.

There was a constant glow of neon light beneath the door, which complimented the flashing numbers that highlighted my loneliness on my monitor. Sometimes I'd hold my breath just to watch the numbers change, hoping I'd be able to trigger the emergency alarm and somebody new would come to my aid. But our bodies aren't built that way, our bodies are built to avoid death at any cost and I'd always end up wheezing as my lungs demanded air. I had so many questions. So many thoughts I needed to tie down. Where was Leo? What were my injuries?

Nobody wanted to tell me anything and I had no idea why. I'd begun to worry that perhaps I was gravely ill, that something was taking over my body whilst I lay here oblivious. Other than bruising around my mid-section and large cuts on my leg, I saw no sign of physical injury. I felt absolutely normal. I had to stop obsessing. I had to stay logical. It had kept me alive for this many years after all.

I knew what everybody around me was thinking. That it was a domestic that went too far. That I did something terrible to Leo. But I didn't. I couldn't. I would never hurt him, not really. It's true that I had a temper, but I would never let it get that far. Would I?

I watched the shadows of feet come and go along the corridor. Sometimes they paused at my door but they never entered. I wished that they would. I needed more distractions. I couldn't just sit here and think. It was terrifying.

Every muscle ached as I forced myself to move. Wriggling my toes and pinching my thighs. Keeping the life going in my body, trying to fight through. Determined to survive. I couldn't believe I ever took for granted how easy it was to bend the arch in my foot or to scratch my forearm. Even just thinking about it now caused me to break out in a sweat of exertion.

I forced myself to try though. To carry on moving as much as I was able whilst confined to this forsaken bed. I may not have been strong enough to walk yet, my one attempt had sent shooting pains burning through my injured leg, but I wasn't going to lie here and fade away. I would be able to walk over to my son and pick him up of my own accord one day.

Waking up one morning, after what felt like months of depression, I found that optimism had taken hold of my heart. I hadn't had any nightmares, no new memories to haunt me, and for once, I'd slept deeply and peacefully. I felt rejuvenated. Today was going to be the day. Today I was going to get out of bed and stay out of bed.

Then I heard a voice come into my room that caused a blinding stress headache at its first syllable.

"Where is my son?"

"I don't remember" I reply, blinking furiously against the bright lights she'd carelessly turned on.

I wished somebody would sort out a spare pair of glasses for me, the world was a soft blur without them. I never wore them as often as I should, but my vision was slowly improving with the course of shots I'd designed. It seemed however, that stress was undoing all my hard work; something to take note of and improve in the next batch.

But there was no mistaking the monochrome shadow that loomed over me. It was my mother-in-law. Regina.

"You must remember something, Paige." She sounded frustrated, as though I was a petulant child.

"I don't remember anything. I'm sorry." Please stop asking me. Please stop making me think about it.

The longer I was left to lie in the dark, the harder it was becoming to separate the memories I did have from the dreams that haunted me.

*Headlights following us down the road.*
*Shouting voices.*
*A rage I'd never felt before.*
*A woman's scream.*
*Not mine.*

My vitals began to rise and Regina cast a professional look over them. I enjoyed the shift in her focus and the pause in the questions. The silence that lingered around us was only punctuated by the electronic sound of my pulse. Right now it sounded like a symphony. She cleared her throat, interrupting my peace, determined to rob me of any optimism I'd awoken with.

"You're lucky you were brought here; my team is award winning as you know."

Nothing could stand in the way of Regina's ego. Not even a missing son and an injured daughter-in-law. Her hospital had always been her true passion in life and her dedication to it showed as staff cowered in shadows when she clipped down the corridors in her ridiculous heels. A woman wasn't a woman without heels, she'd reminded me when I turned up to work in sneakers once again.

Unlike Regina, I valued what others thought of me. You always catch more bees with honey, my mother used to tell me. And I needed my worker bees to stay as busy and as happy as possible. Which is why my team was always the most casually dressed on any given day. Blood samples don't tend to care how you look after all.

Regina was staring at me; her porcelain nose held high, waiting for some display of gratitude or acknowledgement of her statement of grandeur. I didn't have the energy to engage in her sideshow, so instead I stared blankly over her shoulder out of the window. Or at least at the crack of light I could see underneath the blind.

A small exhale of air through pursed lips told me she was furious. To the untrained eye, she would simply look as though she was concentrating. But I wasn't an untrained eye. I was family.

"I'd warned Leo about driving in that storm," she muttered to herself as she flicked through my charts, making her own notes and suggestions with the red pen she always carried in her top pocket. A constant reminder to us that she was in charge.

It was the first time I'd heard Leo's name since waking up in the hospital, he was always reduced to nothing more than 'my husband' on the lips of everybody else. Tears began to spill down my face. All I wanted was to scream and wail. The fear of what may have happened to him was overwhelming. But hysterics wouldn't achieve anything, so I accepted the silent tears escaping that I could not hold back.

"Crying won't bring your memories back. Can't you even remember what you were arguing about?" Her words held a sarcastic edge, as though she didn't quite believe in my amnesia as she returned her pen to its home. She was above all else an extraordinarily smart woman. If anybody was going to extract the blurry memories from my mind, it would be her.

Gently, she touched the sides of her hair, making sure no strands had escaped their imprisonment, but of course they hadn't. Not a hair on her head would dare disobey her.

"I told you, I don't remember anything." Don't make me remember. I'm begging you.

All I wanted was to escape to my home and process my memories in a safe space, but instead, I was being kept in this hospital room and hounded with the same question over and over. If they were trying to break me into admitting half-baked memories, then they were getting close.

"When can I go home, Regina?" I needed to be the one asking the questions, the control would be mine. She looked at me, her gaze ice-cold.

"When I discharge you of course," came her response, so matter-of-fact that had this been a sitcom I probably would have laughed. Of course, she was my lead physician - if she couldn't fix her own family, then how could she claim to be queen bee?

"And good morning to you." She moved to stand over my son's cot. Instinctively I wanted to stop her. Despite the emotional tundra that was his childhood, Leo had insisted we make his mother a part of any of our children's lives. Of course I'd agreed at the time but the idea had rapidly fallen out of favour as soon as I saw that blue line on the test.

When I'd been pregnant she'd treated me as an incubator, asking about my symptoms rather than my wellbeing. Introducing people to my blossoming stomach but never mentioning my name. Speaking constantly about 'our' baby as though she owned a part of him. It made my skin crawl. I could hide most of my resentment behind a smile or a fabricated bout of nausea, but Franklin knew the truth. He'd start kicking me in the bladder frantically the second I set my eyes on her. She took it as a sign that he already adored her. I knew it was nothing more than a physical response to his mother's rapidly raising blood pressure.

At my baby shower she'd gifted me a set of scales to help me bounce back she said. Leo threw them out for me as soon as she'd left and held me as I sobbed angry hormonal tears. She consistently asked us about baby names and eventually turned on the crocodile tears in a last-ditch attempt to insert herself into every part of my pregnancy. But Leo held strong. He knew how important it was to me that this one thing was just our secret, our first one as a new family. Besides, he also knew whatever name we chose would be distasteful to her palate and she wouldn't mince her words about it.

As the main hospital in the settlement, we'd ended up here after my labour began. I'd begged Leo to take me to one of the lesser treatment centres in the zone down from us. To let me give birth at home or even to take me to one of the women on the outskirts, most of whom had midwifery or doula training, but he wouldn't listen. As my labour progressed in our living room, we both knew it wasn't going the way it should. He had to put the physical health and wellbeing of me and the baby above my anxiety. It wouldn't be as bad as I imagined, he reassured me as I squeezed his hand through painful contractions.

Of course Regina had taken it upon herself to oversee my labour, dismissing my chosen physician when I was too vulnerable to fight for what I needed. Appearing at intervals to comment on my dilation or rather lack of. When she'd ordered my caesarean, she looked at me as though I was a failure. I was less of a woman for not being able to birth perfectly like her. I didn't care about her judgement though - either way, I had my baby and so long as we were both safe and well, that's all that mattered to me.

She was there in the operating room, she gasped at Franklin's startled cry as they held him over the curtain for me to see. Then she scooped my fresh baby into her arms and swept him away under the guise of checking his vitals.

The surgeon was inserting the final stitch into my abdomen thirty minutes later when she finally handed him over to me for our first cuddle. Even then, it was a transaction Leo forced under threat of eviction from the room. I watched her misty eyes gaze at me and my son with a longing jealousy as I pulled him close to my chest, letting him fall asleep on my bare skin. In that moment I knew she viewed Franklin as a do-over baby for her. A chance to show off the maternal instincts she'd clearly developed since Leo left home.

Despite my personal feelings towards her however, I couldn't deny that she was a fantastic grandmother. Franklin seemed to bring out a soft side in her that none of us knew existed. She doted on his every blink, sighed happily at his every breath, and spoke to him in hushed tones for hours. I know it pained Leo to watch his mother lavish the attention on his son that he himself had never received, but as he always said, everyone deserves a second chance. Inwardly, I agreed with him as much as the President agrees with the Anarchists, but outwardly, I let bygones be bygones for an easier life. Eventually, the small nice comments I would make about her to Leo and others felt believable even to me.

As if she knew of my inner walk down memory lane, Regina reached down and picked up my three-month-old boy. She cuddled him tight into her chest. "There, there, Franklin. Grandma is here."

Then she turned back towards me, pain painted upon her face so perfectly it could have been makeup. "I wish you would have named him William after his grandfather." There it was. The emotional guilt trip. It had been three months but she still made this appeal every now and again, as though she could force our hand with her soft sighs and small tears.

William would have been a fantastic name. He had been a kind and loving father. The yin to Regina's yang. Where she would smirk at quick wit, he would unleash a belly laugh that would echo through the hospital floor until even the ice queen herself would thaw and could be heard roaring with laughter alongside him. I'd love to have seen that. To watch Regina let loose and simply enjoy life, but when William passed, so did the secret to unlocking her humanity. Fundamentally, I felt sorry for her despite my burning resentment. Up until now, I could only imagine what raising a family without your other half was like. I prayed it wouldn't become my reality.

I'd offered to name the baby William, I knew after all how important Leo's dad was to him. But he wanted our son to have his own legacy, his own journey. Not to be burdened by the path walked by another. So, we'd settled on William as a middle name, a touching tribute. Or so we'd thought. She'd still remind us from time to time that we had up to a year to file for a name change.

As I held my arms out, expecting my son, all empathy I had for her vanished as she walked him towards the window instead, singing gently as she went. If I hadn't found it so soothing, blood may have begun pouring from my eyes. You see, she always allowed her long-forgotten accent to seep into her words as she sang to him. Her perfect English elocution forgotten in those moments. She always sang to him in French, her mother tongue, and there was something so beautiful about her natural tone that I couldn't complain. I could still remember the first time I heard foreign words from her lips. It was like an explosion of human history in my brain.

She knew as well as we did that any language other than the bastardised version of English-American was not State-approved, but she couldn't help herself.

When I was feeling more charitable towards her, I tried to remember how hard it must have been for her as a child to leave everything and everyone behind when the original Earth combusted. And then, when you thought you'd found a new life, to be told that your language, accent and traditions were no longer valid or legal must have been the breaking point for so many of the evacuees who landed on Earth Two. It would explain the initial high suicide rates during the first two years of society's rebuild. Humans are resilient but we aren't wired for a full restart.

Even though she'd been barely a child herself when it happened, she claimed to remember every moment of that historical voyage. When my patience ran thin, I would rant to Leo about what a pathological liar she was, it was impossible that she could remember everything as vividly as she claimed to at the age of five. She even claimed to recall the numbers on the lottery ticket that won her the passage from the burning planet.

Then he'd remind me, in calm and empathetic tones, that I could also remember everything from my childhood, or at least the parts of it that I'd shared with him. That, in fact, I could still tell you what I'd eaten for lunch on any given day over the last thirty-four years. "Sometimes," he would say patiently, kissing me on the forehead, "people defy logic."

"Please let me hold my son," I request weakly. Pitying myself for having to ask and not growing a backbone to demand what I needed. She'd always had that effect on me ever since Leo had first taken me into her home to introduce me as his fiancée. Before then, she'd at least pretended to be welcoming, dismissing me as just another passing figure in her son's endless rotation of girlfriends. For him to tell her I was now going to be a permanent fixture in their lives was quite a displeasing shock. I wasn't the type of woman he was supposed to marry.

I'd never forget the grimace in her smile as she reached out to shake my hand, or the fact she took Leo aside to check he knew the weight of the decision he was making. After all, I wasn't their usual class of company. If it hadn't been for all my successes in the scientific field and indeed within her hospital, I had no doubt she would have refused his intention to marry me. He could have married any eligible woman from any zone thanks to his heritage, and instead, he'd chosen little old me with the wild hair and dark eyes from Nomad's Land.

She looked back at me, finally hearing my request, and the contented smile Franklin always brought out in her faded, replaced by genuine emotion. "Where is my son?" she asked me as she gently placed Franklin back in his cot. I couldn't find the words to tell her what I could remember. I couldn't find any comfort to share with her. Regarding my vitals one last time, she handed me some pills silently and waited as I swallowed them.

"Where is my son? Where is Leo?" There was a hint of desperation to her tone, amalgamated with a large dash of suspicion. "What happened?"

I couldn't help myself. The frustration and fear overwhelmed me. I just wanted to wake up back in my own bed. My husband gently snoring next to me. She couldn't make me admit the horror that haunted me. She couldn't make me remember.

"I don't know!" I shouted, a break in my usual self-control brought about by a level of terror I'd never felt before. If I didn't ever remember, then it never truly happened. None of it happened.

With a sigh, she turned on her heels and clipped out of the room, not even bothering to look back at me. For a moment, I longed to call out to her, any company was better than my own company after all.

The door slammed shut behind her.

I was alone once again.

# Chapter Two

I was sleeping peacefully for the first time in a while. Lost in dreams of better days, rooms full of laughter and beds full of skin. Leo's legs entwined around mine as he nuzzled my neck. The warm skin of his chest pressing against my back as he inched my pyjama trousers down.

"I'll just be two minutes," he whispered. It took me a moment to fully awaken and distinguish her voice from Leo's. I wasn't at home in bed. I was stuck in a nightmare still in the hospital. I thought about opening my eyes and greeting the friendly voice with a smile, but before I could, a second voice burst my content bubble.

"Quite impossible I'm afraid." Regina was there, lurking at the foot of my bed like an incessant breeze. Harmless but annoying.

"I just don't understand -" the new voice tried to object.

"That's crystal clear," Regina shot back, the words oozing patronisingly from between her lips. My fingers ached to curl into my palm as I listened to her condescending tone. However, I decided in that moment that it would be smarter for me to keep my alert status to myself as it would allow me more time to observe the situation.

"At least let me leave this?" the voice pleaded, its tone rising and falling to manipulate Regina's ear. To ask for her blessing.

A frustrated snort of agreement came from within the depths of my mother-in-law's perfect nose.

I listened to the sound of gentle footsteps approaching my bed. Her eyes roamed my situation, taking in the machines I was hooked up to, searching for noticeable injuries and more than likely silently mocking me in jest for the state of my hair. She unleashed a gentle intake of breath as she moved to talk to me, probably to insult me light-heartedly in the hopes I would awaken to return the favour.

"Hurry up." Regina was impatient, I had the feeling my visitor had arrived uninvited and perhaps unauthorised.

Two gentle clicks on my side table as the visitor left the items she had brought for me. I didn't need to open my eyes to know what they were, she had always been there with exactly what I needed when I needed it.

It took every ounce of willpower not to reach out for the familiar hand that brought them. To the voice I'd spoken to all day every day for several years. I had to stay still though, I had to seem weak. It was always better to be underestimated. Always. Even by those closest to you.

I listened to her steady her breathing, biting her tongue in the face of the woman that, at the end of the day, was our employer. I didn't know which of us had more self-control in that moment.

Her name was Violet and she was the best research assistant I'd ever had the pleasure of working with. It always seemed lacking when describing Violet to use her official job title because she was so much more than an assistant.

She was our contemporary in everything other than pointless paper qualifications. Held back by a lack of expensive letters at the end of her name.

We'd offered to fund the courses and exams numerous times, aware that she was just as deserving of the titles as we were but she wasn't interested. It wasn't that she was too proud to accept our help, she preferred to 'fly under the radar'. To be honest, if that choice kept her by my side for more years to come then I was more than happy to support her need for no further credit.

Not many people in the hospital were aware of her intellect or her natural ability to find and fix puzzles that others weren't able to. She had a natural nose for problems, always aware that there was one before it arose.

The rest of the management team often laughed behind my back about my closeness to Violet, referring to her as my 'little project' in a tone so patronising it would make my skin prickle. But none of them ever had the backbone to speak to me in person. If they had, I would have set them straight and explained in impolite terms just how valuable she truly was, especially in comparison to their bloated redundant selves.

In fact, without her input, the eyesight shots I'd been developing may never have been successful. She'd been the only one to spot the minute shadow on a cell that we, in turn, had exploited to build our medication and correct the optic nerve. Without her, I'd still only view the world in blurry vision without my specs.

It was due to be rolled out to the public in the next few weeks and she'd flat out refused to be named in any of the documents, press releases or internal memos. The only place that contained details of her name was in my own private notes that she had no knowledge of. It was important for me to keep the real records of our experiments because if she ever had a change of heart about being so inconspicuous in our achievements, I wanted to have the truth documented and ready to share with the scientific community. I wanted everyone to know how vital she truly was.

Her modesty surprised us every day, although sometimes it did feel a little extreme. She didn't even have a photograph on our website, the image beneath her name nothing but a stock photograph of a microscope. It had taken several weeks to convince her to even let us include her name in our 'meet the team' section.

Once a week, she came to our house for what we liked to call a "family dinner." She was, after all, the closest thing to an aunt that Franklin had. He adored her and she him, the smiles they shared in each other's presence were infectious. We would spend hours eating, drinking and talking, and then at the end of the night, she'd call a car and travel all the way back to the land on the outskirts of the settlement - Nomad's Land.

It was a large area of land that surrounded the city. Left untouched by the government as they concentrated their efforts on the central space of our new planet.

Once they'd completed building work on the last area for occupation, Zone 1; the nearest to Nomad's Land, they'd erected fencing, separating us from them.

We were told in school that the installation of the border was a necessity to protect Zones 1-4 from enemy forces who would seek to destroy all that we had built. The human race had already faced one apocalypse, we were too scarce to face another. On Earth One, it had been mother nature that was our undoing. On Earth Two, our fate was in the hands of the Dwellers. The original occupants of the planet we'd decided to inhabit. At first, everything between our two species had been peaceful, almost friendly.

They'd freely given us some land to claim as our own, helped teach us about the landscape and the new foes of nature we had to fear. Their technology was lightyears ahead of ours and yet they still found us fascinating. Wanting to know all about the history and art we'd left behind. When they found out about the gallery we were planning to build in Zone 4, right at the centre of our settlement, it was even rumoured that our then President extended a personal invitation to their leader for opening night. But then the incident with the treaty happened and war broke out. We had no choice but to erect defences within our own land for the sake of the greater good.

Eventually, they'd at least turned off the laser fencing and allowed the movement of humans in and out of Nomad's Land and the central zones. Recognising that some people chose to live a more basic life. But this had come after many legal battles and blood-soaked protests. I could still remember sitting in our history lessons, listening as the teacher droned on and on about how cruel and vindictive the Dwellers were. How righteous and victimised we were. It never really felt completely honest to me. As I'd always been told by my mother, history is always written by the victor.

The people living in Nomad's Land who had been shut out from our society had explained over and over that they didn't want support from the government. That they were prepared to defend us should any Dwellers arrive in their settlements and that all they wanted was the ability for free movement in and out of the city. They explained it over and over until they were blue in the face and even the newsies, or the media as they were traditionally known, were tired of talking about them.

Finally, it was agreed that free movement would be granted to Nomad's residents under the sole condition that the borders were monitored. All residents of Nomad's Land were required by law to carry an identity chip at all times whereas, for everyone else, it was merely a suggestion. I still have a blister in the palm of my hand from passionately holding onto that damn blue chip every day when I attended my Zone 1 school. Throwing it into the lake was one of the best things I ever did.

These chips contained details of members of our households; last known address, medical records, sanctioned journey history and employment records, and were required to be scanned at the point of entry and exit each time we moved into or out of the central zones.

The leaders of Nomad's agreed to this requirement because they had members of their society who longed to be like everyone else. Parents who wanted a more acceptable life for their children. Children who wanted to grow up and give their future families opportunities never afforded to them because of their address. A lot of residents had never actually bothered to leave Nomad's Land. They were happy enough to keep to themselves and the land they knew. They just wanted the same chances afforded to every other survivor of the human race.

But their bravery and strength over thirty years ago, during what was backhandedly referred to as 'the hardships', meant that we now had amazing people like Violet to work alongside. I was taught when I was very young that people were more than their address, which is why when I'd first been handed Violet's CV, I didn't pick up on my colleague's point about the length of her daily commute.

When they finally spelt it out for me I decided on the spot that she was the one I wanted to assist me. Her covering letter had already won me over but I wasn't about to lose out on the best candidate just because her address wasn't up to the board's small-minded standards. It seemed that my achievements had erased all memory of my birthplace in their minds.

Violet could easily have afforded a modest property in Zone 1 or even Zone 2 like we had but instead, she chose to remain where she'd grown up. Another modesty of hers, being satisfied with what she already had. Something we should all be so lucky to achieve.

One thing that had surprised me about her though was the day she asked me to sign as a character witness on her application for a driver's permit.

I'd never known her to willingly register her name anywhere, so to see her completing a form with the government's logo splashed across it had shocked me.

To try and prevent the pollution that had destroyed our original planet, our government had taken it upon themselves to provide the only vehicles legally available for travel.

Vehicles had to be pre-booked on a sanctioned, or in layman's terms, necessary journey and were provided for all members of the community free of charge. They were doing everything in their power to try and minimise any pollution to our new planet having seen the destruction of Earth One. The pictures of the disintegration of the planet shown to us in class were enough for every younger generation to agree with the law.

You were however, able to apply for a private permit if you could justify it and were considered an upstanding member of society. This didn't mean you were granted your own vehicle, just the ability to hire one once a year. But you still had to declare your journey and intentions. However, a few people saw it as a thrill to control their own destinies through the gearbox, almost feeling free from the shackles of society as they drove themselves along their pre-approved government-sanctioned route.

I never had Violet down as longing for a flight of freedom but she completed the fifty-page form with such care and attention that I could tell it really meant something to her.

Which is why I didn't have the heart to tell her she didn't have a hope in hell. They never granted licences to residents of Nomad's Land. There was always some cock and bull reason as to why but I knew her chances were slim to none before the ink had even dried on my signature. But maybe she'd be the one. Maybe because of all her hard work at the hospital she would be the first exception, especially considering the ten-page character witness I'd sent in on her behalf.

She was devastated when she wasn't approved.

I saw the resentment at the injustice of it all swim across her face every time she had to state her journey and reason for travel through gritted teeth down the phone.

Leo had once used his annual drive to take her home because, of course, Leo had been granted a licence. Regina had made sure of it as soon as he turned sixteen.

We surprised Violet with the journey as a gift for her birthday. He picked up the car from the dealership whilst I cooked dinner, and it was parked on the street when she arrived.

I hadn't ever seen her display such excitement, not even in the lab. Like a child at Christmas she couldn't wait for the journey home, passing up an extra glass of wine and even dessert. I didn't mind really, it just meant more crème brûlée for me. I'd never had any reason to be suspicious of Leo and Violet. That's what I kept reminding myself as they got ready to leave.

When Leo announced that he'd managed to get approval for the longer route back to the border, you would have thought he'd proposed as the happy tears pricked at the edges of her eyes. I never understood the allure of driving but I was pleased it meant so much to her. I knew the route they would be taking, me and Leo had driven it before. It was beautiful. From our house, you were able to follow the central lake all the way through town until the moment it met the lake that ran through Nomad's Land. The water was constantly fizzing with energy and if the sky was clear, as it was that night, you could make out the puffs of evaporation where the two waters met and fought for power. An unending struggle that neither would win but a beautiful sight to witness.

Leo always said that there was something magical about driving somewhere yourself, even under strict guidelines and surveillance. It gave him a sense of freedom. I was happy for Violet to enjoy that with him, though a niggle of jealousy chipped away at me as I loaded the dishwasher and said goodbye to them both. After all, we wouldn't get the chance to go for an unaccompanied drive for the next twelve months. But I was happy for her because she was the family we'd chosen. And sometimes that means more than the one we're born into.

A small cough jolted me out of my daydreams and, once again, I fought to keep my eyes closed. I fought to stay weak and unassuming. All I wanted as I lay in my hospital bed was to open my eyes and see Violet's face, but something told me I was likely to have my meds upped if Regina realised I was more conscious than not these days.

I listened as her soft steps moved away from me, fighting the urge to reach out to her. The clip-clop of Regina's stilettos followed her out of the room and the door was pulled tight shut behind them. I waited a moment, weighing up the risk of throwing my entire plan and nature out of the window and chasing after them. Throwing my arms around Violet and finally releasing the devastation and fear I was trying to bury deep down inside.

A man's cough and heavy footsteps paused at my door. His shadow was large and unmoving. My chances of having any more visitors had receded even further than the President's hairline as I now appeared to have a guard at my door.

I looked towards my bedside table to find my spare glasses from my desk drawer and a shot of the serum we'd developed to help my eyesight return to 20/20 vision.

That woman was an angel.

Putting my glasses on, I pulled myself into a sitting position on the bed, it was time for a clear assessment of my situation.

Franklin was sleeping gently in his cot. I'd never known that boy to sleep so much and part of me worried that it was a sign that something had been missed in his diagnosis. Perhaps a head injury, concussion, internal bleeding. But then his little lungs moved gently up and down and he sighed happily in his sleep. The medical side of my brain rested and my maternal instincts reassured me that he just needed to sleep. He needed to recuperate, even at his incredibly young age his mind wasn't shielded from traumatic events.

*Holding him into my chest.*
*Kicking my legs frantically, my strength fading.*
*Reaching down with one hand to try and untangle myself from the seatbelt.*
*The current grows stronger.*
*He begins to struggle and panic.*
*His eyes pinch closed and mouth parts in a silent scream that I can feel deep in my heart.*

*Losing my grip on him.*
*Desperately reaching out for any part of him as he*
*begins to sink.*
*A dark shadow moving towards him.*
*Engulfing him.*

No. No. I can't think of that. I have to stay strong right now. I have to keep pretending in order to get us home where we can both begin to really heal.

The uneasy feeling in my gut began to recede as I told myself over and over that I had to keep playing the part. I had to keep those memories to myself.

I shook the images from my mind and focused on the drip that was attached to my arm. It had no labels or distinguishable features listed on it, not the best sign. I would also hazard a guess from its tinged blue colour that it wasn't the usual hydration therapy all our patients received, so I had no idea what Regina was keeping me pumped full of.

Briefly I considered pulling it out of my arm, but then she would know how much stronger I was feeling. I couldn't let on just yet, something told me it was better to keep playing the victim for the time being. So, I would continue to let them pump me full of this mysterious liquid until I convinced her to discharge me. After all, despite our differences, I would like to think she wouldn't truly wish any harm upon me just as I wouldn't wish it upon her. We were family after all.

I picked up the small vial and needle Violet had left me - I may as well take the eye serum shot and by tomorrow morning, I would no longer need my glasses. Being able to see clearly would definitely make me feel less vulnerable. For one thing, I would finally be able to see the faces that kept intruding on my peace with that question I had grown to hate.

The label on the vial was loose at one end and I picked at it, there underneath the sticky label were two words in Violet's handwriting: "Stay strong."

It felt as though she was sat with me, holding my hand as I read the message over and over, enjoying the friendly reminder of the world outside of this room.

I knew that I was going to get back to that world. Whatever it took.

# Chapter Three

I woke up once again to the sound of people in my room. I was beginning to think that ninja-like reflexes were part of the hiring policy at the hospital.

"Regina?" I asked, keeping my voice soft and hazy. I'd learnt how to feign weakness at a young age. Once again I reminded myself that it is always wisest to be underestimated. She ignored me instead, keeping her attention on my notes. "Regina?" This time, I made sure to croak her name, a pitiful sound. Letting every syllable crack against my throat, a single word but laced with a thousand thoughts and worries. My mind whirred as it commanded my body to fight against its natural urges to sit up and take control of the situation. It was self-preservation to play the victim, it told my muscles as they quietened down. Most people don't realise how tiring it can be to pretend to be something you're not.

The nurse delivering my lunch looked towards her boss waiting for her response, waiting for some gossip to take back to the break room. I watched as Regina's shoulders rose and fell as she controlled her breathing, aware of her audience. Aware of all they said about her.

"Yes Paige, what is it?" Her tone remained neutral as she turned to look at me with a professional smile. But I could see the corners of her eyes were downturned at having to acknowledge me and what she knew my question would be.

Deep down below my own pain and confusion about the current situation, I had a mountain of empathy for her. Imagining being in her shoes caused a lump in my throat that I feared might choke me. The cruelty of not knowing where your child is, not knowing if they are safe, must feel like a knife to the gut every time you dare to let yourself think about it. The love of my life may currently be missing, but he was her world long before he even made an appearance in mine.

"I just wondered," I paused as if to catch my breath, "whether your treatment plan is working?" I chose my words carefully, specifically assigning my recovery to her capability. If she denied I was improving, it would be an admittance that she wasn't the miracle worker she proclaimed to be. If she admitted I was recovering, she would have to talk about discharging me. She went to dismiss the nurse from the room, not willing to play my game. I couldn't let the only witness escape; her presence was the only leverage I had.

"I'm sorry," that pitiful tone spilt out of my mouth once again. The one nobody had been able to resist. The one my mother taught me. "Could you possibly fix the bottom of my sheet? I can't seem to reach," I gestured at the drip in my arm. "And my feet are freezing."

The nurse smiled at me warmly. "Of course my dear, you just sit back." She busied herself remaking my bed, fluffing my pillows and taking care of my general comfort. She caught my eye, and if I didn't know any better, she shot me a subtle wink. As though she'd seen through my façade and knew I needed her. Impossible, of course, but when the mind is starved of kindness, it begins to dream up its own.

I looked Regina in the eye, watching as her brain weighed up her options. Sometimes when she was lost in thought, I liked to pretend I could read her mind. Inferring meaning into every blink and twitch. People had always been my favourite subject to study.

Her jaw went tight and before she spoke, I knew which decision she would have made. I knew which decision she would always make. Sooner or later, everyone becomes predictable.

"Of course, my treatment is working." She huffed as though I'd insulted her, in a way, I guess I had. "But we still don't understand the reason for your memory loss." It was a clever card to play. One I didn't have an answer for. I could own up about the fuzzy recollections that turned my blood to a panicked lava that threatened to spill out of my eyes. But the idea of speaking them out loud, even thinking about sharing them brought on the start of a panic attack. Triggering my over-reactive fight or flight response. No. I needed to keep those flashbacks to myself. At least until I understood them fully.

Even if her treatment of my overall health was successful and I was physically strong enough to go home, they couldn't in good faith discharge me until they'd checked all possible reasons for my memory loss. What if I continued losing memories? What if something happened to Franklin because of my amnesia? That would be terrible PR for the hospital. I knew in my heart that my mind was healthy, just locked down, but I couldn't explain that to her without sharing what I knew. I had no choice but to let them keep thinking I'd lost my memories and in doing so giving her the excuse to keep me in the hospital.

The nurse patted me gently on the arm and left us alone. I let my façade slip, too caught up in the fact there was no winning for me in my current situation. "Please, I just want to go home."

"I'm afraid it's not up to me," her voice was low and soft. A tone she had never directed at me before. I tried to reach out to her, to make her expand on this quiet declaration, but as soon as the words escaped her lips, she turned on her heels and left. Too afraid of her own honesty.

How was that possible? Who was above Regina in her own hospital? Rumour had it that when the President came in for treatment, she ordered his security team out of the room, and they complied.

Considering that man was so paranoid that he even insisted on a team of guards to watch him sleep at home, it was ludicrous to believe she'd convinced him they weren't needed whilst he was in her care. But somehow, she had found the words to appease him, to soothe him, to lure him into doing exactly what she wanted. She may have liked the credit for being a good doctor, but she also knew that to do her best work she had to be uninterrupted.

If she could influence our President, how was anyone other than Regina the deciding factor in my discharge?

Before I had time to ruminate on the mystery too deeply, the answer came walking into my room.

A vision in black stood before me.

Her skirt was cut just above the knee, showcasing her toned calves which were encased in sheer black tights. Patent black heels with a red bow on the back held her petite feet, a tight leather skirt with corseted sides hugged her perfectly formed hips and the ensemble was tied together with a tight black blouse buttoned to the sharp dramatic collar. She surveyed me with two perfectly framed smoky eyes and pursed her deep red lips.

"Where is your husband?" Her tone was the plummy English our President valued so much. It was so pleasing to my ears. Why this woman wasn't on broadcast with that voice, I did not know.

"I've already told your colleagues. I don't remember." As frustrated as I was by her repetitive question, I was also intrigued by the woman in front of me. A new specimen to study.

She smiled at me, trying to look friendly but failing miserably. She looked like a tiger ready to toy with its prey.

"Paige, my name is Agent Cherry." She took her time on the introduction, her tone becoming soft and honey-tinted. "I'm afraid I can't help you if you won't help me." I considered her point. So, this was another game to play. Another party to appease.

"I'm sorry," I said in my most submissive tone, trying to disarm her. "I really am." I knew I was treading too close to the vortex of sadness that had taken hold of me the moment I woke up in the hospital when I spoke my next words. "I wish I could help. I really do. Nobody wants to find Leo more than me." I tried to gulp down my true despair. I couldn't let it escape. I needed to stay in control. Control is safety.

I dropped my gaze to my hands and fidgeted with my wedding ring. I told myself it was to distract the tears from falling but really, I needed to cling to the only piece of Leo I had with me. I drew strength from the memory of his smile the day he slid this ring onto my finger. The day he became mine. I'll stay strong. I'll stay rational. I'll stay brave. A mantra I'd repeated to myself every night since I was a little girl. "All I can remember is drowning. The water was so dark," I stifled a sob and stole a glance at her to see how my performance was landing, "I was so afraid." I let the catch in my voice linger in the air around us. The true depth of the horror I felt deep inside was beginning to claw its way to the surface.

She sat at the end of my bed with more grace than I'd ever been able to muster and regarded me pitifully. Reaching out, she placed her perfectly manicured hand upon mine. The juxtaposition of her well-painted claws against the stubby gnawed nails of my own aging hands was not lost on me. Where I had callouses from years of handwritten notes, small burns from experiments gone awry and long-forgotten scars, her hands were soft and flawless. Hands of the elite. Hands of Zone 4.

"I can't imagine what you've been through." She squeezed my hand in a show of solidarity. My parched heart drank up her kindness, savouring every last drop. Relishing in human contact. "But we can't let you go home until you tell us what happened. Until you tell us why you were arguing."

"Am I under arrest?" I asked one of the questions that had obsessed me since I woke up in this room.

"Of course not. You're being treated for your injuries. As a patient, they can't let you go until they're happy you have a clean bill of health. Including the cause of your amnesia. We just need to know what happened that night, we need to put the story together so we can find Leo." Her response sounded kind and caring but I was still wary enough to infer the meaning underneath. Either I confessed to half-baked truths or I would be stuck under her control.

"What if my memories never come back?" I was weighing up my options. If I told the truth about my nightmares, they might let me go home. Home to where I could be surrounded by Leo. Home to where he would come and find me. But still, the panic in my bones ached in warning. I had to keep my truths to myself. At least until I had more of them. I could still hear the echo of the woman's scream from my dream if I focused hard enough, a sound just out of reach of my memory. What happened Leo? What went so wrong?

She sighed and let go of my hand. Standing up, she pushed down her skirt, removing imaginary wrinkles.

"Then I guess you won't go home." She looked over at Franklin. "Cute kid." I was jarred by the comment. It was so American for someone who spoke as properly as she did. Looking back at me, her next words were dripping with passive-aggressive energy. "Here's hoping he isn't discharged before you."

The threat was obvious.

Where will my son end up if I don't comply with their wishes and get my memories back? Will they take him from me?

"I'll do anything you need." For the first time since she entered my room, I was being brutally honest. Still, I couldn't bring the truths I could remember to my lips. The words refused to form. My brain shutting them down due to an unknown need to self-preserve.

"Very well." And with that, the vision in black was gone from my room.

I moved to pick up Franklin, no longer caring about the scream-inducing pain that gaped from the injury on my leg. I hobbled as best as I could, trying to take as much weight on one side as possible. Right now, I no longer cared about seeming weak and unassuming. I didn't care if Regina walked in and caught me walking. I just needed my son.

I carried him back to my bed and collapsed into a dreamless sleep with him held tight across my chest.

# Chapter Four

The next few days went by in a blur of tests. I was injected, monitored, scanned, poked, prodded and drawn from. They took samples from every inch of me. I felt like a pin cushion but still, I went along when they came for the next blood draw, and the next and the time after that. There was no way they needed as much blood as they ended up taking unless they were running each test individually. It was just a sadistic way to torment me.

I stayed silent as they put me through machine after machine. I made small talk with the lab assistants I knew, making sure to ask after their families. I laughed at the nurses' jokes, even adding my own humour into the mix. I had to connect with people where I could, I had to remind them that I was human. I was more than just a tragedy. Regina would find it harder to treat me so callously with the hospital on my side. I made sure to mention Franklin as naturally as possible in all my interactions. I wanted it to be unthinkable that he would be discharged without me. I wanted to plant the seeds of uproar if he were. I'd always been taught that people were pawns to be manipulated, but I'd never really played the game until now, always believing myself to be above my mother in terms of morals. When it comes to my child though, no cards are off the table.

Test after test just showed the same result. There was no physical cause for my amnesia, nothing they could find and, therefore, nothing they could solve.

As I lay in my bed worrying about the vision in black's veiled threat, I heard a raised voice outside my door.

"It is utterly ridiculous that you think you can dictate where I drink coffee in my hospital." For once those clipped tones didn't bring on a stress headache.

A man's voice responded, his tone sounded low and threatening but I couldn't make out the words.

"You had better run along and tell somebody then." She closed the door behind her with a kick of her heel. Regina really was a force to be reckoned with.

She came into my room carrying a mug of coffee. She set it down on my side table and nodded towards it.

"I thought you could do with some proper coffee." Her voice was kind and soft, the polar opposite of the one she had used outside my door. I was taken aback by her gesture of kindness and brought the cup to my lips. It was divine, made exactly how I liked it. Milk and three sugars despite the fact I always claimed to take two. I was surprised she'd noticed.

"Thank you," I offered my own olive branch in return. No need to pretend to be grateful, her kindness in this moment warmed my heart. No wonder Leo loved his mother so fiercely. The moments she thawed, you felt like the only other person in the world.

"I'm discharging you today," she announced. The words sounded like music to me. "There is nothing more I can do for you." Her voice sounded so sad at this declaration. Did she feel as though she had failed me? Or was she disappointed she could no longer dictate my every waking moment? Punishment for losing her son.

"I can go home?" I needed to check I'd heard her correctly. That my mind wasn't playing tricks.

"It's not as straightforward as that." She sighed and sat at the side of my bed, close enough for me to smell her perfume. It was woody and floral. I'd never smelt that scent on anybody else. Leo once told me that his father had it specially formulated for Regina when they'd first started dating and he'd brought her a set for every birthday and anniversary since. Morbidly, I couldn't help but wonder how many bottles she had left now and what she would do when her last memory of William ran out.

When I really thought about it, I owed most of my life to a man I'd never met. Regina began recruiting for the research department shortly after his death. She'd hand-picked me as the lead based on my investigatory work into sepsis. She was determined nobody else would lose someone they loved to the disease. It had taken us six long months but, eventually, we cracked it and now every citizen was immunized annually against the infection. Our blood strengthened by Regina's grief. My career exploded after that and soon I met Leo, fell in love and had Franklin. All because of William and the love Regina had for him.

She coughed to try and regain my attention, clearly having noticed the vacant look behind my eyes. "I can discharge you from my care but the end result is up to them."

"Who Regina?" I had the strongest urge to reach out and hug her. I was overwhelmed with gratitude and fear. Whilst I was trapped in the hospital, I had a clear purpose, a reason to keep me going. Now that I was free what did I have left? An empty house? A missing husband?

"They're -" Our conversation was halted by the return of the woman in black. She was as perfect looking as always.

"Dr Hanson," she offered as a way of greeting.

"Georgia," Regina returned coolly, aware of the woman's eyes on the coffee mug I still grasped. The liquid was quickly thawing, such was the tension between the two women.

Agent Cherry stiffened at the use of her name in my presence. Clearly, she believed that naming a foe took away from its threat. She wasn't wrong.

"Hello, Georgia," I offered brightly, smiling up at her as I casually blew on my coffee and took a sip. I knew deep down I shouldn't prod her like this but it was the first moment of fun I'd had in a long time, plus I had Regina on my side now, which only boosted my confidence as I'd had a show of compassion from her.

"I understand you've put the paperwork forward to discharge the patient?" Agent Cherry ignored me entirely, a fact not lost on Regina.

"All the tests have only gone to highlight that there is physically no longer anything I can treat her for." Her tone was clipped and vibrated with a warning. I'd heard this tone too many times in a board meeting. Regina was about to win.

"You know that wasn't -" The woman tried to interrupt but Regina was a force of words and would not be paused.

"Personally," she continued, "I believe she is much more likely to regain her memories in a familiar environment such as the family home. It has been scientifically proven that being around certain triggers can help heal a damaged mind. And we all want her to remember what happened that night as quickly as possible, don't you agree? That way, we can work on finding my son as soon as possible. That is the aim here, isn't it?" Leaving her question in the air, knowing it was an unbeatable hand. Regina's brilliant mind still remained as fierce an opponent as ever. She'd invoked her professionalism, her personal circumstances and science all in one go.

The only way for Agent Cherry to disagree with her would be to admit there was an ulterior motive behind keeping me here. For once it was entertaining not to be on the receiving end of her brilliance.

"I'll have to make a phone call," the woman answered, knowing she'd been put in an impossible position. Clearly, there wasn't a pre-written protocol for this type of situation.

"You do that Georgia," Regina patronisingly spat at Agent Cherry as she moved from the room. Her choice to not use Georgia's official title in her parting shot was not lost on me. It was a sign of utmost disrespect.

"Will you watch Franklin for me?" I asked her, unhooking myself from the drip that had been my constant companion. She raised an eyebrow at my confidence. "I just need to go and thank Violet," I explained, pulling on my jumper.

"I'm not sure Georgia would approve of that." She smiled at me, my partner in crime. She passed me two unmarked pills and held out a glass of water for me to take them. "Last two," she stated with an encouraging smile.

"Good job neither of us care about that then, isn't it?" I smiled back at her, happy to finally have some common ground with my mother-in-law.

Then, without warning, it was as though a wall had slammed down between us and the conspiratorial comradery between us was gone. She nodded at me curtly and moved towards Franklin's cot, her lips tight as though she was holding words back. Probably criticism over my parenting, no doubt. Shrugging off the weight of her resentment, I left her to play mum as I made my way out of the room.

The air in the corridor tasted fresher than it would at the beginning of a winter's day, laced with possibilities and freedom. I paused for a moment to drink it in, taking in the hustle and bustle around me. A world kept just out of my reach for so many weeks. The end game for me may have been to return to my marital home, but the pull I felt to my professional one in this moment was just as strong.

Any thoughts of embarrassment or self-consciousness I may have had wandering the corridors in a pair of hospital-issued leggings and jumper soon inflated as I noticed that whispers halted in their tracks as I passed stunned onlookers. It wasn't so long ago that everyone was eager to know me, the shining star of the department. I hadn't been able to go to the toilet without someone making small talk. Now I felt like something they might find inside an autopsy. The introvert side of me was relieved, the last thing I wanted to do was make conversation. The extrovert side of me just longed for someone to come up, look me in the eyes and ask me how I was. To tell me how terribly I'd been treated. To hug me and tell me that Leo would come home. I needed reassurance more than I needed silence in that moment, but it was lacking from every direction.

Finally, I made my way to the floor that housed my laboratory. What had initially started in a side office on floor six now dominated the entirety of the fourth floor. We'd had to kick countless other departments into other areas of the hospital to be able to comfortably house our equipment and team. Plus, to be honest, we all liked having our own space. The chance to walk around in just our socks if we felt so inclined, or to sing along loudly and terribly to the latest hit on the radio; not to mention the pranks we all enjoyed playing on each other. We wouldn't want to hide around a corner and jump out on a complete stranger now, would we? The sense of relief I felt approaching the door to my office was deafening, all the noise in the world disappeared, all the whispers, sideways glances and insinuation draped coughs as I passed didn't matter anymore. I'd made it home.

Violet was sat at the desk next to mine, her usual workstation. Headphones plugged in as she furiously typed up the day's notes on her computer, her eyes not moving from the screen as her fingers magicked words into existence. At least I knew our projects hadn't halted, we wouldn't be starting from scratch. I leaned on the doorway, enjoying the moment of reality that had been kept from me for so long until she looked up. It was only for the briefest of seconds but the colour left her face as though she'd seen a ghost. She was shocked to see me standing there so brazenly.

Then she let out an excited squeal and came running towards me. Usually, we kept our friendship on the professional side in the office, not wanting anyone to negate her merits as nepotism. But I was more than grateful for her warm embrace.

Before I had the chance to say anything, her hand slipped under my hair and she lay her fingers on my neck. It was an intimate gesture that was out of sorts for our relationship. She tapped out a message on my skin in Morse code, we'd learnt it one day out of boredom as we were waiting for the results from a test to upload. A pointless skill we only ever used to annoy Leo when we'd had too much to drink.

But her message was clear:
*S.O.S*
Something was wrong.

# Chapter Five

"Dr Hanson," an unfamiliar voice interrupted our reunion, causing me to spring from Violet's hug.

"Actually, it's Dr Joseph." I decided to keep my voice light and full of humour, it was always wise to be charming before you'd sized up your enemy. "Two Dr Hanson's in one hospital is quite enough already." I turned towards the doorway, expecting to greet the owner of the voice, ready to flash them a dazzling smile.

"Up here," they spoke again, and Violet pointed to the corner of the room. Haphazardly installed up there was a camera and speaker. I'd been too excited to return to my lab to notice them. "Interesting that you chose to practice under your maiden name." The voice sounded more accusatory than interested, yet another person assuming the worst.

What the voice didn't know, however, was that Joseph wasn't my maiden name.

I'd left my true surname behind many years ago, before I'd even met Leo or come to work at the hospital. A way to distance myself from my mother and her actions once and for all. A way to escape her hold over me.

Joseph had been my grandfather's name, the person who'd raised me when my mother was no longer able to. He spent our days together encouraging my natural interest in science and making me laugh at his ridiculous jokes. I was never more carefree than when I was with him.

When he passed away he made sure I was still taken care of, the money he left me had enabled me to start my further education and apply for a new identity. I'm sure he wouldn't have approved of the shady dealings I had to partake in, or the flirtation I had to undertake in order to secure a new life for myself, but I knew that deep down he would be happy I was finally out from my mother's shadow. I couldn't decide which gift had been greater – my education or my freedom, so it seemed only fitting to me that I took his name as a way to honour his memory. That way, he was still there for every achievement. Still my greatest supporter. Forever a port in my storm.

"It's actually quite boring," Violet spoke up in my defence before I had a chance to formulate a reply. "As she said, having three doctor Hanson's in one hospital would have been an administrative nightmare." Between Leo and his mother, there were quite enough of us practising under that surname.

Plus, after all the times I'd teased Leo over his surname when we'd first met, I wasn't about to give him the chance to return the favour.

*"Doctor handsome, eh?" had been my opening line. He'd turned to look at me, one eyebrow raised, sweat light on his forehead from the unusually hot day in the ward and his face had broken into the warmest smile I'd come across in a while.*

*"Well, if the name fits." He replied and like that, our story began. Textbook.*

"Who gave you permission to install surveillance in my lab?" I tapped my foot irritably, forgetting it was encased in a pair of fluffy socks and I myself was in hospital standard pyjamas. Thank God I wasn't still in a gown. I'd feel marginally more ridiculous than I did right now. I felt just about as far from intimidating as a person could get, but I was still going to give it my best.

"We don't need to ask permission." His voice was condescending.

"Right," I drew the word out sarcastically and rolled my eyes at Violet. "I'm just going to grab my project notes and go home." I couldn't help the victorious smirk I flashed at the camera, I was poking the bear and I liked it.

"Paige -" Violet took the three short steps to the filing cabinet alongside me. The drawers were bare. My in-tray was empty. A dust stencil on my desk was all that remained of my laptop.

"Do you have any idea what you're interfering with? Do you even know what we do here?" My ego longed to list off my alphabetical list of qualifications, but I was able to quell that passion with logic. Inflating my own sense of self-worth would only alienate people from me, it wouldn't achieve anything.

Besides, I'd never have told the full truth behind my achievements. Due to my photographic memory I was able to learn in two years what it took everyone else to absorb in twelve. I always thought of it as cheating, but Leo pointed out that it was just using my natural ability in the same way he used his charm on his tutor if his grades were less than adequate.

"We're more than aware of your qualifications, Mrs Hanson." Dryly he admitted to knowing exactly who I was.

Violet looked at the camera in disgust, they'd intentionally ignored my professional title in my own laboratory. She went to speak but I stopped her before she said something they could make her regret.

"I don't think you understand. This is my lab. Not the State's. This is mine. I built it. I've been here for every experiment, every finding, every cure. I hand-pick the staff, the projects and the funding. I sign off on every decision from the paper clips to the scientific reports. So, please don't tell me you don't need my permission to monitor my laboratory. I make the decisions here." There was a pause. I'd gotten through to them. Finally, after all this time, someone was actually going to take me seriously.

"Not anymore," came the response. An ominous click as the microphone turned off.

Burly security guards turned up in the doorway. Violet shouted at them as I quietly allowed them to escort me back to my hospital room. Those two words had disabled any passion or confidence I had remaining. My heart was breaking all over again. The lab was my baby long before I'd had Franklin. I'd poured everything I had into it for so many years. And now it was gone. Stolen from me. Just like Leo.

Georgia was sat in a chair at the side of my empty bed when I returned. "Time to go home," she declared, tossing a plastic bag onto my stripped bed.

"Franklin?" I asked nervously. I couldn't lose him too. He was all I had left.

"Yes. He can go too." For a brief moment, her face was soft and I saw her humanity. She never wanted to separate us. Not truly.

I picked up the plastic bag that contained the personal belongings that had been recovered from the accident, my jewellery and Franklin's mud-stained comfort blanket. Just two keep sakes from a life we had known. Then I bundled my son into my arms and made a move towards the door.

"Your car has been ordered and the programmed journey sanctioned. Do try not to lose anybody this time." She smirked at me, willing me to break. Wanting a show of my rage so she had a reason to keep me here. I was wrong. The woman had no humanity.

"Thank you," I uttered with a sickly-sweet smile and made my way to the hospital exit, head held high despite the eyes of suspicion hitting me from every corner. The woman with the missing husband. The woman we can't trust.

I climbed into the automated vehicle, strapped Franklin in and settled down for a silent journey.

Finally, we were going home.

# Chapter Six

Walking through my house, it was as though Leo had never lived there. My heart was echoing with his memories, yet the tears couldn't escape. I couldn't let myself grieve when I knew he was still out there. I had to stay strong. My tears would be wasted the moment he walked back into the house.

His office was completely barren of any trace of him. Years and years' worth of notes vanished. Checking his top drawer, my heart sank as I realised they'd even taken his sketch pad. It had been full of mindless doodles and half-finished cartoons he'd created when his mind was too blocked from work. It was his escapism.

The bookcase now only held my choices, a wide-ranging collection of genres, most only half-read. His coffee tin had been left without a lid where someone had rifled through the expensive bitter beans he preferred and the TV guide with the crossword he'd completed had vanished. What were they trying to achieve? Trying to find? Surely, this wasn't standard protocol in a missing person case.

In our bedroom, his side of the wardrobe was stripped bare. An odd sock tangled in a mess of wires behind the TV was the only item belonging to my husband that I'd been left with. My home had been pillaged and I had no idea why.

After I settled Franklin in his bed, I moved to the kitchen, pausing to take in the atmosphere of my once busy and happy house before I poured myself a glass of wine from the bottle we'd brought to celebrate the night of our anniversary. Leo was right, it was delicious and would have complemented the dish he had left chilling in the fridge perfectly. But now that food was mouldy. Now my home was empty.

Fruitlessly, I picked up my phone and dialled his number. It went straight to voicemail. I listened to his outgoing message twelve times as I finished my glass, only leaving a message the very last time.

"Call me. Please." I hung up before my sobs grew too loud. My soul was beginning to warn me that he might never hear my message.

After everything in that bloody hospital and the eviction from my own laboratory all I'd wanted was to come home to find him. Find my normality. Find it had all been a terrible mistake. They'd hospitalised the wrong woman, the wrong wife. Instead, I'd come home to find our safe space devoid of any physical sign of him. He'd been scrubbed from existence.

I wasn't paying attention to the time when I switched on the television, too desperate for some noise to drown out the silence around me. By the time the broadcast started, I was too tired to get back up to switch it off at the monitor. Our remote control had been an innocent victim in a standard domestic one evening long ago.

I couldn't remember for the life of me what had happened to make me angry enough to launch it at Leo's head, but I remember feeling relief when my husband ducked and it shattered against the wall. I'd regretted throwing it the moment it left my hand but life's like that sometimes, we all do stupid things. Leo joked he'd never replace it in order to give me less firepower. Truth was, I never replaced it for that very reason.

There on the screen in front of me was the face of our gracious leader, complete with his big Hollywood grin as he showed off the day's kill card.

I could practically see the saliva seeping from the corners of his mouth as he spoke about how many enemies we had mutilated, those we kept to torture and those we would hunt down tomorrow. The war had been going on for decades. As a nation we'd grown numb to the horror that took place just outside of our settlements' border. Families would sit and eat tea with the broadcast playing in the background, it was just another standard part of life.

Then with a pause and a quick personality change, he sombrely introduced the short section of the people we had lost that day. Each face given less than a millisecond, names plucked from a hat to be read out loud on air for the world to hear. For us all to remember how much our glorious leader cared. To understand how much their civic duty meant to him personally.

I'd never voted for the man and nor would I. In fact, I'd donated to any rival politician who had dared to stand against him. Regina had voted for him, and of course, the other members of the hospital board had joined her. All proudly wearing their branded pins on their jackets whenever a vote was due. A subtle way of influencing their staff members into trying to win their approval with their ballot. The one they'd given to me was collecting dust somewhere on a landfill. There were a lot of things about myself I was prepared to hide but my distaste for our president was not one of them. I may not be willing to go to the same extreme lengths as my mother to make my distaste known, but I had my own subtle ways to fight the power.

I could still remember when he used to be beamed into the homes of millions every Friday night at seven. People back then used to choose to spend the night in, curled up on their sofa with a big ol' bowl of salted snacks and listen to him wine and dine the biggest names in showbiz. It was a treat at the end of another long week. An escape from the drudgery that was life into a land of beautiful people and scripted spontaneity. I'd found him mildly amusing to watch as an adolescent, but pre-written wit wasn't a strong position for a leader.

Now he interrupted our days as and when he pleased via State-mandated broadcasts. Taking delight in torture, showing us videos of corpses or screaming bodies and all but dismissing our dead and dying troops, but hey, at least he still had that charming white smile.

Listening mindlessly to his drivel, I moved back into the kitchen to pour myself another glass of wine. My tablet was still in the kitchen drawer where I left it. The tattered pink case with my name engraved upon it a reminder of our first anniversary. Leo had worked so many extra shifts at the hospital to buy it for me. It was the most extravagant thing I'd owned at that point in time and I treasured it.

Since then, whenever he'd received a promotion or bonus, he offered to buy me an upgrade. It was true that the software on it was about six years past its best but it was a reminder of a simpler time. I shoved it under my arm as I carried my now full to the brim glass and a bar of chocolate back to the sofa. Before I sat back down I made sure to turn the television off. I'd had quite enough of the grand leader for one night.

Thankfully, my tablet was password protected and they hadn't bothered to take it with them to try and crack it. Dismissing it as ancient technology, no doubt. I felt a surge of relief. I didn't need anyone watching the numerous lip sync videos in my gallery that I'd recorded for my own amusement.

I had to stay sane. I couldn't just sit here and do nothing. I sat with the browser open, fingers hovering about the keyboard, unwilling to type what I needed to know into the search bar.

Logic would be my saviour here. Logic had always been there for me, it's what I lived my life by. Every day of my life was ruled by logic, all of my greatest breakthroughs were led by it. I just had to examine the evidence and pick it apart. I had to reduce what had happened to evidence, dismiss the fear that had wound its tendrils around my stomach since I woke up in the hospital, and concentrate on the stone-cold facts.

From what I could remember, we'd been in the water. The car had crashed. I could remember the feel of the steering wheel under my skin, but any surrounding memories were just out of reach. Frustration caused me to slam the case of my tablet closed. This was hopeless.

I looked at my name engraved on the cover; I remembered the shy pride on Leo's face as I unwrapped it. I couldn't give up. I wouldn't do that to Leo.

'Found Missing Person Cases' I typed into the search bar, desperate for a piece of hope. Taking a large gulp of wine I opened the first result, the government's website of crimes since we arrived on Earth Two. It turned out our governments success rate in finding missing people was rather lacking, they stated that our population was still too small for somebody to be easily squirreled away. Taking another large mouthful of wine, I clicked on the 'unfound' tab and waited for the results to load.

Murders. Crime deals gone sour. Spousal arguments that escalated beyond repair. The list was at least four times as long as its twin. Names upon names of people who went missing and were now presumed dead. No bodies recovered. Would Leo be on this list one day?

No. Stop that. Don't think like that.

Facts. Remember the facts.

If Leo was injured, they would have found him. If he had died in the crash, he would have floated to the surface by now. Something in my gut told me he hadn't been stuck in the car. Closing my eyes, I picked through the hazy memory I had.

> *The car below me was empty.*
> *My only concern in that moment was Franklin.*
> *I was afraid but not full of grief.*
> *There was no sign of Leo.*

I pressed the back button three times until I was back at the search bar. Someone out there could help me; I knew they could.

'Unsolved missing person cases' I typed into the blinking bar, taking a deep breath as I clicked enter. Her name appeared everywhere as I knew it would.

Bailey Miree, a private investigator whose reputation spoke for itself. She had helped bring many missing people home. One way or another. She worked tirelessly becoming an extension of each family she was hired by. Only to disappear once the work had been done. I'd read enough blog posts, news stories and non-fiction books about true crime to know she featured in some capacity in most of them.

But that's not how I originally got to know her.

I knew who she was from the time before Paige Hanson. Before Paige Joseph. I knew her from the time I spent with my mother.

The two of us had never met, my mum made sure I met as few people in her inner circle as possible. A way to keep me innocent, I suppose. But I knew her name. I'd heard the hushed half conversations when my mum had snuck to another part of the house to discuss delicate plans I couldn't be knowledgeable of. I'd read the emails on the nights my mum stayed out too late; her password had been so easy to guess - my date of birth. I knew how involved she was in my mother's plans, knew how guilty she truly was of stocking an unstable fire.

Yet she was never called to trial when they found my mum guilty. She was never called as a witness, an accomplice or a partner. Her name never made its way into the papers or onto a judge's tongue. She was a ghost. Only I knew the truth of what she'd done and there was no way I would tell the authorities. It would only mean more trouble for my mum. More trouble for me. I just wanted it all to go away, so I never made Bailey pay for her crimes. I never made sure that their victims had full justice.

The level of desperation I felt superseded all of the ill will. All of the resentment that still festered in my heart even after the decades that had passed. Bailey Miree was my only option, the only one who would actually investigate Leo's disappearance and not just hold the wife as suspect number one. I didn't even know if the police were investigating any further leads or if they were just using all their time to incriminate me somehow. An easy win for their department that way, I supposed.

She wouldn't allow that. Bailey would find him and bring him back home to me. Alive. She would leave no stone unturned; I knew after all first-hand just how thorough she could be. I could also only imagine that her contacts and influence had grown in strength and reach since our paths crossed that lifetime ago.

I searched for her name and found her official website. "Investigator for hire" was the headline. No further information, no blog, no additional tabs. Just an email address.

Needing some more Dutch courage, I moved to the kitchen and refilled my wine. Pausing at the counter, I watched the light on my tablet fade as the screen auto-locked. I could just leave it like that. Nobody was forcing me to contact the woman, I could quite easily never revisit that part of my past. My chest turned to steel as I took a deep breath. I had no choice.

Bringing the rest of the bottle back into the living room with me, I placed it carefully on the table. Then lifted it and placed a coaster underneath. Leo wouldn't be happy if I stained the table and I didn't want to argue when he came home. Without any more chances for hesitation I unlocked my tablet and hit the button to send an enquiry. Maybe I'd end up finding her as useful as my mother did. After completing the form with my relevant details I sat back and stared at the wall, taking sips of my wine as I waited for a reply I knew wouldn't arrive anytime soon. Before I'd noticed what had happened, it was midnight and the air outside was full of artificial sounds.

Mum had told me about the time before those sounds. When they'd first arrived on Earth Two after our home planet combusted, people had complained that it was too quiet at night. It was unnerving apparently to have streets devoid of traffic and revellers. They weren't used to the silence, they found it oppressive.

So, every night around 10 pm, the speakers on the streets began to play recordings of a world long-lost until the sun rose. I'd always been a light sleeper, my insomnia usually caused by a ghost of a lifelong sacrifice.

But not tonight.

I sat awake on the sofa, not wanting to lay down in our bed, staring at the photographs on the wall.

Us on our graduation day.

Leo in his first uniform.

Me winning my second and third awards.

Our wedding day.

Franklin's birth.

I stare at the walls until my eyes glaze over and dry. I'm surprised they'd left me the pictures considering everything else of Leo's had been stolen from my home. Perhaps someone somewhere had a heart after all.

I woke up on the sofa to the sound of Franklin gurgling upstairs. My mouth felt furry and I had melted chocolate in my bra. If only my mother-in-law could see me now. A smile nearly cracked through the numbness that had taken hold of my features, Regina would be distraught to see the true state of me.

Standing up I noticed for the first time that the picture of Franklin was crooked. With a sigh, I lifted it from the wall and straightened the nail.

Moving to hang it back up, my finger snagged at the corner of the frame. It was slightly misaligned, and I could feel a hardened glob of glue in the joint. I didn't remember it breaking let alone putting it back together. We would have just bought a new one, much less hassle, and it wasn't like Leo didn't love an excuse to browse the homeware aisle.

I ran my hand across the joint, hoping for an epiphany to kick in. Hoping that Regina was right and I just needed to come home to piece my memories back together. But there was nothing.

Forgetting things wasn't something I was used to. Leo would always say that my memory was a superpower. I could remember buying the frame. Picking up the prints on our way home. Spending an afternoon making sure they were all hung with precision but without it looking like we were trying too hard. We didn't want to seem like perfectionists after all. Accidental perfection was the phrase we'd coined about our decorating style. What pompous asses we'd been.

I could even remember what we'd had as a takeaway that night. It had been Leo's turn to choose and, as usual, he'd chosen pizza. One large pepperoni with garlic butter, a side of popcorn chicken and two large beers.

The pizza joint had even cracked their usual joke about the variation in our order. Leo had walked to the store to collect and returned with two extra beers on the house. My husband could make lifelong friends in the time it took to pay for a pizza, that's the kind of guy he was. Is. The kind of guy he is.

I could remember all of that. Every detail.

But I couldn't remember the frame ever breaking.

Franklin's gurgles became more of a protest, and I placed the frame on the table and proceeded to start his morning routine. I waited for a more reasonable time to start making calls to see if anyone could put me in touch directly with Bailey.

I made Franklin a bottle and left it cooling on the counter as I climbed the stairs to his room. Counting them in my head as I went, bringing my brain back to logic. Focusing my grip on the handrail and feeling the sanded wood beneath my palms. It had been the first thing we'd installed when we'd brought this house.

Leo, of course, had wanted to paint it something bright and whimsical, and I had wanted it bare.

We'd argued for hours, going back and forth, trading stories of childhood as our reasoning. I'd grown up in a house where every inch was busy and full of knickknacks that never matched, whereas he'd grown up in a house that may as well have been a laboratory.

Each sentence we fired at each other was more passionate and trauma-filled than the last until I stormed from the hall into the kitchen to call for a car.

The argument continued as we wandered through our local hardware store, passing strangers throwing us concerned looks until store security was called to have a word with us about our language and the volume of it.

Everything was quickly forgotten between the sheets when we returned home, and he conceded to my wishes to keep it bare and I believed I had compromised by allowing him to choose an off-white paint. I'd won that battle but now it just looked unfinished. Barren. He'd been right all along.

I stole a glance through our bedroom door as I headed to Franklin, expecting to see a sleepy Leo sat on the edge, running his hands through his hair. I was about to tell him to arrange a trip out to the store for whatever paint he fancied. But he wasn't there. Of course he wasn't.

My son shot me a beautiful smile as I opened the door to his room and I couldn't help but return it. In all this madness and halted grief, he was my saving grace. I was going to find Leo for the both of us. I'd do whatever it took and I sure as hell wasn't going to sit back and rely on the State to find him for me. Not when I had so many potential contacts I could call upon, should I want to delve further into my past. I was hopeful that Bailey would respond in the first instance so I wouldn't have to take any further trips down memory lane. I'd spent my whole life avoiding the path my mother chose, now I was moving towards it.

I carried him carefully down the stairs, picked up the bottle and moved back to the sofa. He softly drank and his little uncoordinated hands knocked at the sides of the bottle as he tried to gain control. He was going to end up being as stubborn as his mother. I smiled to myself, content, and reached to the side table for my coffee.

But it wasn't there.

Of course it wasn't.

Leo always made the first pot of the day and would bring me a mug of piping hot caffeine as I fed Franklin before he jumped in the shower to get ready for work.

My sense of contentment vanished, and I fought back the tight lump in my throat as I cuddled my son into my chest. His hair was finally beginning to grow properly and looked like it might be as wild as my own. He seemed less and less like a baby every day. Leo deserved to witness every one of these changes. Frustration replaced despair. Why hadn't they found him yet? Why weren't they talking to me? My ego began to inflate. I was smarter than them. I'd never failed a test nor forgotten a password. I would be the one to succeed. I would be the one to find my husband despite their inept handling of the case so far. I would do it all for Franklin.

Finally, he fell asleep in my arms and I carried him back to his bed before moving to our bathroom. There were two toothbrushes in the pot and I picked his up absentmindedly. Taking the time to stare at the bristles, he went through toothbrushes like no one I'd ever known. His gums were constantly sore from over-brushing, sometimes it was as if he was trying to scrub the memory of words from his mouth. As though the minty fresh paste would help keep his secrets. Secrets I thought I'd known. But where was he? Where could he have gone? Wasn't I his safe space?

The shower took a while to heat up, so I switched it on and looked at myself in the mirror. My skin was pale, which was unusual for me, my eyes were dark and there was a stress rash across my chest, but overall, considering everything that had happened, I wasn't physically in bad shape. Only my leg displayed any sign of physical injury and even that was beginning to heal. If only my skin could crack and display the emotions I held inside. Maybe then people would stop treating me as a suspect.

The toothpaste tube was almost empty, I knew I'd put it on the shopping list, but it had obviously been forgotten. Squeezing out the remnants, I cleaned my teeth thoroughly to try and remove the fuzzy hangover that had taken residence on my tongue. The powdery taste of pain pills dry-swallowed.

The mirror was now steamed with the heat from the shower, so I stripped out of the clothes I'd lived in for weeks and stepped under the water. The pressure was perfect, as always, and I let the water beat down on me as I took three deep breaths. In for four. Out for eight. In for four. Out for eight. In for four.

I didn't breathe out.

I broke the pattern.

The water cascaded over my face and although I knew it was warm, it felt frozen as it beat against my skin. My lungs burned now, desperate to rid themselves of the old oxygen having depleted it of its usefulness. But still, I held on.

*Gasping under water. Lungs filling with dirt. Reaching out in desperation for Franklin.*
*Seeing his lifeless body floating away from me.*
*I kick and I kick but I'm stuck.*

*Tangled in the seatbelt.*
*My brain hurts.*
*Panic raises my heart rate.*
*I'm going to die.*
*A shadow moving towards me.*

The oxygen rushed out of my mouth violently and I leaned on the shower wall to catch my breath. My chest heaved with violent sobs as I slipped to the floor and placed my head on my knees. Naked and alone my vulnerability came crashing down upon me. I couldn't do this without him. I'd built my life around him. Time meant nothing as I finally unleashed my sorrow and fear from deep within my bones where it had taken residence as a matter of self-preservation. Eventually, the shudders subsided and I felt my mind begin to clear. I had to stay focused. I had to find Leo. I pulled myself back up onto my feet and shook my head to remove the depression. Focus. Focus and logic would bring my husband back to me.

I picked up the shampoo bottle and began to wash my hair. I knew they did it in the hospital but it never really felt clean. The scent was floral and pleasant and, for a moment, I forgot what just happened. I forgot the horrific memory that had taken over me. My hands automatically massaged my scalp as I watched the shampoo circle and disappear down the drain.

Smiling, I picked up my conditioner. I'd missed conditioner and my hair felt the same. Its curly nature did not appreciate the cheap two-in-one they supplied at the hospital. I squirted a pea-sized amount into my palm and worked it through my ends, leaving it to settle for a few minutes.

Why can't I remember what happened that night? I've never not been able to remember something before.

A foreboding feeling descended upon me and I didn't bother to rinse my hair nor turn the shower off as I stepped out and wrapped a towel haphazardly around myself and my hair.

Leaving wet footprints on the carpets, I moved downstairs. Something wasn't right. The photo frame was still on the coffee table where I left it.

Instinctively, my fingers picked at the dry glue oozing out from the joint as I twisted the frame back and forth. It came apart in my hand.

There, in my husband's handwriting were two words:

"It worked."

# Chapter Seven

What worked, Leo?
What worked?

*I hear an echo of myself asking the same question on an
evening forgotten.
I'm angry.
I'm scared and frustrated.
He hands me a bag and takes Franklin out of my arms.*

Holding the fragment of the frame in my hands I
willed the memories back, finally prepared for the
horror they may bring. Hoping that this clue would be
enough to unlock them. But it was not.

I moved to take another frame from the wall and
then it hit me. I froze like a politician under oath. If they
took the time to bug my lab, there was no doubt in my
mind that my home was bugged too. It wouldn't have
been a stretch to leave behind a few cameras and
microphones whilst they were clearing out every
physical memory of my husband. Given that they kept
me in a hospital bed for a month, clearly, I was a person
of interest to them.

Purposefully, I threw the broken frame into the
bin, making a show of sighing to myself and shrugging
as I removed the photograph and left it on the coffee
table. I tried not to linger over the wood that contained
Leo's handwriting, but it was hard given that it was one
of my last physical links to him. Aware of eyes upon my

skin, I grasped my towel a little tighter as I took my attention away from the bin.

I continued my façade as I plugged in the bottle steriliser as though forgetting this simple task was the reason I left my shower unfinished. I had to maintain normality, at least for now.

Leaving the tap to run cold for a few seconds, I drummed my fingers on the counter to show my frustration with time. To give the air of a mother trapped in a mundane routine. Measuring out 70ml exactly of water, I filled the machine, loaded up the clean bottles and paused. I would only have one shot at this.

As I turned the machine on, it short-circuited the fuse box. The lights went out, the TV stopped recording and I heard the shower stop running.

The steriliser had broken the night before our anniversary, shorting out all our electricity every time we tried to run it. We hadn't been able to replace it as the store was closed, and then I left the purchase of a new one and the disposal of the old one in Leo's capable hands as it was his day off. But evidentially, he had forgotten both tasks. For the first time in our relationship, I was grateful for his lack of memory.

Ten minutes.

That was all the time I believed I had. That was how long the journey from the hospital would take and I knew that Georgia, Agent Cherry, would be connected to this somehow.

Dropping my towel to the floor, I had no time to consistently rearrange it. I raced back into the living room being sure to grab the frame that contained Leo's message from within the bin and shoved it deep into my wet hair below my wrap.

I lifted each frame from the wall and checked for signs of damage and repair. There were none. I crawled on my knees, looking under the coffee table, around the wooden sofa legs, behind the TV unit and at the underside of every shelf and ornament. But there were no more messages. There was nothing more from Leo.

A heavy and frantic knocking began to beat at my door. They were earlier than I expected.

"Mrs Hanson?" a voice boomed. "Mrs Hanson, I'm going to need you to open up."

"Just a second, I'm not decent." I managed to pull my towel back around me as my front door got kicked open.

Franklin started to scream out at the sudden noise, his sleep disrupted. I stared at the man in my doorway, and instead of speaking to him, I directed my question to the black heels I could see behind his feet.

"Do you mind?" I asked, gesturing up the stairs towards the sound of my baby. He listened to instructions I couldn't make out, shrugged and nodded.

I raced up the stairs to Franklin's room and scooped him into my arms.

"I've got you. Mamas got you," I whispered into his ear as I held him close. The lights flickered back on and the boiler began to hum as it tried to correct the draught caused by my missing door. He snuggled into the warm groove where my neck and shoulders met, his crying slowing as he took comfort in my familiar scent.

He fell back to sleep easily in my arms but I was in no rush to go back downstairs. I sat in the rocking chair and tucked him into my chest, taking my time to enjoy the rhythm of his soft breaths. I'd nearly forgotten about my unwanted visitors when a soft knock came at the nursery door. It was opened before I could offer a response.

Georgia stood in the doorway for a moment, regarding me and Franklin in the chair. There was a look on her face I couldn't get a read on, but as she met my eye it was gone. She held out an arm with my dressing gown draped over it. The furry grey cat print looked ridiculous in her hands, but it was my favourite thing to put on after a hard day at work.

"We need you downstairs." She left the gown on the side of the crib and I listened to her soft footsteps retreating down the stairs. She'd removed her heels just to walk on my carpet. Almost as if she was a respectful guest.

I lay my son down, pulled on the gown enjoying its comfort, then made my way downstairs. I awkwardly paused behind her, waiting for her to finish tightening the straps on her shoes as she sat on the bottom step.

She stood and regarded me. "We have to talk." I nodded and followed her into the living room. Her male companion had already made himself at home on my sofa, legs spread wide apart, but she waited for me to gesture at a seat before taking a place. Showing me a level of consideration I wasn't expecting. What had happened to the woman who threatened to take my son away from me? Had she finally gained some empathy?

"Why did your power cut out?" she asked hands on slim knees, legs crossed at the ankle. Composed. Graceful. In control.

"How did you know my power cut out?" I countered. She raised an eyebrow, viewing me as a worthy opponent.

"We have surveillance in your home," she said in a bored tone, but I noticed the twitch at the side of her mouth - she was enjoying herself.

"Something shorted the fuse box," the man interjected and she nodded curtly at him. Annoyed that our game of cat and mouse had been interrupted.

"Any idea what that could have been?" turning her attention back to me, she offered me a new move.

"No," I lied. "But it was a cheap house, maybe the wiring isn't as solid as it should be." Checkmate.

Georgia looked up at the photos on my wall, spotting a bare nail "Why is one missing?"

I shrugged, not wanting to indulge her in this game anymore. I had always been a sore loser. I had no doubt that they'd seen me break the frame, dispose of it, and then use the steriliser. She knew everything, so what was the point in answering?

"I found this in the trash." From his pockets, the man laid out the pieces of the frame. "One piece is missing." He looked at me suspiciously.

"I'm afraid I don't keep an account of every piece of rubbish I throw away." I resisted the urge to roll my eyes at him. Confidence was one thing in the face of adversity, cockiness was another.

She smiled at my response. "We'll be sending someone to fix the door, of course." She stood to leave, extending a hand out for me to shake. It was all very civilised. Someone was clearly twisting her arm behind the scenes, causing her to treat me as a fellow human and not just a case number. Could it be that Bailey was already weaving her webs after receiving my request for help?

I stared at her hand blankly until she returned it to her side. I knew I was being petulant but I couldn't shake the resentment from our shared time in the hospital.

Motioning at her colleague, he stood slowly on her command, trying to dominate me with his presence. I stood and attempted to look intimidating myself in my age-stained dressing gown with a damp wrap on my head. As she made to leave, she threw out her last parting shot, "We'll send you a new steriliser as well."

That was a mistake, revealing all of her cards. I couldn't help myself as I retorted, "I assume you have a legal justification for installing spyware in my home?"

"Mrs Hanson, I don't need a justification for anything I do." She turned to me, satisfied to have gotten a rise out of me. Something about this woman brought me out in angry goosebumps.

"I think you'll find that, unless I'm a suspect of a State crime, then this sort of monitoring is illegal."

"Are you not a suspect in a State crime?"

I was speechless. I had no response to offer so, instead, I sat back down and dropped my eyes to the floor. A show of subordination.

I heard her exhale with disappointment, she'd expected more of a fight from me. I listened as she walked out of my house, down the path and into their waiting vehicle. Putting my arm between the sofa cushions, I pulled out my tablet and opened an icon I rarely used.

My social media site, the place where we're all supposed to share our thoughts and feelings openly and honestly, despite it being constantly monitored for any sign of insubordination. It had been strongly suggested to me several times over the years that I needed to engage with it more regularly, but I always had the excuse that I was a busy professional to explain my disinterest in it. If it was a choice between my research and my social media presence, I knew which the State would prefer me to put my time into.

I performed to the bare minimum acceptable. Posting photos of my engagement ring, a single snapshot from our wedding day and lovingly crafted updates on Franklin's arrival. To the online world, I was still accessible just not as accessible as others.

I opened up the tab where we were expected to write updates on our life, hesitating over the keyboard, formulating the words I knew there would be no turning back from.

"It's times like these you really need family." I typed.

I stared at the words for a good while, not quite wanting to put them out into the world. Knowing the havoc they would bring.

I heard Franklin begin to stir upstairs. I had to do this for him. I hit post and headed back towards his room, pausing briefly to throw some clean pyjamas on.

As I untied the wrap from my head, I made sure to keep my fingers tightly wrapped around the piece of wood concealed there. I threw the wrap on the floor, still containing Leo's message within, confident that the cameras wouldn't have picked anything up out of the ordinary. It could wait there until I could safely retrieve it again.

Walking into Franklin's room, the question was still on my mind, louder than before.

What worked Leo?

What worked?

# Chapter Eight

The next morning, as I went about the mundane circle of activities that parenting a child entail; nappy changes, feeding, burping, cleaning and working out the new steriliser that had been delivered as promised, repeat times a thousand, my mind drifted back to my own childhood.

The one before I went to live with my grandfather. Looking into Franklin's beautiful brown eyes I knew that no matter what, even with Leo currently missing, I would never allow his life to descend into chaos the way mine had.

My mother was a whirlwind.

Usually, when I hear people use descriptions like that, I can't help but think it's a little too poetic to be realistic. A tad dramatic perhaps.

But when it came to my mother, there was no other description.

She came and she went as she pleased with little to no warning, leaving a trail of devastation and eventually death behind her.

It's not that I wasn't loved. I was fiercely loved. She loved me like I was the most precious thing she ever owned. It was obsessive at times, and then a switch would flick and I wouldn't hear from her for weeks. Off on a new adventure, following a new calling whilst I was left in the care of my grandparents or whoever was her most devout friend at the time.

My mother believed life on Earth Two was unfair. She believed the government held too much power and that the President was corrupt. Their erasure of cultures and languages was criminal and the new laws they kept introducing were inhumane. In essence, she believed the world we were forced to inhabit was evil.

Mother was a big supporter of 'the way things were' - a movement to highlight old laws that had never truly been removed from legislation. Laws that supported basic human rights. Using these to circumvent what they believed to be unjust restrictions on our lives. In particular, she violently disagreed with both the Repopulation Act and the subsequent Marriage Act - two laws that had been written in stone on the day the human race landed on Earth Two. They were supposed to help us survive but, in reality, did nothing more than steal freedom from us.

She never really understood how terrifying the ongoing war was to those of us who weren't idealistic. Every day our troops were being slaughtered by the natives, or Dwellers as we called them, whose planet we'd begun to take over. Whenever I tried to confide in her about my fears, she would preach that the war was solely the government's fault. She would scream it in our garden on the nights when she found the alcohol I hid in my room. If they'd just stuck to the original treaty and hadn't tried to grab the extra land, we'd all be living in peace and harmony. She'd hold me as I had panic attacks, my young mind unable to comprehend mortality, hatred and violence, and then she'd sit with me until my breathing was steady once again. In for four. Out for eight. She'd whisper to me, tenderly stroking my hair.

It was like having two mothers; one who belonged to the rest of the world, the passionate, fiery, violent, and political one. But then there was the private side of her, reserved just for me. The side who would sleep on my bedroom floor if I had a nightmare. Who would hold my hands tightly as we danced around the living room, creating routines that only made sense to us. Who cleaned my face after a bully had kicked mud into it and taught me how to stay strong in the face of adversity. But every time I let myself hope that my mum would come back to me and stay, she was off on another flight of fancy. Another protest to attend, speech to give or disruption to plan.

She'd wax poetically about the brief period in time we'd lived side by side with the Dwellers, mingling with each other, sharing histories and cultures. Her passion for their culture and cause only grew the more she fell in love with my stepfather, Kyan. The day he left was the day my mother changed for good.

So misguided was she that she didn't even care to listen when I tried tirelessly to repeat the facts to her face. I brought home textbook after textbook, would leave documentaries playing in the background, all of which proved that we tried to do things the right way to protect our growing population. Applying for an extension to the treaty, arranging a meeting with the Dwellers' leader, only for our team to be ambushed and slaughtered. She even refused to partake in the one minute silence every year to remember those that had been lost, preferring instead to sing a low and heavy Dweller song about grief and betrayal. It was embarrassing.

She was blinded by hatred for a life she shouldn't have been living had she not held a winning lottery ticket in her hands back on Earth One. Now I was older, I thought perhaps a lot of her rage stemmed from survivor's guilt, a way to release the anguish over the horrors her loved ones must have faced.

Leo never knew the truth about my past. I couldn't share with him the life and woman I'd stemmed from. He'd only ever known me as Paige Joseph. He would never have understood the full extent of the background I grew up in. He'd decide, just like everybody else had back then, that the apple never fell too far from the tree.

I gave him a watered-down version of the truth. I let him glimpse the chaos and the disorganisation. I showed him the moments of love. Those were the important things to know about my childhood that, try as I might to fight, have shaped me into the person I am today.

So, I told him what he needed to know and explained away the absence of my parents by saying they'd passed right before I started school. Which was only half a lie.

My dad died when I was young, I never really knew him as he'd left just before he got ill. Unable to put up with my mother's anarchy any longer. I never bothered to get in touch because what kind of man would leave a child in a situation he himself could no longer stand?

But all of that was in the past. It didn't matter today. What mattered today was caring for my son and finding out what had happened to my husband. Which is why, when our entire street blacked out, I knew I had made the right decision. My gut relaxed, my survival instinct was sated.

As the sun set and the stars came out, I reached for the electric cigarette I kept hidden at the top of my books on the shelf. They hadn't eliminated the risks from them completely, so it still felt like a guilty pleasure. Another secret I'd kept from Leo. Although I'd hazard a guess that he knew but had filed it away in the 'things we don't talk about' drawer of our relationship.

I stepped out into my back garden and slid the door closed behind me. The air was humid, a storm was on its way and the wind was picking up. I could hear recycling bins begin to clatter down the street as the clouds set in.

Taking in a lungful of vapour, I felt at ease with the world. The weather suited my mood. With the power being out, I'd given thought to retrieving the piece of the frame I'd saved. All I wanted to do was stare at it and drink wine as though that would bring Leo back home to me.

But it was safer for it to remain concealed underneath the discarded towel. That way, when the power was turned back on, nothing would have moved and they would have no reason to be suspicious.

The shed at the end of our garden was creaking with the growing howls of the wind. I hadn't stepped foot in it in years, it was Leo's sanctuary as he called it. When he fancied some alone time in there tinkering with his miniature buildings, I was more than happy to indulge him and enjoy an evening's peace reading.

The air went still and silent. All I could hear was the sound of my own breath as I supplied my bloodstream with nicotine.

My legs moved automatically towards the shed. I supposed now was as good a time as any to have a look. There was no one around to watch me and I was certain that it had been stripped of any remnants of him anyway.

As I placed my hand on the handle, the first crack of thunder loomed ominously in the distance. The sky lit up purple and the rain was painfully warm. It wouldn't be long until the centre was above me, so I moved to get back inside. A rustling came from within the shed and my heart stopped.

"Leo?" I called out nervously as I pulled the door open slowly, unsure of the state I'd find him in.

As the rain moved to a scalding temperature and the sky began to light up in an abundance of colours, there before me stood a shadow I barely recognised.

My mother.

# Chapter Nine

"Jesus Christ!" I exclaimed as she grabbed me roughly by the arm and pulled me into the shelter of the shed.

"Well, hello to you too," she countered with an infectious smile. There was always something so warm, enigmatic and charming about her, but she could turn off the magic just as easily as she turned it on. It's what made her such a powerful foe to those she had in her crosshairs. If she hadn't been my mother, she'd probably be my hero.

I couldn't help myself as I threw my arms around her and began to cry. All the emotions I'd kept bottled in since I woke up in the hospital came pouring out. She patiently stood and held me, rubbing my back and whispering in my ear.

"I've got you agabi mou. Mama's got you."

Eventually, I eased my tight grip around her and took as much of a step back as the space would allow. The rain was beating down so heavily on the roof, I began to worry it was going to cave in.

"Can you run?" I asked her. She nodded and smiled mischievously.

"You better be quick!" she replied, darting from the shed, ignoring the sizzling rain beating down on her. She threw the backdoor open and stood in the warm glow of my kitchen.

I remembered being three years old.

Standing out in the rain under nothing more than a newspaper that was beginning to melt in the heat as she picked the lock of somebody's back door.

She always managed to find us shelter, even when we were far from home. At the time of her arrest, the newsies painted her as a master manipulator. Someone who gave orders but never got her own hands dirty. I knew that wasn't true though. I'd been there from the beginning when she only had herself to rely on. She'd never asked anyone to do something she'd never done herself.

I had stood in my favourite wellies, dripping on the stranger's kitchen floor whilst she quietly tapped away on their keyboard. Then, as quickly as the storm had arrived it left, and we went with it.

She'd grabbed me an apple from their fruit bowl and passed it to me as she closed the door behind us without a sound. That evening, we ate one of the best roast dinners she'd ever cooked and watched an old movie she'd managed to get a copy of. An animated tale of good triumphing over great evil. That's who she was back then, a plucky underdog trying to right wrongs.

It had been one of my favourite days.

And now I was standing in my own kitchen, dripping wet, watching my mother root through my fruit bowl. I couldn't help but smile as she picked an apple, some things never changed.

"I've seen all your photos online." She paused; aware she was teetering the line of the boundaries I lay down many years ago. "Can I meet him?" Her eyes were wide and eager, and I couldn't resist. No matter what had passed between us, she would always be the first love of my life. We crept upstairs together, discarding our soggy shoes along the way. Her hand found mine and I didn't pull away. Grateful to feel like her child again. She was here to protect me. Everything would be okay. Gently, I pushed Franklin's door open and the light from the hall highlighted his sleeping frame.

"So peaceful," she murmured, proud tears at the edge of her eyes. She used to look at me like that. I remembered how those looks became sparser and fleeting as I grew a mind of my own and she realised I would never blindly drink the Kool-Aid like those she surrounded herself with.

"We need to talk, Mum." Letting go of her hand, I pulled the door to and she nodded, heading back down the stairs, taking in the photographs along the wall. A life she had been erased from. Part of me felt such guilt for all she'd missed out on. But she had been the one to make that choice, long before I changed my name.

We sat awkwardly on my sofa maintaining as much physical distance between us as possible, my breakdown from earlier forgotten. "I wish I could offer you a coffee but the power is out." I looked at her accusingly.

"I'll take a beer," she replied with a cheeky smirk. Sighing, I stood up and moved to the fridge. I pulled one of the green bottles from the rack and, with a shrug, pulled myself one out too.

The sizzle of the carbonated liquid soothed me slightly as I opened both the lids and noticed the storm outside had passed its crescendo. We didn't have too long before the power was restored.

"How long have you got?" I asked, passing her the beer. She tilted her head back taking a long drink, savouring the flavour.

"I'm due out of solitary tomorrow, so probably until the morning." She shrugged innocently.

"I don't know how you do it."

"I have friends everywhere, darling." She elongated her last word in a plummy accent that didn't suit her and then laughed at the absurdity of it.

She wasn't wrong.

Since her trial, she'd become the poster child for the anarchist movement. Featured on protest banners, graffiti and mentioned in pretty much any article that claimed to tell the truth. It meant I never really had to miss my mum too much; she was everywhere, you just had to look for her.

I did look for her more often than not, explaining away my interest in her trial and her fellow 'believers' with sarcasm and disdain. As if I couldn't believe that people could exist who were so delusional. Still, to this day, I had to fight an onslaught of memories whenever I noticed her initials plastered on bridges and the like. She was omnipresent. Exactly what she'd always wanted.

In my first year at college, I'd sit around at many parties and listen silently as my mother's name became dirt amongst my fellow students. I joined in as they laughed at her beliefs and I disparaged her actions alongside them.

All the while there was a hidden part of me that was proud of her. At least she had the passion in life to stand by her beliefs, which was more than I could say for some of the spineless members of my study group. They couldn't even find it in themselves to stand up to their professors against unfair grading, something I myself never struggled with. I had, after all, learned from the master.

That had been the takeaway from my childhood at least. To always stand up for what you believed to be right. Which was why sometimes I found it hard to bite my tongue as she became the punchline to more and more vicious jokes. But I did. I always did. My self-control had always been stronger than hers.

It had been her celebrated status that had saved her from the death sentence in the end.

The prosecuting attorney, a fierce man named Jack Wright, argued that to kill her would just further the cause, giving the Anarchists a political martyr to stand behind. Something factual that they could hate the government for.

I watched with bated breath as the judge deliberated his point. Knowing that as well as Jack's passionate argument, my mum probably had friends inside the judge's quarters just to be sure. Even though I was sure she wouldn't be executed, my heart still hammered as I awaited the judge's sentence.

My mother was sentenced to life imprisonment with no visitors or chance for parole. A life without meaning. Considering her actions had caused the deaths of a dozen people, that seemed fair to me. My heart broke for the mother I'd lost but the logic in my bones knew it was the best possible outcome. For her and me.

She and Jack started communicating via secret letters a week after she began her sentence. They were wed by video conference six months later, with Jack handing in his resignation for the State the week before the nuptials.

He was disgraced, of course. There was talk of disbarring him but he managed to talk his way out of that one. He was the only person I'd ever known who could match my mother when it came to the gift of the gab.

Now he spends his time defending the types of crimes he used to prosecute. My mother claimed it had been love at first sight. I still believed it was more convenience than romance, at least to her anyway. From what I'd read about him, he seemed like a good man and a brilliant lawyer, who now, at least thanks to his involvement with my mother, fought to protect those that the Repopulation Act found lacking.

As I'd taken my trip down memory lane, she'd finished her beer and picked mine up from the table. She took a swig and looked around the room, this time not with the eye of an estranged mother but with the eye of a rebellious mastermind. "So, I guess you're under surveillance?"

"Throughout the house." I sighed.

"Well, thank goodness for the power cut." She chuckled, proud of herself. "That's criminal." Her tone immediately flipped at the heavy-handed way the State was bullying me.

"Not if they suspect me of being a criminal of the State. Which, apparently, they do."

"We'll see about that. Either they have to provide valid reasoning as to why you are a suspect, which I doubt they will reveal, or they have to remove the devices. Besides, anyone who knows you knows you aren't a killer." Her voice was soft, I couldn't tell if it was pride or disappointment in her tone.

"They won't listen to me." I felt defeated and lost, half the woman I used to be. If I could at least remember what had happened that night, maybe all my problems would disappear.

She cast a sad eye over me, disappointed that her daughter lacked the passion to fight for herself in this moment. Bailey's name was on the tip of my tongue. I wanted to prove to her that I still had some fight left in me. But to reveal that I knew who Bailey was would let her know just how compliant I'd been in her crimes. It would let her know that I could have stopped her but didn't. It would let her know that I was more like her than she realised. I couldn't deal with the guilt from my childhood right now, I'd worked so hard to lock it away, and this moment was not the right time to take out the key. Not with Leo missing.

"I'll send Jack," she said with a nod.

The street lights began to flicker back and she looked sadly out of the window.

"I'll see you again." Standing to leave, she placed a gentle kiss on my forehead and left through the kitchen door without turning around to look at me again. She never turned back when she said goodbye. It killed me just as much now as it did on that awful day decades ago.

Credit where credit was due however, my mother may have been chaos incarnate but she always took care of her young.

# Chapter Ten

Jack arrived at my door promptly at nine in the morning, dressed in a dark navy three-piece suit with a pocket watch chain hanging across the waistcoat. I knew without a doubt that this man was a showman, but just like my mother, I knew that sometimes a girl needed a show.

"Mrs Hanson," he began, offering his hand which I automatically shook. I'd taken care to still be in my pyjamas with unwashed hair. Even going so far as delaying Franklin's nap by half an hour so he was on my hip when the doorbell rang. If he was the picture-perfect image of a showman, then I was the duckling on the edge he had to take under his wing. "I understand your husband is missing." And with his opening lines, he began the most important improvisation of my life.

"I'm really sorry but I'm not interested in talking to the press." It was time to remember all the lessons of my youth once again. Stay oblivious, act naïve, do anything you can to appeal to their humanity.

"Oh, I'm not the press, Mrs Hanson. My name is Jack Wright and I'm a lawyer who specialises in your kind of case." I looked at him with intrigue, my bloodshot eyes hoping for salvation.

"My kind of case?" I gestured for him to follow me as I placed Franklin in his bouncer. He paused at the threshold, awaiting a formal invitation. He was as dedicated an actor as me. "Oh, I'm sorry, Mr Wright, was it? Would you mind if we talked in the living room so I can get the baby to sleep? He's been a nightmare all morning." Not a lie. The half-hour of screaming those monitoring me would have had to endure prior to this meet-cute had sadistically filled me with joy.

"I couldn't help but notice the cameras outside your property." He briefly looked into one of the corners of the room, pointing at a mark I hadn't noticed before, "And inside your property."

"I'm under surveillance," I replied flatly. He sat down in the armchair opposite me and I gestured at him to shush as Franklin's eyes closed. Once I was sure he was asleep, I nodded my head towards the kitchen and he followed.

I moved to pick up one of the dining chairs so I could sit, but he placed a kind hand on my shoulder and did it for me. Wearily, I sat down and pulled my dressing gown a little tighter around myself. Running my hand through my greasy hair, I sent a silent prayer out into the world that this song and dance would work.

"Do you mind if I ask what you're under surveillance for?" He quietly pulled out a chair and sat opposite me. We had no trouble maintaining eye contact, both aware that we were being scrutinised and that a car would already be on its way.

"I'm suspected of committing a crime against the State." I allowed my voice to weaken with defeat and I placed my head in my hands.

For a moment, I thought about crying but decided that perhaps it was better to go for understated depression rather than melodramatics. Best to stick as close as possible to my true character lest the footage ever be used in a court of law or reviewed by character witnesses.

"And what -" He paused for dramatic effect, knowing that this was our starring moment, "crime was that, Mrs Hanson?"

"I don't know," I speak into my hands at first and then slowly look up at him as though a revelation had hit me. "I don't know," I repeated, my voice now stronger.

The knock at the door came as we knew it would. Franklin stirred but thankfully didn't wake.

"Don't you think that's something you're entitled to know?" He delivered the punchline with such emotion that, for a moment, I forgot this was all a pretence. I felt a sense of righteousness swell in my chest. I had been wronged. It was my husband who was missing and yet I was the one who had been wronged by the very people who should be striving to reunite us.

The door knocked again.

"Excuse me," I said as I moved towards the door, already knowing who would be stood behind it. Subconsciously, I tightened the belt on my dressing gown. This time, it wasn't for show, it was for vanity.

There on the other side of the door was Georgia in all her gothic glory. Today, her lips were blood-red, deep and powerful. I was surprised to find that the shoes and nails matched. She was clearly experimenting with her signature look, adding in splashes of colour to dramatize her void essence wardrobe.

"Georgia," I greeted her, knowing she'd hate that I'd used her name. Sure enough, her eyebrow twitched, I'd gotten under her skin.

"Mr Wright," she ignored me and glided through my living room. "You have no reason to be here."

"Ah, Agent Cherry, so nice to see you again." She made no move to return his handshake.

"As I said, Mr Wright, you have no reason to be here."

"I'm afraid you'll find it is actually you; who has no reason to be here. No lawful reason anyway." He reached into his pocket and pulled out a small purple device that wouldn't look out of place in a decorative rockery. "Unless you are willing to give my client a copy of the warrant, listing her supposed State crime, she is legally able to use this as part of the Protection Act introduced three years ago."

She cast her eyes down to the device and rolled them upwards towards the ceiling before returning her steely gaze towards him, her irritated hand tapping her fingers on her pleather clad hip. "That information is classified."

"Well," he began with a smile. She'd given the exact answer we'd needed. "As I'm sure you're aware, Agent Cherry, it is an offence to install spyware in a private residence unless a warrant stating the suspected crime is presented to the suspect or their representative." His smile now turned indulgent and patronising as though talking to a stroppy child. As a woman, I felt my blood pressure rise at his tone. Looking at Georgia, I knew she felt the same. But she wouldn't give him the satisfaction of a reaction. "My client is, therefore, legally entitled to run this device in her own home to counteract your technology. But then again, I believe we've had this dance several times before, haven't we?"

He thumbed the small purple rock, enjoying the game of poker that was stacked in his favour. It looked so innocuous that it was hard to believe it would interfere with any and all surveillance equipment. It would fit in with just about any home décor and nobody would know any different. The Anarchists had worked tirelessly to create this device. My mother's lackeys campaigning on every level to show the unjust level of control the State could yield over any of us it fancied. It had been a long and heavy-handed road for them to fight but, eventually, they had the public on their side, thanks in part to more than a handful of celebrity endorsements. Everyone fell under her spell. Everyone except her own daughter. Now wasn't the time for resentment, it was time for admiration. If my mother hadn't been the manipulative leader she was, then I wouldn't have access to this technology to defend myself.

For the first time since Georgia's arrival, she turned her attention towards me. I could see the silent plea in her eyes but her words remained professional. I had a sense of unease in my stomach. Was this all a mistake? Is that what she was trying to convey to me?

"Mrs Hanson, if you hire this man as your defence, it may be taken at a later date as an admittance of guilt." She'd decided not to rely on a subtle look between us. She laid the cards out straight in front of me, desperate to give me a chance to save myself. I wanted to trust her, something inside me ached to turn to her, believing that there may be more to her than met the eye. But my survival instinct wouldn't let me waver from the plan. It growled in defence at her as her eyes grew kind and soft.

"Guilt of what?" I asked, desperate for her answer. Needing to know exactly what I was suspected of. To feel that sense of relief as everything fell into place.

Just tell me what I'm suspected of and I'll comply with you, Agent Cherry. Just trust me enough to be honest with me and I'll trust you enough to be honest with you. Just believe in me. Please.

But she stayed silent and stone-faced, her jaw tight once again. The glimpse of compassion now locked away. My frustration bubbled up from my stomach and spilled out of my mouth.

"The only thing I am guilty of, Agent Cherry, is having amnesia and a missing husband. Quite why either of those things would constitute the breaking of a State law is beyond me." The time for playing naïve was finished. "As the records from the hospital will show, I have complied at every opportunity. All I ask now is to be left to recover in the privacy of my own home."

"Very well." She moved towards the front door but, as usual, couldn't resist a parting shot. "This won't be the last you hear from us."

Before I could spit a retort back at her, Jack stepped in. He moved towards the door where she was stood, expecting a snippet of anger from me that she could exploit at a later date.

"Any further contact will be conducted at my office with myself present. Do you understand?"

"Yes, Jack. I understand." With a curt nod, she disappeared up the driveway.

Closing the door on my nightmare, he turned to me with a wide grin, making sure to activate the device he pulled from his pocket.

"I think that went rather well, don't you?" He was beaming from ear to ear, I believe it was pride on his face. Pride over my performance.

I felt as though I wanted to embrace him in celebration, but given that this was our first meeting, it would be overstepping my internal boundaries. He was, after all, just my mother's husband. It's not like he was a father figure. It's not like he was Kyan.

"How's your mother? I understand she paid a visit last night?"

"She's good," I answered absentmindedly, moving to pick up Franklin as he stirred.

"I don't know how you do it, Paige. Even I sometimes wonder why she doesn't just stay out?" His shoulders relaxed for the first time since he arrived, desperate for a normal conversation. He'd asked me the question I'd spent most of my younger years asking. The truth had been hurtful but one day, he'd come to accept it too. Clearly, he'd been told a different version of the current state of my relationship with my mother.

Unsurprising really, telling people we were beyond estranged didn't tie into the story she wanted to weave about herself.

"You know why," I couldn't help the impatience in my voice. Why was he turning to me for answers and comfort? Did he think I cared about their marriage? "If she stays incarcerated, she'll always be a martyr."

He nodded absentmindedly having clearly been given this answer time and time again. One day, it would be enough to satisfy him as it did eventually me. What state their relationship would be in by then I didn't know. Maybe he'd grow to hate her as I briefly had in my teenage years. As I grew, however, that hate ebbed away every year and was replaced by acceptance and simmering respect. As I saw more of the world and the way things worked, I began to understand her passion for her convictions further. But I'd never understand her choosing them over me. I could never forgive her for that.

"She gave me another set of strict instructions." He took a step towards me, arms outreached to take over parenting duties. "She told me to order you to take a long bubble bath whilst I get to know my grandson."

I flinched at the term of endearment.

Grandfather was not a title he deserved, having never met any of us before. But I knew protesting would achieve nothing positive and would only get him into trouble with my mum. Something neither of us wanted.

Nodding, I passed my son to him, I watched them together for a moment, willing Franklin to start fussing in the face of a stranger. Instead, he reached up for Jack's tie and flashed him a gummy smile.

Thanks for having my back kid.

I sat on the edge of the bath as the water ran, steam filling up the small bathroom and settling into the corners of the ceiling that would soon be full of mould.

Leo had never gotten around to installing the extractor fan that lay discarded in the cupboard under the stairs.

Leo.

I missed him so terribly.

As I sunk into the steaming water, I let the tears escape. Howling sobs left my lungs and the lump in my throat that had been there for days started to soften. I forgot that there were still people in my home and I let myself simply feel. Now I knew my house was a safe space again, another weight had been lifted, but each weight brought with it distraction from reality, and distraction provided emotional protection.

I put my head under the water and opened my eyes.

The world was a blurry mess and my eyes stung with the heat and bubbles.

Come back to me, Leo. Come back.

*I feel his hand on my arm.*
*Fingers wrapped around me so tightly, I'm sure they will bruise.*
*He pulls me with all of his strength.*
*But it's not enough to free me from the seatbelt.*
*With my last bit of strength, I push him away from me and point to the distant shadows where I last saw Franklin.*
*I can feel the dirty water scratching at my eyes as I keep them forced open.*
*He tries again to pull me upwards.*
*Why doesn't he understand?*
*Save Franklin.*
*He deserves to be saved.*

The water had cooled in temperature as I sat back up. My fingers were puckered, and using my foot, I pulled out the plug. I felt the tug of the water around me as I remained lying down in the draining bath. Listening to the glug of the pipes as gravity did its business.

With a sigh, I stood up and wrapped a towel around myself. I took my time to get dressed, choosing a black dress both in homage to Agent Cherry and as a symbol of my stilted grief. After all, I could neither play the role of wife or widow for the time being. Stuck in limbo.

Jack was sat comfortably on my sofa, two cups of coffee cooling on the table next to him.

"I hope you don't mind," he offered awkwardly. I shook my head with a smile. It was quite nice to have coffee waiting for me in its usual spot.

"Where's Franklin?"

"Upstairs asleep. I've also made us some lunch if you're hungry?" My mother had obviously given him strict caregiving instructions, and to be honest, I was more than happy to be cared for right now. I sat down in the armchair and waited whilst he brought me my sandwich.

We sat in semi-comfortable silence as we ate in union. To be honest, I was surprised he managed to find anything resembling food in my kitchen, I really needed to get to a shop.

"So," I began, willing to engage him further in this charade, willing to show him this kindness. "How often do you get to see my mum?"

"I go to visit about once a month when we can bribe the right person, and she comes to see me every other week just about." He smiled to himself at the memory of her. I guess, for him at least, it really was love.

"How's she doing?" I took another bite of my sandwich and regarded him. Wanting to get a measure of my mother's true hold over him.

"You know what she's like. Up one minute, down the next. Always angry at the world." For a moment, I wondered if he was about to speak ill of her, if he would dare. "Such a passionate woman." Nope. Still as besotted as the rest of them.

"Yeah." I had nothing further to add to the conversation so carried on picking at the last few bites of my sandwich.

"How are you doing?" He turned to me; his face full of genuine concern. I recoiled slightly at the emotion in his eyes; he was, after all, basically a stranger.

"I'm okay." He continued to stare at me in worry. "It's hard. It's really hard." I offered this nugget of truth to try and please him. It worked, he felt he had done his part.

"I can't imagine. But at least you're not alone anymore. As you said, it's times like these you really need family." He went to give me a fatherly pat on the knee, I stood up quickly and held my hand out for his plate. He nodded his thanks and I escaped to the kitchen.

"She really misses you," he called to me across the open-plan room.

"I've been missing her my whole life." I couldn't help my retort. It was unfair to bring him into my resentment when all he was trying to do was help.

"All she ever wanted was for the world to be fair. For you. For your children." So, she'd given him the same rationale I'd been subjected to growing up. I gripped the washing up liquid tightly in my hands and squeezed it far too hard. It spurted all over the counter.

"But all I ever wanted was a mum," I replied, hating myself for being drawn into this conversation.

"The greatest thing she ever did for you as a mum was accepting you cutting her out of her life." He was standing next to me now, holding a tea towel and gesturing at the dripping clean plate in my hand.

"I didn't cut her out of my life." I wasn't about to be painted as the bad guy in this.

"You changed your name. You moved away. You never once reached out to her. You deny any and all relation to her."

"I don't deny it." He was good, I'd give him that, he was persuasive. But he wasn't my mother. His attempts at emotional manipulation fell to the floor at my feet.

"You've hidden it so well that nobody would ever think to ask."

"I had to." I wanted this conversation to end before I said something I couldn't take back. I liked Jack despite appearances, he'd helped me out greatly, he was good to my mother and he'd been kind to me when it was most needed. But I wasn't about to welcome him into my family. I wasn't about to take advice from him about situations he had no knowledge of.

"I know." He paused for a moment, knowing he'd overstepped his place. "She knows too." He took his time hanging the hand towel back over the drawer, straightening the edges as though that could bring order back to his life. "That, in my opinion, is what makes her such a good mum." He walks back towards the living room, closing remarks made.

I couldn't argue. I didn't have the logical words to disprove him. For the second time today, he'd shown me just how convincing a lawyer he could be.

As I dried my hands on the towel, making sure to straighten it behind me, I heard the distinct voice of our President booming out from the living room.

"Jack, I don't tend to watch -" My voice stopped as I turned to look towards him.

Jack was sat in shock on my sofa. He didn't acknowledge me as I moved to sit next to him.

Our knees were touching and, instinctively, he reached for my hand as our President continued. I didn't pull away.

"I give a very simple instruction. You must stay at home. People will only be allowed to leave their homes for the following very limited purposes: shopping for necessities once a week or for medical needs. That's all. These are the only reasons you should leave your home. You should not be meeting friends. If your friends ask you to meet, you should say no. If you don't follow the rules, we have powers to enforce them. We will get through this, but your compliance is vital at this time. This is chemical warfare and believe me when I say that we will not stand for it."

My phone rang as I knew it would. Violet's number flashed on the screen. She didn't even greet me; I could hear the shock in her tone. "We've sent a car."

"Jack, I need to go." I couldn't believe I had to leave my son with this stranger. But I had no other choice.

Jack barely managed to nod at me, unable to tear his eyes away from the scientific advisor that now filled the screen. He was a former professor of mine, I trusted him. As I pulled on my coat and shoes, I listened as he outlined what they knew so far.

Chemical warfare.

An airborne virus.

Incurable and vicious.

Placing my keys in my coat pocket, I walked down my path into the waiting car.

"Computer," I asked the car. "Play the broadcast, please."

"Dr Joseph, you usually require silence on your journeys," the car responded in its attempt at a friendly female voice.

Why they always insisted on making artificial intelligence female I didn't know. I'd hazard a guess at it seeming less threatening somehow.

"Play the broadcast," I asked again sharply, in no mood to be questioned by another government drone.

It complied, and as we took the short journey to the hospital, I listened as reporters spoke over each other, desperate to have their questions answered. The words entered my brain but they never really registered.

All I really understood in that moment was that our entire world had been turned upside down.

And it was up to my team to fix it.

# Chapter Eleven

It was chaos outside the hospital. The President's address had ended up having the opposite effect on the general populace from what I could see. Nobody was staying at home as ordered.

Members of the public were banging on the hospital's main entrance as security guards held the doors closed from the inside, their faces covered with masks.

There was a camera crew off to the left of the car park, a short woman with an even shorter blonde bob gave her best serious smile down the lens of the camera as she reported on the scene in front of us. I recognised her from one of the many live interviews I gave on behalf of the hospital and our work. If Gayle caught sight of me, I'd be plastered all over the news.

Leo and I had found ourselves clashing more often as people began to recognised me in the streets. It wasn't that he was jealous. With his charm and a dash of nepotism, he could easily have been the spokesperson for the hospital. He was never interested in that. Me? I found it fascinating. How I could influence an entire room of people just with words and well-chosen inflictions. A simple hand gesture could manipulate everyone into believing me, it was like magic. I treated each interview as though it was a thesis. Something new to be trialled and tested. In one, I'd make the interviewer cry with laughter. In another, I would cry on command. In another again, I was going to use as much alliteration as possible to measure its effect on the audience. It was all a game to me. So, it wasn't jealousy that caused us to argue. It was fear. The more attention I gained, the less likely it would be that Leo could carry on with his side work, his true passion to help those who were denied a family by the Repopulation Act. I wish he'd known how much I agreed with his work.

Now was not the time for me to play a game, Gayle would have to wait until I had time cleared in my schedule.

"The public are demanding protection, demanding answers," I overheard as I passed her, picking my way through wailing bodies as I went to the staff entrance on the outskirts of the madness. Keeping my head ducked low for fear of being recognised. Suddenly, being the public face and shining star of healthcare didn't seem as appealing to me.

I swiped my pass on the entrance panel, but the light remained red. Thinking it an error, I rubbed the electronic chip on the card with the edge of my coat, inspecting it for damage and dust before swiping again. Still, it would not grant me access.

Swinging my bag across my body, I began to rummage inside. I was always amazed as to how much its small stature could hold. Finding my phone, I dialled my office number from memory. I didn't have time to go through my contacts, and Violet answered with her usual professional tone. Although, as a close friend, I could detect an undercurrent of panic in her voice.

I explained the situation with my access card and I could hear her pulling on her shoes before we'd even cut the call to a close. Impatiently, I tapped my foot as I waited for her to make the journey from our lab down to the entrance level.

The crowd began to grow louder and more violent, frustrated that they were being ignored. Then the entire car park was plunged into neon light as helicopters circled us with spotlights. Sirens filled the air and before I'd even had a chance to work out what was going on, I heard the soft sound of darts being fired. All around me I could hear available flesh being pierced, bodies slumping to the ground no longer able to stand and the march of military-grade boots.

Footsteps approached me from behind. Slowly, I raised my pass into the air without turning around. The approaching party paused and then retreated just as Violet unlocked the door and pushed a mask into my chest.

She was already wearing hers and, begrudgingly, I slipped mine over my head. I couldn't quite get my head around the absurdity of having to cover my face in my own workplace, but as soon as I slipped it on, I realised that it really was quite a contraption. My entire face was covered in a lightweight metal and the air I was now breathing tasted fresh as though I was chewing gum. My eyesight wasn't impaired in the slightest by the encasing, in fact, if anything, it felt a little sharper. I briefly held my hand out to inspect it.

"A lot of people haven't noticed that, you know," she said to me as we walked the corridors towards our laboratory. "They're too busy enjoying the AI we installed," she continued as I feigned intelligence on the matter, computer programming wasn't really a subject I enjoyed. "Or the programming that provides patient data, industry research and expert suggestions at the blink of an eye." She tilted her head towards me awaiting my reaction, desperate for a bit of friendly praise. It really was revolutionary and would help save countless lives. I wanted to find the words to tell her how proud I was of her, to offer her a celebratory high five or even to flash her a reassuring smile.

But I didn't. My mind was already processing everything at warp speed. I didn't have time to consider anybody's emotions right now, not even Violet's. I only had the capacity for logic.

"How does it know what power to correct the vision by? It took us three months to finalise the serum and even now it has to be created on a patient-specific basis." I knew I sounded jealous and a part of me was, but I hoped she could see through my question and take it for the only level of genuine interest I could currently express.

She laughed, always happy to have baffled me. Technological development wasn't one of my strong suits, whereas it was an area she was expressing more and more interest in.

We both knew that Violet would be better off transferring to a different lab to work with one of my colleagues who specialised in the technical side of medical advances. We never spoke about it though. All too aware that, like most people, our friendship revolved around our proximity to each other.

"Well, it was actually Leo -" She paused her sentence, realising this was the first time we'd spoken about him since he vanished. "You know I'm always here for you to talk to," she offered. It was one of the first real acts of concern about my wellbeing I'd received since the day I woke up in the hospital bed.

My throat constricted with emotion, so I nodded in what I hoped was a kind way at her. There was a flash of concern on her face in reply as her jaw tightened. Before I could explain just how much I was struggling to hold myself together, the automatic doors to the lab opened and we were surrounded by people I barely knew.

"Excellent work on the masks, Dr Joseph." A man I recognised from the board eagerly shook my hand. "Couldn't have come at a better time."

"Well, actually -" I turned to look at Violet who shook her head subtly at me, refusing once again any acknowledgement of her achievements. "It was a team effort." I added, unwilling to take unearned credit.

My words mean very little to him. I was, after all, the hospital's wunderkind. Even if I'd declared the truth, that I'd had zero input in the mask's design, they'd still slap my name on it. It was good PR after my many years of successful treatments. The name Paige Joseph held a lot of weight in certain circles and would always guarantee a bidding war from manufacturers.

He smiled widely at me, and I could see the glint of currency in his pupils. Having paid his lip service, he and his minions left my lab and peace was restored. I watched his retreating back and fantasised for a moment about throwing a textbook at his head. It was the least toads like him deserved. Their humanity traded for their cheque book as my mother would conclude.

Sometimes I played a game in my head where I dreamed up outrageous scenarios to weigh up the likelihood of any ramifications. It helped pass the time when I was waiting for the computer to analyse data, and quite often, it brought a smile to my tired face. I would definitely be adding his face to my rotation of victims. Hitting a board member with a book was quite low risk as far as I'd weighed up, it would be a slap on the wrist and a boring meeting with Regina. I doubt they'd even make me apologise.

Oh, but when I daydreamed about leaving the hospital and taking all of my work and research with me, when I dreamt about walking out of this building with my head held high and never returning, that always ended in the same result. Certain imprisonment for betraying the State. For robbing them of their profit. It would never be worth the risk, despite how satisfying even thinking about it felt nor what my contract stated. In writing, everything I worked on belonged to me. Something I'd insisted on adding after they asked me to sign a twenty-year contract, but in reality I knew their lawyers would hound me until my dying day if I was to make use of that clause.

As I hung up my jacket and reached for my lab coat, I realised that an uncomfortable silence had fallen between the two of us. This may be the first time it had happened since we met many years ago. Usually, myself or Violet chattered mindlessly as we prepared for a day at work. But not today.

Today was different in every possible way.

"Why don't you ever let me put your name on the patents? It could change your life," I scolded, desperate for something to say but already wearily knowing her response.

"I don't want my life to change. Besides, if I file it under your name, at least I know all the proceeds go back into our work eventually. After the board take their cut, of course."

She'd never been comfortable with the way our work was monetised. And the hospital had never been comfortable with the fact we always filed copyright for the exact length of time it would take for them to recoup any losses, our treatments and findings becoming much less valuable once they were in the public domain for the poorer treatment centres to replicate.

I'd told her during her interview that we weren't here to make money but that we had to play the game. At the time, she'd been happy with that answer, but over the years I'd seen the resentment build as she lost friends to diseases she knew she could cure. Sometimes people didn't have the time to wait for a patent to run out, she'd begun to tell me.

"If you sat the exams, you know you could set your own rules on your work. Go independent if you like," I parroted the sentences I'd tried to get across to her so many times in the past.

"If we get out of this alive, I'll take any damn test you want." Out of anyone else's mouth those words would have seemed harsh but it was merely a sign that our relationship was back on track. I smiled sarcastically at her as we pulled our masks back on.

"When have we ever not made it out of something alive?" I jokingly asked her.

She went to fire a witty remark back at me and there it was. The sadness had taken her over because should pessimism be believed, there was somebody absent from our group, someone who may not have made it out alive. I didn't have the emotional energy to deal with her grief over Leo in that moment, so I stood up straight and marched into the heart of our lab with my head held high.

My technicians were sitting around on stools, some of them swinging themselves around out of boredom. A gentle murmur of conversation buzzed between them, a few light laughs peppered the atmosphere.

The room fell silent when they noticed me.

I saw the sentences of condolence form on their lips. Not here. Not now. I couldn't accept their pity or sorrow. Not when, deep down, I had to believe that Leo was still out there somewhere. He had to be.

"Where are the samples?" I asked, needing to start a conversation before anyone else spoke. I was here to work, not to talk about my personal life. Momentarily, their looks of pity were replaced by shock, I even spotted a few raised eyebrows around the room.

I gathered from their reactions that my behaviour in this situation was unusual. I knew that I was expected by society to stay home, regain my memory and wait for the inevitable call from the police. But that wasn't me. I wouldn't sit around waiting for my world to cave in. I wouldn't grieve somebody who wasn't dead. Society needed me to pull myself together more than it wanted me to fall apart.

"There is not one available at the moment," one of the male technicians spoke up nervously. I didn't recognise him. He must have been hired after the accident, without my agreement.

"Why not?" I placed my hand down hard on the workstation, causing a row of test tubes to rattle. "How are we supposed to undertake our work without samples?" I was on edge now. How could I be expected to help people when the State wouldn't help me?

"Maybe it's too soon for you to be here," Violet whispered as she put a hand out to steady the test tubes.

I looked at her with disappointment. Had she given up on me too? Was I not behaving in a palatable manner to her?

"I am exactly where I need to be." I turned back towards the team, forcing a soft smile onto my face. "I'm sorry, I just don't understand how we could be expected to work on something that doesn't exist."

"They said they're sending them by courier," he spoke again. I went to read his name badge and then realised that, in this moment, I had zero interest in learning who he was.

"Who are they?" I tried to keep the irritation out of my voice at his half-responses. I wished he would just cut to the chase and tell me the full story. This back and forth was draining.

"The government advisors Dr Joseph." He smiled at me, proud of himself for being the one to mention the importance of our work first.

I couldn't help the angry sigh that escaped my lungs. "And how long do they think that will be?"

"We don't, uh, currently have an ETA," he shrugged, now willingly accepting his fate in my crosshairs. It was inevitable that somebody had to be a point for my rage. Rage always needs a target. Mother taught me that.

"If we can't study this virus then we can't help. Did you explain that to them?" My question was rhetorical and we both knew it. I swore I saw his colleagues physically shrink into themselves as my voice grew in volume. "No. Of course you didn't. You complied with whatever they wanted, of course, the good little citizen you are. But in my lab, in my lab, you aren't a citizen, you are a scientist and a scientist always needs to know why. Call them back and demand the sample." I thumbed one of the test tubes into my pocket as I made my impassioned closing statement. Sometimes, you just have to take matters into your own hands.

Storming out of the lab, I left Violet and my team behind, twiddling their thumbs. They could wait around all they wanted for the samples to arrive. I, on the other hand, had decided to collect my own.

I knew we would have at least one cadaver in the building. We were the only large hospital in the settlement so, logically, at least one patient with the virus would have passed through our doors and sadly never walked back out of them.

As I made my way to the lift, I took in the wards as I passed. Staff members were all wearing the same mask as me, along with aprons and gloves. Even the receptionists were dressed for battle. Leo's colleagues regarded me with a mix of compassion and suspicion, but none of them stopped to talk to me.

I listened to snippets of conversations as I picked my way through the bustling staff members going about their duty.

"The Dwellers -"

"Yeah, her husband -"

"We're all going to d -"

"It's war -"

"She says she doesn't remember -"

As the lift doors closed, I glanced at my phone. No new e-mails. No contact from Bailey. The brief distraction of hope paused my realisation that the people around me didn't seem to know whether chemical warfare or my missing husband was the hot topic of the day, and so they seemed to have settled on indulging in both.

Even a pandemic couldn't eclipse the forgetful woman with the missing husband.

# Chapter Twelve

As the lift moved downwards, I enjoyed the onset of silence. I placed a hand either side of the lift walls as it shuddered to a halt. The doors slowly opened and the darkness of the corridor was a stark contrast to the warm neon light in the lift.

A lot of people were scared of this floor, a natural fear really as it was the place we were all destined to visit one final time. I, however, wasn't afraid.

I'd gotten over that fear the day I had to come and identify my grandfather, a formality as he'd passed in the hospital but, nevertheless, they'd brought me down to a place like this to sign the paperwork.

The finality of it all had struck me at a relatively young age. One minute you were up there blissfully anaware of what was around the corner, and the next you were down here. Just another item on somebody's action points for the day. Now I found that visits to the morgue were no different to visiting the maternity floor. Just another ward doing its service in the circle of life.

Since the day I lost my grandad, I'd made it my mission to give people as many opportunities to stay away from this floor as possible. It was the driving force behind each achievement. I may have gotten over my fear of death the day I'd seen his body laid out on a slab, but I still lived with the pain of the loss. I would do anything to stop others from feeling that for as long as feasibly possible.

It was the reason I drove myself to the brink of a breakdown towards the end of every project, working more hours than the rest of the team combined. Driving Leo mad with constant chatter about any anomaly or problem I had encountered whilst being glued to my microscope, looking at slide after slide. He used to joke that I was the only doctor who physically brought their work home with them.

I knew though that if he was able to bring home some of his patients, he would have. It wasn't unheard of in our house for him to spend night after night hunched over at his desk pouring over medical journals and scouring the internet to try and find a diagnosis for some mysterious ailment. He was just as passionate about his work as I was. It was one of the things that made us unbreakable as a couple, we both knew nobody else would understand or accept our never-ending work ethic.

I smelled the unmistakable scent of tobacco smoke and made my way towards the fire door I knew would be ajar. "Where did you get that?" I asked, extending my hand for the cigarette.

The man standing outside didn't flinch at the sound of my voice and there was no fear in his face when he turned around to look at me. His mask was pushed backwards, exposing his lips. I followed suit.

"Wouldn't you like to know," he countered with a smouldering grin.

If Violet knew about how gorgeous he was, she'd definitely overcome her fear of the morgue.

Fed up of waiting for him to offer, I leaned forward and pulled the cigarette from his hand. I took a deep inhale and allowed the smoke to swim about in my lungs and the nicotine to penetrate my blood cells.

"I've managed to grow a plant," he finally revealed as he took it back from me, his fingers lingering on my palm as he did. "I heard about Leo, I'm sorry."

More kindness.

More sympathy.

"You're aware there's an airborne virus out here?" I said, returning my mask to its rightful place. I still didn't know what people expected me to say when they apologised for Leo's disappearance. Thank you? It just doesn't seem right.

"If there is one thing I've learnt from my line of work," he carefully stubbed out the cigarette in the grass, making sure to bury the end under a little mound of mud. "It's that we all have to go some time."

We walked in step with each other into his office, it was about two degrees below comfortable and, to be honest, that was how we both preferred it. I'd been sneaking down here for a nicotine fix for years. Most of the time electronic but, on the rare occasion, he managed to procure the real thing a cigarette and we'd spend the afternoon smoking and talking.

"If they catch you with that, you know there'll be trouble," I half-heartedly warned him. Knowing implicitly that I'd likely be asking for another before I left.

"Two issues with that love," he held the door open for me. "No one other than yourself ever makes it down here, they just send everyone down tagged and unaccompanied like unwanted post. Secondly, I hardly think a small synthetic tobacco plant is the worst thing they'll hang me for."

"They wouldn't hang you," I protested.

"No, not for the tobacco they wouldn't." His name was officially Honorius but everybody here just knew him as Rus. He'd taken his leave from the upper-class family that afforded him such an obnoxious name as soon as he was able.

We often made fun of the privately born babies and their legally given names. I'd only ever known one woman in all my time at the hospital who had a public birth that tried to use a name above her station. The birth application was rejected and the baby had been given a standard name, just like the rest of us.

I'd only heard Leo go by his full name of Leopold on our wedding day. To be honest, compared to the way those in Regina's standing tended to name their children, he'd gotten off lightly.

Violet, on the other hand, quite enjoyed rolling his full name off her tongue in the plumiest accent she could muster after her third glass of wine. She would tease him mercilessly some evenings.

"Paige," hearing my name shocked me from my memory trip. "Are you okay?" He stood close enough for me to feel the body heat rising out of his skin, it was comforting.

"Sorry, my head's all over the place." He was one of the few people I felt I could be honest with. "But I'm sure you've heard all about that."

Stepping away from me, he disappeared into the kitchen and returned with a can of iced coffee. If my mother-in-law knew I enjoyed canned coffee, I'd never hear the end of our class differences. With her in mind, I cracked the seal with a satisfying pop.

"Claire sends her love," he offered in a warm tone as he took a sip from the mug perched on the edge of his desk. "Rebecca too. And Theo." His face broke into a genuine smile.

"How was Theo?" I was relieved to not be talking about myself. About Leo. I could keep my footing in small talk.

"He's good. Really good, actually. Just finished his latest novel, his agent believes that this could be the big one for him." Pride seeped out of him as he spoke.

"That's brilliant news. And how are Claire and Becky?" I always called Rebecca Becky despite how much she begged me not to. It was the basis of most of our social interactions. It was fun to have someone to wind up in good humour.

"Enjoying deployment as much as they possibly can be. Luckily, they've both been transferred from the epicentre to the front line so at least we don't have to worry about them so much." We continued our small talk until I caught sight of the clock, I'd already been down here for nearly an hour.

It was so tempting to stay in this little bubble of normality away from the health crisis, away from suspicious stares and away from my empty home, but hadn't I just stressed to my team about the importance of time?

"I'm going to level with you Rus. I need a favour." Taking the can from my hand, he threw it clean over his shoulder where it rather impressively landed in the bin. He sat and regarded me, weighing up his options.

"You want the cells, don't you?" he asked without surprise. I nodded. He knew me completely and utterly. The second he'd heard footsteps in the corridor, he'd known who was coming and what I would ask.

"I assume you have a test tube?" Without pause, I threw my arms around him and pulled him into a tight hug. I slipped the test tube into his back pocket. I'd never felt more paranoid about being on the hospital's CCTV, all too aware of the mechanical eyes watching me and their blinking red lights of judgement.

The test tube was one of Violet's prototypes, no need to worry about the addition of liquid nitrogen, temperature controls or vacuum seals. Somehow, she'd devised a way for the glass to measure the sample it contained and provide exactly what it needed to survive.

Just like the masks!

I couldn't help but grin over Rus's shoulder having figured out Violet's mask design.

"Your hair smells good," he said as we pulled apart.

"Don't make me tell your wife you talk to me like that," I jokingly shoved him on the shoulder. "Or Theo!" I added.

His eyes glazed over with frustration. I'd spoken without thought.

I listened for the sound of anybody else in the basement, he might usually receive no visitors other than me, but it would be Sod's law for this moment to be the one that broke that rule.

Silence. Blissful silence.

He let out a long slow sigh between pursed lips.

"I thought you only got sloppy after your second bottle of wine," he tutted.

Rus's living situation was a little complicated.

He and his wife, Claire, resided in a beautiful State-supplied home that was part of the compensation package for Claire's job in the war.

The property was very, very large and so they shared it with another married couple, Theo and Rebecca. The two women served together in the same unit and could be posted onsite for up to six months at a time.

To the outside world this living arrangement was convenient simply because it made sure the husbands weren't left completely abandoned. They had each other to lean on for emotional support and it saved the State from funding two houses and sending a therapist to two separate homes weekly. Plus, it was everybody's assumption that lonely men would stray from their wives. But I'd never known four people so loyal to each other.

There were two couples living in that home. Just not the couples that existed on paper.

'Project Repopulation' was one of the first laws put into place when the survivors of Earth One arrived here. Their population stood at 8,000 on that first day, and now, thanks to the Repopulation law, it stands at nearly 45,000 give or take, depending on the relevant day's casualties in the war.

The survival of the human race was deemed the most important civic duty any of us could undertake. Therefore, the pushback on the removal of LGBTQ+ rights hard fought for was dismissed as selfish, short-sighted and an act of terrorism against the State. Who you loved wasn't more important than procreating.

Of course, they had the science in place that would have allowed for artificial insemination, which, in turn, could have allowed people to be with whoever they chose, but for reasons unknown to the population this was deemed an unacceptable route to repopulation. So-called 'natural' couplings were worthier for the cause. I guess it was just another way to control us.

There were doctors who still offered the insemination service under the radar, Leo included, but as the years passed, the punishment for breaking this fundamental State law became more and more akin to the dark ages. Public floggings for anyone assisting and potential hangings for those found to be reproducing using unnatural methods.

No matter how bad the punishments grew, we never once discussed Leo stopping his treatments. We both knew deep down that this law was wrong, though to say that out loud even to each other was a step too close to rebellion for us. So, we remained silent, each pretending that it wasn't happening so we could put on the façade of being happy, law-abiding citizens.

'Project Repopulation' had been the driving force behind my mother's decision to found the movement she was in prison for. She herself had found she had to marry a man she didn't love and carry a child she hadn't planned for. In fact, I could remember that being one of the first things she ever spoke to me about when explaining her political stance.

"I'm not saying you aren't loved Paige," she'd say to me, pulling me into an embrace so tight that every inch of me knew she was speaking the truth. "I'm saying you didn't come into the world the way I'd hoped."

That's the way I'd always been taught to view myself, as someone who deserved to be here but didn't necessarily belong here. If I'd ever spoken honestly to a therapist, that would probably be a key point they'd like to unpick.

My mother's trial and imprisonment was directly linked to the fight against 'Project Repopulation', and as such, it was a cause secretly close to my heart. Which was why I'd introduced Leo to my friends.

Rus had wanted to marry Theo the moment he laid eyes on him. He'd told me that on the drunken night he'd confessed his truths to me as we smoked in solitude in his kitchen. Their love was passionate and instantaneous, much like mine and Leo's, which was why, once again, I found myself questioning the laws of our government. Just as my mother had always taught me.

But being unable to be with the man he loved, he fell into an awkward flirtation with Claire, a young army cadet. They went on a few dates and even though there was no physical spark between them, they got along fiercely, sharing the same sense of dark humour and love of old movies.

They moved in together into their current home, and soon enough, he proposed. It wasn't grand or garish. They were sat on the sofa watching their favourite film when he turned to her and bravely confessed his secret. He promised if she married him that he would be a faithful husband who would protect her and make her laugh every day. But on the flip side, he apologised for the fact that he would never be able to love her the way she deserved. It was the bravest thing he had ever said to anyone, knowing full well she could have had him executed for his confession. That's how much he loved her though, he trusted her with his life in that moment.

Claire had burst out crying and for a moment, Rus felt the imaginary tug of a noose around his neck. However, they were tears of relief at having found a kindred spirit and the two of them sat, newly engaged, discussing the real loves of their lives.

So, a plan was born.

Theo and Rebecca followed standard protocol, sharing public dates and affection until they too got engaged. The two couples had a joint wedding due to the closeness of the women who had been serving alongside each other on the frontline for years.

Everybody celebrated the nuptials of our brave soldiers and their handsome husbands and wished them well on their futures together. They even had a brief interview on the news about their romances. So, it made perfect sense to share the large living space between the four of them. After all, they were all best friends and wouldn't it be cute for the inevitable children to grow up alongside each other?

Which was why Leo offered his services to them should they ever need it. He didn't want to know the details of their lives as he said, they were my friends, but he wanted them to know he supported them and that was his way of showing that. They told me it was the best wedding present they had received.

They all knew that eventually, one or the other of them would have to go through with the deed to avoid any suspicion and I'd been present at a few alcohol-fuelled nights debating who should pull that metaphorical short straw.

Having a child was a big decision whatever route you went down. A shiver ran down my spine as I heard Leo's voice.

*"What do you mean we're in debt?" My voice is shaking with rage.*

*"I had to take out a loan -"*

*"Ah, so you mean **you're** in debt." I can't help the nasty, condescending tone that drips from my lips. How could he do this to us? How could he risk everything?*

*He stiffens and his jaw tightens. There is only so far my righteous horse can carry me. "I had no choice. They needed my help," he responds.*

*"Having a child isn't a right!" I can't help but parrot our President with my retort. I never liked to agree with that man, he was vile, but on this one point of his I can concede in this moment. Having a family is not a right. It's a 'nice to have'.*

*"Of course you would say that, you have a child. You had a child so easily you could never understand the longing others have for one." The truth stings. He's right, I was privileged when it came to this argument. I could never understand how others felt. And worse than that, in this moment, I don't care. I don't care about the pain and suffering others are facing, the sadness they feel at another negative test or the physical pain their bodies have withstood when things go wrong. I don't care about the fact the State keep the laws on artificial insemination in place simply to deny citizens the right to be who they truly are.*

*I. Don't. Care.*

*I care about myself. About the son I've been so lucky to have. I care about the security of my family. If that means others can't have what I do, then I don't care. Then Franklin coos in his sleep. Love crashes over me. It replaces the hatred and anger in my heart. I can't be selfish. I can't disregard the desperation others feel. I can't ignore the cruelty of the law. It isn't right and, most importantly, it isn't how I was raised.*

*"How can I help?" I ask, my eyes meeting his as I watch the worry and anger melt out of him.*

Rus's voice snapped me back to reality.

"This is off the record I gather?" His voice was light-hearted again, my slip of the tongue forgiven.

"Can you bring it over later?" I asked, knowing full well he would do whatever I asked of him. He was such a good friend.

"It's a date." He winked at me.

Despite knowing about his love for Theo, his flirtation still sent the occasional shiver up my spine after all, I am only human.

Planting a simple kiss on his cheek, I turned and headed back to the lift, no need to drag out the goodbye. Before I stepped into the lift I fired Violet a message, letting her know to call me when the samples arrived, and then I headed out of the hospital, away from the suspicious stares, away from the thickening air of fear and headed home.

# Chapter Thirteen

I closed the door behind Jack, having thanked him endlessly for stepping in to babysit in an emergency.

The empty beer bottle hidden at the back of my recycling told me that my mum had visited, but I let them think they'd gotten away with their secret rendezvous. I didn't have the energy to ask him about it. All I cared about was closing the front door and enjoying the silence until Franklin woke up.

My mobile and tablet both kept crashing, so I was unable to distract my mind with an endless refreshing of my e-mails to see if Bailey had been in touch or to indulge in an endless supply of short user-created videos on the latest app. Instead I found myself simply with the time and space to think.

I was never very good at sitting and clearing my mind. My mum used to try and teach me to meditate, to focus only on the sounds in the world around me. To relax and let the universe wash over me. But thinking about not thinking became an obsession and I always ended the session more stressed than I began. In the end, I used to sit with her and pretend to be calm and clear, it pleased her and it cost me nothing to do. She never knew that I spent the time mentally working my way through whatever problem my homework currently posed. Still to this day, I thought she'd be annoyed if she knew the truth. Teaching me to meditate was one of the few parental duties she felt herself successful at. She truly believed she'd given me a way to feel at ease in a world that was so confusing.

Desperately, I tried to remember her teachings. Focusing only on my breathing. In for four, out for eight. In for four, out for eight. God, this is boring.

Staring at the wall, I remembered the photo frame with Leo's writing hidden upstairs in a clump of used towels. Treading as softly as possible on the stairs, I moved to retrieve it, rubbing it absentmindedly through my fingers as I returned to the living room.

What worked Leo?

What the hell worked?

I traced the grains of his handwriting with my index finger, over and over I followed the letters until they begin to feel like a scar on my skin.

The sound of a horn being pushed continuously distracted me.

Looking out of my window, I found that the street was empty. Devoid of life.

*There is a woman screaming.*
*It's as loud as the horn.*
*Maybe louder.*
*I'm blinded by headlights.*
*What does she want, Leo?*
*What does she want?*
*Brakes squeaking under pressure.*
*Knuckles white on the steering wheel as I try to control the direction.*
*Franklin whimpering.*
*A gunshot.*

I woke up with a start on the floor to the sound of my kettle boiling. I didn't remember turning it on. Rubbing my head I stood up slowly, unsure on my feet. I'd never fainted before but with all the stress I was under, I guess it could be expected. Plus, it was hardly like I was taking great care of my physical health. I couldn't even remember the last time I ate.

My brain began whirring through my to-do list as I straightened out my top and rearranged a loose bra strap. I really needed to get around to adjusting them, but at the end of every day, it was just a relief to throw it into the corner of my room and forget about it until another hectic morning. A constant annoyance but one I never bothered correcting.

Surely, it wouldn't be long until my lab received the sample from the State. Violet had promised to call as soon as she had confirmation it was on its way. I checked my phone for messages, there was a missed call from Regina that I didn't the capacity to return.

Just as I was heading to the kitchen to make myself a coffee, there was a soft tap at my front door. There were very few people in my life who were respectful of a sleeping baby, so I headed towards the door with hope for a friendly face. My head was beginning to ache and I suspected I may have knocked it when I fainted.

"Doctor Joseph," the voice on the other side of the closed door was softer than usual but still unmistakable. Agent Cherry. Georgia.

"Is my lawyer with you?" My hand paused on the latch as I wrestled with the decision to open the door or not. I was perfectly within my rights to turn her away. The law was clear on that, it was on my side if I wanted to be stubborn. Silence was my only response. Clearly Jack wasn't aware of this visit.

"We need you to come in for questioning." Her voice was stronger now, its authority returning at the mention of Jack.

"I don't believe I have to go anywhere with you." I was trying to sound strong, trying to ignore the gentle crush of a headache that was taking hold of my sinuses.

"I'm afraid you have no choice." She paused and clears her throat. "Mr Wright is already waiting for you at the station."

It felt like the door handle had scalded me as I took a step back. Being called in for official questioning could only mean one thing, there was a case to be built.

My mind ran to the worst-case scenario. If they now believed they had a formal case, that must mean there was some form of physical evidence. Leo.

No wonder her approach was softer than usual.

She was here to escort me to the room where she would break the news to me that my husband was dead. That Leo was dead.

I wouldn't go to that room.

I couldn't go to that room.

"I'll wait for you in the car whilst you make arrangements." I listened to the muffled sound of her heels clicking up my pathway. The pathway me and Leo lay together one boiling hot day. It had been a stupid decision to perform such manual labour in the middle of a heatwave but he'd insisted. We'd spent the whole afternoon sniping at each other as our muscles began to ache and our skin began to burn.

Occasionally, I wondered if anyone who visited noticed the chip missing on one of the slabs. A victim of our frustration with each other. Still, all had been forgiven as we sat on the floor in our hallway, staring out at the path we had lain, the entryway to the home we were building together. Enjoying a cold beer each.

I gave thought to packing a bag of essentials, grabbing Franklin and escaping through the back garden. But that would just delay the inevitable conversations. The stone-cold fact of my situation. Running away wouldn't bring Leo back to life.

My phone beeped three times.

Three messages.

One to confirm our usual sitter, Laura, was on her way. I guess Agent Cherry had arranged that.

The second was Violet alerting me to the arrival of the samples.

Third was a reminder to buy Leo a birthday gift ready for next month, sent automatically from my calendar.

I remained in my spot, a step back from the front door until the doorbell rang. My feet were heavy as I moved forward to let Laura in. It felt like the longest distance I'd ever faced. Behind that door lay the answer to the only excuse I had keeping me from that room. Keeping me from the news.

As the door swung open, I saw the sadness on Laura's face. She'd assumed the same news awaiting me as I had. She opened and closed her mouth wordlessly like a fish, not mature enough to express her feelings or concern. I almost felt sorry for her.

"He's asleep," were the only words I could speak to her. I was halfway down the path on autopilot when I felt a tap on my shoulders. Laura passed me a pair of shoes and gently nodded down at my bare feet. I took them from her but before we could exchange pleasantries, Franklin began to cry in his cot and she disappeared inside to do her job.

No longer caring about the stares I could feel from my neighbours, I sat down on the path and pulled on my shoes. My fingers were lazy with the laces but, eventually, I tied the knot and with a sigh began to pull myself to my feet.

And there it was.

The chipped slab.

Always there. Ever present. Our never-ending memories.

I heard a car door open and Agent Cherry offered me her hand. "It's time to leave, Doctor Joseph."

"Please call me Paige."

She nodded softly. If she was about to implode my life then we were beyond formalities at this point.

We walked in silence to the car.

We drove in silence to the station.

The sound of my heart breaking filled the space around us.

# Chapter Fourteen

The first thing I noticed when we walked into the room was the tightness in Jack's shoulders. Warmly he smiled at me and pulled out the chair next to him for me to sit, but the tension in his body told me the truth of my situation. This was not going to be a pleasant meeting.

He gave my hand a small squeeze under the table away from prying eyes and then pulled away, pinched his cuffs up from his wrists and laid his hands on the desk. His monogrammed cufflinks looked dull under the sparse overhead lighting.

So, this was Jack in action.

I'd read about him and watched him at my mother's trial on television but never had I witnessed him turn into a full-blown lawyer in the flesh. Even though I knew what a kind man he really was, I began to feel intimidated by the energy coming from him, he was ready for a fight.

"Agent Cherry, would you mind explaining to myself and my client why we have been dragged down here?" His tone was professional, emotionless.

She sat down opposite us and took her time pouring a glass of water. Then, maintaining eye contact with me, she pushed it across the table towards me. She hadn't even acknowledged Jack. She only had eyes for me.

Grateful to have something to do with my hands, I picked it up and held it close to my chest. In that moment, I didn't want her to speak. I longed for some kind of emergency that would call her away. I'd happily sit here in this tiny room for the rest of my life if she just wouldn't reply to Jack's question.

"There has been a development in the case," she finally responded.

My knuckles were white as I held the glass as tight as I could. Holding onto my grip on reality. Please stop talking. Please. Just stop.

"Would you care to elaborate?" he pushed.

No, she wouldn't, Jack.

She wouldn't care to elaborate.

She doesn't have to.

It would be better if she didn't.

I couldn't bring myself to look at him to try and convey my reservations, my desperate need for silence. Instead, I kept my eyes focused on a scratch on the table. It was deep and had jagged edges as though someone had clawed desperately at its surface for hours. I wondered if they'd reacted like that after hearing similar news to mine. Maybe I could add matching damage so my pain would be on display permanently.

"We've found the vehicle. We need to ask Paige - " she softened the first letter in my name, preparing me for what was about to happen. "What she remembers from that night."

"She's told you before, she was drowning. That's all she can remember." He made a move to stand, to dismiss the situation we all found ourselves in.

"I meant what she can remember leading up to the accident." He sat back down as she finished her sentence. There was more to this meeting than he initially assumed.

Accident she'd said. There was my first clue. This was being viewed as an accident. Something that could have been avoided had sensible precautions been taken. Had the risk been assessed and controlled.

"It was our anniversary," I began before Jack could object and ask for some formal request for my questioning. As long as I was talking, she wouldn't be able to tell me the truth. She wouldn't be able to tell me that Leo was dead. "We'd managed to book a table at The Waterfall."

The Waterfall was one of the most popular restaurants around, situated in a part of Nomad's Land that had accepted its inevitable gentrification and decided to exploit the natural beauty available to the inner-landers desperate for a taste of something different. Prices were reasonable other than when a storm warning was in place. It was probably one of the few businesses in history that built its price model around the weather, but it was for a very good reason.

The water in the lake that surrounded the restaurant was ice-cold. Too cold to even dip your toes into and it was crystal clear, you could sit and watch the well, fish I suppose we'd call them, go about their day in perfect vision.

If one looked hard enough, you could even see the gills located on their backs and tails open and close as they turned the water into their life force. The stark contrast of their ink-black skin against the white sand at the bottom of the lake only added to the beauty. Scientists had theorised as to why these creatures had evolved to having their gills; the most sensitive part of them to attack, on such easy to reach positions and had come to the conclusion that the fish had no predators to fear. I remembered Leo scoffing when he read the paper. It was obvious to anyone who had seen the fish in real life that they had nothing to fear. Such was the size of their bodies and jaws. But science always liked to have an answer written down in a journal somewhere.

At the centre of the lake was the waterfall from which the restaurant drew its name and the best seat in the house was located in a cavern directly behind the cascading waters. Guests were accompanied to their table by a staff member in a small shuttle that could withstand the cold power of the water, and anyone lucky enough to reserve the popular table was advised to dress warmly with the restaurant selling branded jumpers, scarfs and gloves in its side shop for those who forgot.

"Which table did you manage to get?" Agent Cherry sounded genuinely interested, spots in the main restaurant were hard to come by and booked months in advance.

"Our friend knows the owner, she managed to get us the table behind the fall." I felt embarrassed as I admitted one of the perks my life afforded me. We'd never struggled to get a table anywhere thanks to Regina's and, therefore, our connections. It was, however, Violet who knew the owner of The Waterfall, an old flame she'd kept on friendly terms with. Clever girl.

The reason the prices increased when bad weather was predicted was the natural theatre a storm and the lake provided. It was a hypnotic ballet as the boiling hot rain drops hit the ice-cold water. The lake sizzled, popped and bubbled as it tried to retreat from the heat, but eventually, the two opposites joined into one and for a brief half an hour, the lake became warm enough to paddle in.

Brave patrons would sit on the edge, sipping a glass of wine and letting the scales of the inquisitive fish tickle their feet. Occasionally, there were bites that required medical intervention but that couldn't deter the upper-class population from the experience. It was a bragging right in social circles to have reserved a table, which could only be trumped by someone who had the chance to bathe in the waters. The pissing contest was always ongoing.

Agent Cherry regarded me with undisguised jealousy. She knew as well as I did that one of the biggest storms of the year had been predicted for that night. It would have been amazing had we made it.

"If you had a table for dinner booked, why did we find prepared meals in your fridge?" I had to keep her intrigued enough to ask me questions rather than tell me the truth.

"That evidence is not admissible." Jack's interruption wasn't appreciated. He was breaking the spell I was trying to weave.

"I'm not using it as evidence. This isn't a courtroom and I am not here to make an arrest today." She hung on the word today, it made my skin crawl.

"Leo was a very fussy eater," I couldn't help the small smile that twitched at the edge of my lips as I remembered our early dating days.

The way he'd force himself to eat dishes as they were served instead of asking for amendments, not wanting to seem demanding. After a few months of dinner dates, he confided in me that he was often ill after eating out and from then on, we decided that to accommodate his social anxiety and to make sure we didn't have to cook again when we got home, we would stick to restaurants and takeaways where he could comfortably eat directly from the menu.

The only exception being special occasions, such as our anniversary, where, instead, we would order some form of sharer dish that I could pick at whilst he enjoyed a glass or two of wine, and when we returned home, he would cook us both a hearty meal that pleased him.

But to explain all of that to an outsider felt like a betrayal.

"Leo always got hungry after a few glasses of wine," was the only answer I could offer her.

She shrugged her shoulder and accepted my response, at least on the surface anyway. "Why was

Franklin in the car?"

> *I can remember speeding along in the car.*
> *Franklin crying in the back, unaccustomed to the panic in the air around him.*
> *Driving past our usual babysitter's home, committing the blur of her house to memory, longing for a return to normality.*

"He was fussy and clingy that evening. As we had the private table, we knew he wouldn't disturb anybody else." She nodded this time. Her responses becoming more animated as we moved through her questions.

"You were found in the lake by the hospital, the one that feeds from the before mentioned restaurant." A statement rather than a question this time.

The water was so dark and dirty, I couldn't see Franklin as he floated away from me. The water was cold but not uncomfortably so.

"I believe that was the case, yes." I had no choice but to go along with her facts, I wasn't about to start tearing down the theatre of my amnesia just to correct her.

"So, you agree that you were drowning in the lake?" She was trying to trick me; she was trying to prove some kind of point.

"My client doesn't remember specifics about the night, you know that," Jack interjected, desperate to include his own voice in our conversation.

"Logically speaking, if I was found by the lake, it would be correct to assume I was drowning in the lake." I couldn't argue with logic, despite my hazy memories pulling me in other directions.

"Correct. That would be the logical assumption." She took in a deep breath and her entire body tensed. Here came the news I was dreading. I hadn't managed to speak for long enough. Time had caught up with me. My chest began to burn as I held my breath, waiting for her next words. Waiting for her to break my heart.

"If you were drowning in the lake, why did we recover your car today in the large river on the outskirts of Nomad's Land?" A quizzical look was on her face.

My heart literally skipped a beat. It hurt when it restarted, my arteries and chambers burning with effort. My body wanted to give up in that moment but my brain wouldn't let it.

I couldn't remember that night clearly but what I could remember was the dirt of the water. I could barely see my hand as I tried to untangle myself from the seatbelt. I remembered watching Franklin disappear into the darkness in front of me. It clicked together.

I hadn't been drowning in the lake I was found by. Those waters were crystal clear. It would be impossible.

"All I can remember is drowning. I don't know where I was," I offered up my usual defence.

"What can you remember about drowning?" she pushed.

Jack scoffed at her question. I looked at him kindly, he only wanted to protect me from invasive and emotional questions.

"I remember being scared." I turned my attention back to her. I wasn't about to reveal the few truths I'd managed to piece together. Something in my gut told me to guard the truth with my life. "I remember being surrounded by water. My lungs burning as I held my breath. I lost my grip on Franklin." I let my real emotions seep into my half-truths. "I watched him float away from me and I couldn't get to him."

"Why couldn't you get to him?"

For a moment, I could feel the seatbelt tight around my ankles again, holding me to the ground.

"I'm not a very strong swimmer," my voice

dripped with guilt at not being able to fend for myself. I'm the victim in this room. She will see me as one.

"How did you end up on the shore by the hospital?"

"I drowned Agent Cherry. That's all I know." I extended my hands across the table, palms up, a sign of honesty.

"How did your car end up in the river? If you crashed into the lake, surely, we should have found it there?"

"I'm sorry, I can't help you any further. Surely there must be surveillance footage you can check? If I had the answers, I would give them to you. Nobody wants to find Leo more than me." She couldn't argue with that statement. It was the absolute truth of the matter. Nobody wanted a husband home more than a wife.

"Unfortunately, the night of your accident, there was a State-wide blackout. We lost four whole hours of footage across the city." Silence descended on us in the room.

This was the moment she was about to play her strongest hand. This was when she'd tell me they'd found Leo's body. I couldn't delay it any longer, I had no more words to give her. "Thank you for your time today Mrs Hanson." A return to formality, her sympathy for me had vanished. She stood to leave.

"Is that it?" I couldn't help the words as they rushed from my mouth before my brain could stop them.

"What do you mean?" She turned back towards me with genuine interest.

"Aren't you going to tell me you found Leo?"

"Why would you think we've found Leo?"

"I just assumed."

"Did you think I'd brought you here to tell you

he'd died?" There was a glint in her eye I didn't like. "Why would you think he was dead, Mrs Hanson?"

"It's a very reasonable thing for her to have assumed," Jack interjected before she could pull at that thread any longer. "I myself thought the same when you called us both here."

She nodded at us both curtly before leaving the room without any further statements or questions. No parting shot for the first time.

Jack stood, offered me a hand, and together, we walked out of the station into the sunshine and back into hope.

Leo was still out there.

I could still find him.

# Chapter Fifteen

I'd hoped to return home to some much-needed normality, but luck wasn't in my favour. An awkward tableau awaited me in my living room.

Laura was there, which was expected, nursing a cup of coffee. She always helped herself to the good brand I kept hidden behind cereal boxes rather than the cheaper alternative I left out on the counter for guests. Leo used to call it selfish. I'd always point out that it was frugal. He'd never had to live a life of hard-won luxuries, so he didn't understand how important named brand coffee could be to someone.

Sat in the large comfy armchair was Violet. She'd taken her usual spot in my home and had her feet curled under her as she regarded the people around her with heavy eyes over a half-drunk glass of wine. I always kept a bottle of red in especially for her, and she always knew where to find it.

Finally, sat awkwardly on one of the dining chairs he'd dragged into the room, was Rus. A bunch of flowers hanging limply from his arms and an unopened bottle of wine at his feet. He looked stressed and dishevelled but, somehow, it only seemed to add to his handsome features. The lucky bastard. I noted that he had no drink nor had he been allowed to sit comfortably like the two women who always made themselves at home.

"Your friends welcomed themselves in," offered Laura with little emotion in her voice. She tilted her mug towards me and I nodded. "Is everything okay?" she asked, concern and grief leaking into her infliction. I mustered a tight smile and tried to fix my features into a reassuring expression. Always playing a part, always doing as I should.

"Leo is still out there." I couldn't bring myself to say the word alive, it would tempt too much fate. Her shoulders relaxed and she moved into the kitchen to make us both a cup of coffee.

Violet and Rus both went to speak at the same time, then both fell silent. She was staring at him with a mixture of attraction and contempt. In another world, this would be the beginning of their top-shelf romance novel.

"Vi, what's up?" I turned towards my best friend first.

"They've closed Nomad's Land." Her voice was hollow and shell-shocked.

"What? How is that -"

She interrupted me before I could finish my question. "They turned the fence back on."

We'd all been under the impression that the laser fences had been permanently disabled when the agreement of travel had been put in place between the mainland and Nomad's Land.

The occupants of Nomad's Land had sworn to protect the outskirts from Dweller forces to prevent them from moving into the mainland to launch an attack, the whole basis of the treaty had been built around that promise.

In return, the government had allowed the relatives free travelling between the two areas; with the correct ID. They'd offered financial incentives to companies who hired the so-called Nomad's and they'd permanently disabled the lasers that had once been a deadly barrier between the two of us.

Their 'positive discrimination' bill had angered people on both sides of the property lines. The people who lived in the closest zone to the centre repeatedly stated that it should be the best candidate who received the job and that positions shouldn't be given out just because somebody happened to have a Nomad's address.

The people who lived in Nomad's Land just wanted equality and they viewed the governments' bill and agreement as another way to highlight their differences. It's why so few of them actually ventured out of Nomad's, happy enough with the life they'd already built for themselves away from government intervention.

Having been born in Nomad's Land myself, a fact I'd opted to keep on my new birth certificate, I could see all sides of the argument as could Violet. Which was how we both knew she'd been truly the best candidate for the job when I'd first hired her. The fact she lived in Nomad's Land only really bothered the board and some of my more closed-minded colleagues. Until I reminded them that I, their star researcher, also hailed from that land.

The idea that the government had not just lied about the permanent destruction of the barrier between the lands but had, in fact, reinstated it only shocked me mildly. After all, my mother had consistently drilled into me that the government was never to be truly trusted, learnings that were harder to erase than my old identity. But I could see that Violet was shaken to her core. Despite her passionate dislike of some of the aspects of government, she still believed them to be good on a base level.

"You can stay with me as long as you need." I made the offer although I knew it went without saying. She was family, after all. I watched as she drank the rest of her wine in two big gulps.

"I'm going to get a refill and take a bath. We'll talk about him," she glared at Rus, "later."

Laura placed my coffee on the table next to me and wandered upstairs to the spare room that she'd turned into her new home in my absence. What choice did she really have? The government had forced her from her own home into mine with an undefined eviction date.

My house had gone from feeling empty to feeling ready to burst. You might think I'd be grateful for the company but you'd be wrong. I already felt claustrophobic.

Rus and I were finally alone in the living room. I gestured for him to move from the chair to the sofa next to me. As he did so, Violet stalked back through the room and thudded up the stairs. That woman really had a temper when it suited her. Obviously turning her anger at her family's situation into jealousy that I had a friend besides her in the world. It was a coping mechanism and I didn't begrudge her it. Sometimes you just needed someone to be angry at.

He handed me the flowers. "I thought it might make you laugh if I turned up with these." As I held the bouquet, I felt the hard glass tube held within the ribbon. "Now I realise it was rather stupid of me."

"No, it would have been funny." I placed the flowers on the coffee table. "I've just had a rough couple of hours."

"Want to talk about it?"

"Not really." We both knew that if the worst had happened to Leo, he'd already know. There was no way Regina would allow Leo to be examined by anyone other than her own mortician. He nodded grimly, aware that someday soon, the moment could come where he'd know my husband had died before I did. "Did you want me to open this?" I picked up the bottle of wine, it was my favourite brand and grape, I wouldn't have expected anything less from such a good friend.

He shook his head. "I'd better not." His eyes glanced upstairs; Violet had put him on edge. One evening soon, I'd have to arrange a dinner for the three of us so she could get to know him as I did. It would be a much-needed distraction for us all.

I followed him towards the front door and he pulled me into a tight hug.

"Take care of yourself love." He kissed me gently on the cheek and left me standing alone, holding a bottle of wine. Closing the door, I looked at the coffee waiting for me on the table. Walking past it, I grabbed a bottle opener and a wine glass.

Sometimes caffeine wasn't the solution.

# Chapter Sixteen

*Leo's hands are on my shoulder. Despite the dirt in the water, his eyes are wide open, unblinking, and he smiles at me softly before placing his lips on mine.*

*The burning in my lungs is relieved as oxygen returns to my bloodstream for a moment.*

*I gesture towards where Franklin floated away from me. He is the one who deserves to be saved. That needs to be saved.*

*Leo keeps smiling at me and gestures towards the surface. Franklin is safe. Finally, I smile back at him, squinting through the debris-laden water.*

*At least I'll die knowing my son is safe, with Leo by my side. One last time, I try to pull my legs upwards, to release them from the seatbelts keeping me attached to the slowly sinking car. But it is no use. Soon, I'll be at the bottom of the lake, my eternal resting place.*

The room was pitch black as I woke up from my dream. There was a body next to me in our bed. Leo.

Just before I reached out to him, I remembered that it was Violet. The smell of her perfume and the red wine on her breath brought me back to reality.

Leo was still missing. Dreaming about him did me no favours. It gave me no answers.

I thought about waking Violet to tell her about my dream, to confide in her all the puzzle pieces I had so far. But once again, my gut told me to guard my secrets.

Besides, I very much doubted she'd appreciate

being woken at three am especially considering the cross words we'd exchanged before bed.

I thought she was a little put out by Laura's now permanent presence in my house, presuming the spare room to be hers when she'd arrived at my doorstep. It wasn't fair, however, to ask a virtual stranger, a girl just approaching the end of her teens, to share a bed with her employer. There was probably a law against that.

So, we went to bed at the same time and lay back to back. Each fuming about hurtful words we'd thrown around. In some ways, it was comforting to go to bed with someone to be angry at, it felt like Leo was home again.

She'd accused me of hiding Rus away. Consistently, she stated that I'd lied to her but wouldn't expand on the accusation. Asking me if Leo was friends with him too. Her jealousy was ridiculous. Clearly she'd painted this second life for me and Leo that didn't include her, something she couldn't stand.

In turn, I'd called her needy. Ungrateful. Naïve. My sympathy had evaporated incredibly quickly. I didn't want to understand the true meaning behind her anger. I didn't care. I was tired of having to say the right words to keep people onside. I don't know how my mother had the energy to keep it up for so long.

When she'd started expressing her sadness at being cut off from her family thanks to the fences I scoffed, telling her she was stupid for believing something like this would never happen.

It was cruel.

An apology immediately formed itself on my tongue.

Then she'd shot back that she had secrets too. Leo had secrets too. Before I could press her for more information she stormed off to bed and refused to talk any further.

I'd pushed her button and she'd stamped on mine. That's the problem with loving people. You always know how to hurt each other.

So I lay there wide awake, listening to her soft breaths as she slept. For a while, I watched her eyes twitch as she dreamt, wondering where she was and what she was doing. Then a soft murmur came from her lips.

"Leo," she spoke out loud.

It was as though I had been slapped. Wherever she was in her dreams, she was with Leo. Jealousy filled my veins and I wanted to shake her awake and insist that he was mine alone to dream about. However there was still a tiny rational part of my brain that reassured me and calmed me as it reminded me that dreams are subconscious and we have no control over them. She herself had her own grief and worry about Leo to process, and who was I to take that away from her?

I knew I wouldn't be able to sleep after that. My adrenaline was too high. So I gently slipped out from under the duvet, pushed my feet into my slippers and moved towards the bedroom door, intending to read on the sofa until sleep eventually took me.

As I pulled the bedroom door to a close, I heard her whisper again.

"I'm sorry."

I closed the door a little more firmly than I'd first intended, hoping it would disturb her even lightly, throw her brain off its current path. But as I listened at the door I heard no signs of life.

I made myself a cup of chamomile tea. Leo always insisted on keeping some in the cupboards despite us both being avid coffee drinkers. But he kept them in the cupboard for moments like this. Nights when he knew I couldn't and wouldn't sleep. It was his way of helping.

The pack was nearly empty. I didn't know if I'd be

able to bring myself to replace it when it ran out. I'd rather wait for Leo to do it.

*"We have to leave." He passes a backpack towards me. "Pack light." He stinks of burning plastic. What has he done?*

*I was back in my mother's kitchen. Just ten years old the first time I heard that sentence. What books should I pack? What could I part with?*

*The anxiety rose in my chest just as it had before. Once again, somebody was telling me I had to leave my life behind. I knew that I had to break his heart just as I had my mother's. I'd worked so hard for this life. I'd worked so hard on becoming the person I'd grown into. I wasn't about to lose it.*

*"No." I refuse to take the backpack from his hands, it hangs limply in his grasp. I watch as a range of emotions filter across his face had he really expected me to blindly go with him? To comply just because he commanded?*

*They'd both underestimated my resolve at the exact moment they should have relied on it. If she'd just explained to me the reasons behind her request, if he'd just explained to me before demanding my submission, then maybe my response would have been different. Maybe I would have given them what they needed. But they'd both underestimated my love, my logic. Both decided I was too fragile to understand whatever the situation was. They'd both lost some of my heart in that moment. A piece that would never grow back.*

The sun was beginning to rise as I drifted back into reality. It was hard not to hear my mother's voice ranting about the convenience of the virus, to hear her whisper the thoughts I was trying desperately to keep locked in. I couldn't let any more of her poison into my veins.

It was the Dwellers. That made more sense, they'd finally had enough of us encroaching on their land and they were angry. So angry that they'd taken the war to this extreme. That I understood. That I could relate to. Sometimes people, even Dwellers, get so angry they just want to watch the world burn.

I placed the flowers from Rus in a vase and held the test tube in my hand. Here was the sample I needed to help everybody. But as Violet had confirmed earlier, the State had finally delivered their samples, so the whole exercise with Rus had been for nothing.

Instead of putting the tube in my work bag to add to the samples in the lab, I went into the garden. The air was cold with the first morning frost, a sign that we were in for a hot relentless day. I wished I'd thought to bring my inhaler outside with me, nicotine when the world was quiet and still really was magical.

But I didn't go back inside the house to fetch it. I could already hear the stirring of life creaking through the floorboards upstairs.

There was no explanation for what I did next. I just knew I had to do it. That voice in my gut again was telling me how to act. 'Don't trust,' it repeated.

We had a loose slab on our patio, it was barely noticeable but it was where Leo concealed his insemination tools. I lifted it out of its place and sure enough, his tools were still there. Agent Cherry hadn't discovered our one safe space when she'd erased my husband from my home.

I placed the tube inside the old battered bag that contained his tools. Taking a moment to hold the handles in my palm as though I could feel his touch again through them.

Then replacing the slab, I made it back into the kitchen just in time to be greeted by a still angry-looking Violet.

Flicking the kettle on, I pulled two mugs from the cupboard and pointed them at her. She nodded curtly and I made us both our first coffee of the day.

"What time are we heading into work?" she asked. The first words she had spoken to me since revealing Leo had secrets. I knew he had secrets. I just thought they were all my secrets too.

"In an hour?" I offered. She took her coffee, and with a nod, headed upstairs to shower.

If she stayed in this mood, it was going to be a long day in the lab. I made the decision to apologise as soon as she came downstairs. I could use the chat with Agent Cherry to excuse my words and my worries about Leo to guilt her into forgiveness. She'd be back to normal by the time the car arrived. My mother's words floated through my head:

That's the good thing about loving people.

You always know how to get what you want.

# Chapter Seventeen

The car ride to the lab was pleasant as we resumed our usual banter. Forgetting her pettiness last night, it was easy to remember why I loved Violet so fiercely. Not everyone understood why I valued her friendship so much, but they hadn't been there the many nights she held me as I wept whilst in the midst of post-natal depression. Never trying to pacify me with words or push me to seek help. She'd just simply existed by my side, offering me her strength when I had none left of my own.

The excitement in the air this morning was thick between us, it always was on the first day of a new project. And this project was unlike anything we'd ever faced before. She told me how the samples had turned up, hand-delivered by a female agent dressed all in black. No doubt Agent Cherry, she'd called into the hospital before coming to my house to question me about the car.

The agent hadn't released the samples from their protection until Violet had signed several release forms. Not having the time to read through them all, she had agreed to keep them under lock and key. She even had to demonstrate how our safe worked before the agent entrusted the samples to her and left our lab.

Before she'd had a chance to run them through our analysis machine, the lockdown of Nomad's Land had been announced and she'd rushed to the border, desperate to make it home.

When she'd found herself turned away, she immediately made her way to my house. Crying with every step that she took as she heard those she left behind her begging to be released from the other side of the fence. They were terrified of the virus and their imprisonment. Certain they'd been sacrificed to save the luckier population. I couldn't tell her that they were wrong to fear that. My brain had reached the same conclusion upon hearing the news for the first time. They were lambs for the State's slaughter.

So our first job on arrival would be to run the samples through analysis and wait for our systems to do their work. I didn't mind the delay. Contrary to yesterday's panic, today I felt calm. I was confident that we would find the answer before the end of the day.

We laughed at each other as we pulled on our masks and headed towards the entrance. The car park was bare, unsurprising really when you considered the entire population was on State-mandated lockdown. But it was still an unnerving sight to behold.

By this time in the morning the visitor bays were normally all booked out, empty vehicles gently buzzing their engines as they waited for their fares to return. The automated front doors would provide poetry each morning as they performed their duties to a melodic pattern. Staff members would be arriving for their shift, being wished good-natured luck by their departing colleagues as the shifts changed over.

This morning however, the doors remained closed, the visitor bays were empty and the staff we did see milling around kept their greetings to themselves. Heads hunched down in horror, warm smiles replaced by masks.

Our good mood however, carried us through the corridors. Past the suspicious stares that always seemed to come my way, through the oddly quiet halls and past the empty cafe. Violet offered to get the first round in, and so with cheery agreement I made my way towards the lab. I had a new challenge to keep my mind off Leo, a hot coffee on its way and a group of like-minded people to bounce ideas off all day. Soon, we would have a cure, Bailey would be in touch, the lockdown would be finished, Leo would come home and all would be right in the world. I was sure of it.

I found my footsteps to be the only noise in our once-bustling workspace. Peeking through the glass doors into the central lab, I noted that every chair was empty. Where is my team?

"State orders, I'm afraid. Cleared personnel only." Regina's clipped tones stroked their way up my spine, causing it to involuntarily shudder. I could still remember how helpless she'd made me feel as I lay in a hospital bed under her care.

"Sorry I missed your call yesterday," I offered in way of conversation as I pulled on my lab coat.

"Call? What call?" She made a show of leafing through some paperwork on Violet's desk as though she had interest in it. "It must have been a misdial."

"You know they found the car?" I didn't see the point in prolonging the inevitable confrontation. She'd probably known about the car hours before I had, her connections were like spider webs throughout the system, matched only by my mother's. I prepared myself for an onslaught of accusations, over-exaggerated tears and whispered insults in her native tongue.

"Yes," she lowered her voice a tone. "How did your meeting go?" I was taken aback by her question. There was no hatred in her tone, no anger or distrust. She actually cared. About me. She hadn't assumed the worst of me upon hearing the news.

Before I could answer her question, Violet joined us in the room. Placing the two coffees on her desk, she regarded Regina as though she was something she'd stepped in. I knew Violet disliked Regina, she'd heard enough impassioned rants from me to colour her opinion that shade, but this time, Regina didn't deserve contempt. In reality, I wasn't sure she deserved any of it in the past either. We all make mistakes.

"Authorised personnel only I'm afraid, Doctor Hanson." She smirked as she spoke, finally able to speak to Regina how she'd always been spoken to. A victory granted to her by the virus and her new elevated status due to it.

Regina looked taken aback but had the grace to leave the room without any biting remarks. As she left, I noticed a wrinkle at the back of her silk shirt. I kept my eye on it as her retreating back disappeared through the corridors, committing her faux pas to memory for a later date. For a time I felt less forgiving.

"I forgot to tell you that it's just us. We're the only two people in the whole of the hospital who are allowed to work with the samples. Pretty neat, huh?"

It made sense given the contagious nature of the disease. Plus, it had been set upon us by enemy forces as an act of war. We couldn't trust anyone other than ourselves with the information or our findings. You never knew who was secretly a sympathiser. The irony wasn't lost on me.

Even though our lab was located at the centre of the hospital, we could hear the beginning whistles of wind upon the ceiling. A storm was starting. Violet was never a fan of thunderstorms but if she felt unnerved by the first rumblings setting in, she didn't show it. Too caught up in the task at hand.

She shrugged her white coat on and scanned her pass to open the doors to our laboratory. It was eerily quiet without the usual morning's rabble. I didn't have to scold anyone for bringing in a box of pastries whilst simultaneously helping myself to the cinnamon swirl. It was rather difficult to press the point that we had to keep the environment sterile with a mouthful of sugary goodness, but I made a show of trying daily.

Usually once we'd all eaten and caught up on pleasantries, we would have to step out of the room and press the incinerator button. Truly, it was a dreadful waste of resources but the team seemed to like the routine and it humanised me in their eyes. Plus I never tired of watching the flames lick across the surfaces and furniture that would forever remain unscathed by its touch.

They were all specially designed to withstand the heat that would rub up against them and the fire that would dance along their varnish. It was routinely run before we arrived for the day and by the last person to depart in order to keep the environment spotless, so it was a novelty for most people to watch the process.

But this morning, there was no need for the extra theatre. I missed it.

Violet was already unlocking the safe and I watched with excitement as she pulled out the sample case. Like a child at Christmas, I couldn't wait to see what was inside. She spun the case towards me so I could have the honour of opening it. I was touched by her gesture.

Then I remembered it was simply my turn.

We had a tally going as to who got to input the data of any new project into the machine. She was up by one point, which meant that no matter how she felt, today was my lucky day. Fair was fair after all.

I opened the box and there in the case lay two samples. Disappointment plummeted through my stomach like a rock. We'd need so much more information than this to reach a conclusion. How could we work out how to stop something with only two examples of it? Did they not realise how large a test scale we would need to save everyone? Before I could say anything to her, Violet handed me half a stack of paperwork.

"All the documents I had to sign yesterday. I guess we should read them."

So, we did. It took roughly two hours for us to take in every sentence, clause and mitigation. Without realising what she'd done she'd essentially signed our lives away until we achieved a result.

We were to only return home to rest. We had to wear the new State-issued ID chips at all times so our whereabouts could be checked. We were unable to socialise with anyone except for each other. She'd agreed to our phone calls being monitored, the reinstallation of CCTV in the lab and even to an ongoing non-disclosure agreement that, if broken, would lead to immediate imprisonment without a trial. She'd complied with it all and had taken me along for the ride too.

I could feel the sallow shadows of dread under my eyes as I looked up at her. To her credit, her eyes were watering as she took in the magnitude of what she'd done. If I had known that Regina was the last person outside of my household I'd get to speak to for a while I'd have, well, I wouldn't have really done anything different but I might have insisted on buying the first coffee round if only to chat to the barista.

How did this paperwork affect my relationship with Jack?

Did I have to ignore Laura now even though she was living in my house?

What about Agent Cherry, was I now exempt from talking to her? Every cloud I guess.

I had so many questions racing through my mind and there was only one true answer. We had to get the job done as quickly as possible to have these sanctions lifted from our lives. They were only applicable whilst the samples were in our care, therefore, we had to ship them back to the government as soon as we could to reach some level of normality again.

There were no kind words to express to Violet the feelings I had towards her in that moment, so instead I picked up the two samples and placed them into the system. As the machinery clicked and whirled to life, I let the gentle buzzing of the motherboard soothe me. This wasn't so bad. Of course they had to be this careful. Nothing could slip into enemy hands.

She handed me a single sheet of paper that had been at the bottom of the delivery box. It outlined our sole directive. We were to identify what was different between the two samples.

They had been taken from identical twins, so by all accounts, they should be exactly the same. However, one twin had died from the disease and one had survived. It was our job to work out why.

"So, they don't want a vaccine?" I asked her.

"No."

"Or an antibody test?" I couldn't help but try to make sense of the directive in front of us.

"No."

"They want a, I don't know, a death predictor?" It seemed such a ridiculous request that I must be reading it wrong. Misinterpreting their needs.

She shrugged her shoulders, as baffled by the directive as I was. "I guess it's to stop the hospital and the treatment centres from being overrun by those who don't stand a chance."

"So, people can choose who lives and who dies? That's awful. Everyone should be treated the same."

"But if we waste resources on someone who can't be saved and lose someone who could survive, isn't that awful too?" The logic she displayed with that sentence shocked me. Hadn't we always been on the same page about saving as many lives as possible?

"It just doesn't feel right." My words were pathetic and pointless but I wanted to send them out into the universe. To let it know that I didn't agree with the actions thrust upon me. I didn't get into medicine to take treatment away from people. I wanted to throw a hissy fit, to refuse to undertake the work thrust upon us as a show of solidarity to the rest of the population. To show them that I was better than the State, that I wouldn't partake in something so cruel. There it was again, the voice of my mother echoing through my brain. The State was cruel. This task proved that beyond a doubt.

"I know. But we should just do what's asked of us." It wasn't like Violet to be so compliant. She sounded so very lost and defeated. I knew she had the same moral struggles as me in that moment, all we'd ever wanted to do was help people and improve their lives. Now we were about to hand over a death predictor to the government that would give them all the information they needed to simply stop caring about those who wouldn't survive if they caught the virus. As if they needed any further excuses to push those at the bottom further down.

If one of the board members was found to fail the death predictor there was no doubt that they would be whisked away, provided every treatment available, and when that failed, they'd be given the comfiest ending a person could wish for. It was one of the perks of being a soulless money drone.

I couldn't spiral like this. I couldn't allow negativity to impact upon our work. We had a job to do. It might not be the job we wanted, but we had to accept it. The paperwork made that clear enough.

At the end of the day, there would be other teams just like us working in other zones most likely on the vaccine or antibody tests.

We were just creating another cog in the treatment machine. When all the puzzle pieces were put together, we would all emerge victorious. I knew it.

# Chapter Eighteen

The day hadn't been as successful as we'd hoped, so the car ride home was a lot quieter than the one we'd taken in the morning. We'd both realised by about lunchtime that we'd been naïve and perhaps egotistical in regard to how easily we'd solve the problems before us.

Our samples hadn't been as straightforward as we'd expected, and without having a sample of the virus to study, it was hard trying to find the difference that meant someone was more likely to survive infection. We were playing an overpriced game of spot the difference for nine hours before we called it a day. My eyes were square from squinting at the screen solidly and my head ached from all the information I was trying to hold in.

Laura had left a lasagne in the fridge and Violet put it on to warm whilst I took over the bedtime routine from my now in-house nanny. Franklin was a wriggling ball of smiles as I gently washed his hair, face and in between the chubby folds on his thighs that I adored. I sang nonsense songs as he tried to coordinate his limbs to splash in the water. Every day he was changing and the fact Leo was missing it all caused an ever-growing lump of grief in my stomach. I thought Franklin was too young to realise his dad was missing, but he'd definitely become a fretful sleeper the last few nights. There was clearly more going on in his brain than I realised. I desperately hoped he wouldn't grow up with a memory as vast as mine. I didn't want him to remember this time in his life. I'd pay any amount to stop that from happening.

I took my time getting him dressed in his sleepsuit. I hadn't checked to see which one Laura had left out and tears threatened to spill when I read "Daddy's little man" on the front. Quickly, I undid the poppers and put him into a plain one instead. I couldn't face those words again in the morning.

Breaking one of the much-lauded 'parenting rules' from the leaflet passed out to every new mother, I let Franklin fall asleep in my arms, and after laying him down, I sat watching him in his cot until I heard the timer on the oven beep through the floor below me. I had no interest in eating but could definitely do with a glass of wine from the bottle I knew Violet would have set out on the coffee table.

Just as I expected, she was already sat in her usual armchair, legs curled beneath her, a pair of fluffy socks stolen from my drawer on her feet and a plate of lasagne lounging haphazardly on her lap. She was staring blankly at the wall, lost deep in her own thoughts.

"Penny for them?" I asked as I sat on the sofa and picked up the glass of wine she'd poured for me. Glancing at the lasagne, I felt my stomach contract with hunger. I guess my body and my mind weren't quite in sync. I picked up a forkful of food and let it sit in my mouth, my throat froze as though I'd forgotten how to swallow and I coughed slightly as the cheese sauce got stuck in my throat. It was no use, it wasn't moving. As subtly as I could, I spat the food back onto my plate. If she had been paying attention to the scene before her, then my friend may have thought slightly less of me. I guess no matter what my mind or body thought, my anxiety would always win the battle.

"Worth more than a cent." The level of frivolity in her retort was lacklustre. She was trying to act as though everything was normal. Perhaps she found being in the home I shared with Leo too strange. Even with all the additional houseguests, it still felt empty without his presence.

"It must be hard being here without Leo," I offered. Willing to concede to her the ability to grieve for one evening at least.

"He was the last thing on my mind," she sounded defensive. "I'm sorry." She chewed a mouthful of lasagne and regarded the living room. "But yes, it is strange being here without him butting in every two minutes." She smiled warmly at me, making fun of him as we normally would.

"He'll be gutted he's missed out on lasagne."

"It's one of the few things someone else could make him!" She laughed but behind my smile, my tongue was at the roof of my mouth, tense and ready to strike. How did she know about Leo's fussy nature? We'd only ever all eaten together in our house where he would prepare a dish everybody would like in order to avoid Violet teasing him. He would always joke that he didn't need to give her any further ammunition.

"True." I agreed, biting down on my mistrust. We were stuck together by law until the project ended and there was no sense in making the situation any harder than it had to be. So I filed my observation away, ready to obsess over it as she slept that night. "Have you managed to speak to anyone back home?"

"No. Even if my phone would let me dial out, the rules on this new project means I'm unable to." She took her fork mindlessly to the top of her lasagne and twirled it repetitively until it was covered in melted cheese. Then she laid her fork down at the side of her plate. "I still can't believe they shut it down." Speaking to herself now, she leaned forward to pick up her wine. I sat back and waited for the words to spill out of her as they always did when she had something on her mind.

She never wanted someone to talk to, just someone to talk at.

"I miss Ada. God, I miss her so much." She took a long sip to steady her nerves. Even after all these years, there were parts of herself she didn't like to share with me. I'd pieced together as much as I could over time and knew that Ada was her baby sister, a surprise addition to the family fifteen years after Violet was born. Because of her mum's age Vi had pitched in a lot over the years, acting as a secondary parental figure as much as she was able.

"Why has no one fought back? That's what I want to know? Where are the Anarchists now?" The mention of my mother's group pulled my attention. What did Violet know about them? "They always said they'd stand up to injustices and where are they now? Cowering away in their homes, safe and sound in the inner zones I bet." She was angry, but still, I did not engage her in conversation as she stalked out of the room and returned with another bottle of wine. If I engaged, she'd stop sharing. It had happened to me so many times in the past. I was desperate to get to know more about her and this was the only way to keep the information coming. If I reminded her she was sharing, then she'd shut down. Forever protecting secrets I may never know about.

As she filled her glass to the brim, she carried on addressing the room. "Do you know why I was so mad at you yesterday?" I shook my head, too afraid to verbally respond. "My marriage ended because of cheating. And it just sucks that you would do that to Leo."

I couldn't hold in my words any longer, shock caused me to reply. "I have never cheated on Leo!" My voice was a little higher than I expected. She raised an eyebrow at me.

"Right."

"Rus is a friend. Nothing more."

"If I had a friend like that…"

"If you had a friend like that, you'd know I haven't had an affair." I stopped myself from continuing, aware I was teetering too close to a truth that was not mine to share. "I can be friends with an attractive man without having an affair with him you know? You manage it perfectly fine with Leo, don't you?" I didn't mean to spit the last point across the room so violently, but between the whispers in her sleep and the knowledge of Leo's secret, I was irked. I'd never been a woman who had doubts or insecurities but I had so much on my plate, they'd decided to join in.

She scoffed at my unspoken accusation. "Leo isn't quite as attractive as you think."

We both took a sip of our drinks before simultaneously letting out a barking laugh. Leo would have steam coming out of his ears at that comment. He wasn't vain per se, but he definitely knew how attractive he was.

To my surprise, she apologised first. "I'm sorry I assumed the worst. I should have known better."

"That's okay. We're both under a lot of stress." The second bottle was starting to empty and I decided to brave my chances at a conversation. "I'm sorry you had a rough time."

"Every marriage is rough." She shrugged nonchalantly, parroting comforting words she'd heard a hundred times.

"When were you married?" I recognised the fear in her eyes, it always seemed to creep in when she opened up. Maybe I'd finally gotten to the source of it. Maybe her ex was the reason she kept herself hidden in the shadows.

"I was very young. Too young. The day of my sixteenth birthday, in fact. But I was in love and I thought it's what had to happen. It's the next logical step when you're in love isn't it? To promise to do it forever." She shifted in her seat and I assumed she was making a move for bed, desperate to avoid further conversation. "I really did love him though. Still do probably."

"Why did it go wrong?"

"He wasn't built for marriage. It was a foreign concept to him. He cheated regularly and there was only so much I could forgive. We were deeply flawed together. Completely different people with opposing beliefs." She shrugged sadly and wrapped her hands around the nearly empty wine glass. "I still see him sometimes. It was tough for him to not be part of the family anymore. He was very close to Ada."

"That's very mature of you."

"It's the fairest thing for everyone."

I wanted to ask her more, get to know this part of her history whilst she was an open book. But she just looked so defeated. The trip down memory lane had just reminded her of what she'd lost and what she was missing whilst Nomad's Land was on lockdown.

"You know that I'll do anything I can to get Nomad's reopened?"

She smiled at me, stood and motioned for me to follow suit. Pulling me into a tight hug, she whispered, "I know you will."

# Chapter Nineteen

*Leo's leaning over me, calling my name.*
*The world around us seems so dark.*
*But he's there and I feel safe.*
*I can hear Franklin gurgling beside me.*
*Leo looks tired. His chest is heaving.*
*There are long and ragged lacerations on both sides of*
*his neck but, thankfully, no blood.*
*I look at him properly. Trying to convey my thoughts,*
*lungs burning too much to speak.*
*His eyes look different.*
*The pupils are narrow and grey.*
*Head injury.*
*I try to reach up to him but my arms are deeply bruised*
*and the muscles ache.*
*He leans down close to my ear and whispers.*
*"Don't trust -."*

I woke with a start before he could finish his
sentence. Sweat dripping from my brows, chin and the
small of my back.

Violet turned over sleepily towards me. It was still
dark out and the fake sound of ambience in the street
seemed louder and more offensive than ever.

"You okay?" she asked in a murmur, not really
awake.

"Bad dream. I'm okay." She nodded with her eyes
already closed and turned over and fell back into a deep
sleep.

I pulled the duvet around myself tighter, despite
my high body temperature. So, that was the voice in my

gut that kept me silent. It was Leo. But who did he mean? As I lay there running through the images over and over, I came back to the words he left me. What worked? What worked and who shouldn't I trust?

Leo, what have you gotten us into?

I lay there until the sun came up and Violet stirred. I heard Laura pad into Franklin's room to check on him. Life was continuing as normal whilst I felt like my whole world had been knocked sideways once again.

Going through the motions was something I was a dab hand at now, so nobody questioned how I was feeling as I made small talk over coffee, got Franklin dressed for the day or as I mindlessly scrolled through my phone in the car. Any verbal queues I missed were dismissed by the two women in my life as a symptom of my tireless work ethic and I didn't care enough to correct them.

It was an easy routine to stick to as we slid on our masks and made our way to our lab. All staff were under the strict instructions not to interact with us and that suited me fine. Our usual coffee order was waiting for us on our desks.

"I guess there is a perk to this whole situation," Violet remarked as she took a sip from her cup. I nodded and checked the lab's logs. The new nightly routine had been adhered to, hourly remote incineration and zero access from any personnel.

My screen asked me to review the CCTV footage. I couldn't think of anything I wanted to do less, but as per the agreements Violet signed, I had no choice. The past twenty-four hours were played before me in quick speed, the whole process taking less than twenty minutes. I added my fingerprint to the sign off sheet to state that I'd complied with all requests, and finally, our day could begin.

It was the exact same routine as yesterday. We stared at the computerised samples on-screen until our eyes ached and our brains stopped. We laughed at ridiculously unfunny things out of despair. Then, at lunchtime, a bell rang out in the lab. We stared at each other, it was a totally new sound to us.

"An agent is here to see you, Doctor Hanson," came an electronic voice from the ceiling. Female, as usual.

As expected Agent Cherry stood next to my desk. Somehow she'd managed to find a black mask with red accents. This woman's coordination knew no bounds.

"Agent Cherry."

"Doctor Hanson."

We exchanged new found formalities and she placed a locked case upon my desk.

"New samples. Once your current assignment is complete, this is your next task." She gritted her teeth. Knowing that for once I had the upper hand. That right now, in our current situation, I outranked her. "Please," she added.

"Do we need to leave a tip?" Violet called from inside the lab. I didn't need to turn to look at her to see the smirk on her face. I felt it in her words. We felt untouchable and we were both growing to like it.

"Make sure you lock it away." With that she turned and clipped away. I picked up the case and did as commanded. If it hadn't been for the CCTV, I'd have opened it before we finished our current project. The excitement was back in my stomach, these would be the virus samples. We could start working on a vaccine as soon as we were done. If we weren't being monitored, I would have brought in the sample Rus acquired for me, I could have given us a head start on the work on a cure. But how would I explain it to the State? What punishment would they dish out to us for stealing a sample? It was okay though. Now we had the official sample. Soon the real work could begin.

Violet felt the same as me and it was with renewed energy that we returned to our task. Three more hours of silently staring at a screen passed before Violet let out an excited gasp.

"There. There. Look there." She jabbed her finger against the screen passionately. It quivered under her touch and the image momentarily disappeared.

We held our breath as we waited for it to reboot.

"There." Her voice was an excited whisper, as though she was afraid adding volume would cause the machine to malfunction again.

I peered towards the image that had caused her such excitement. She was right. There was a difference. A teeny tiny shadow of a difference in the cell. Anybody else would have dismissed it as a speck of dust that had infiltrated the sample, but she knew better. She'd won the game.

The bell rang again.

"An agent will be here in an hour to collect your findings."

It was unnerving to realise that we were being watched in real-time. That somebody had overheard our mindless jokes to keep morale up. Violet looked up at the ceiling crossly. Clearly, she felt irritated that her moment to celebrate had been interrupted. Me? I was relieved that, finally, we could get on with the real task at hand. Saving lives with our vaccine. If we were quick enough, we could outpace the State's plan to use what we'd dubbed the 'Death Test'.

Two fresh coffees and a pile of sandwiches had appeared on our desks and we tucked in as we typed up our findings ready for collection. With every word I completed I found the excitement in my chest growing. Task one would be complete as soon as the handover was done. Looking at the clock, we only had two hours until we had to be finished for the day.

I'd never had someone dictate my working hours before, it was strange. Normally, after a breakthrough like this one, we'd order take away and stay late into the night checking our findings and hypothesising about their implications. But not today. Not tonight.

We were to be ejected from our lab at exactly five pm and weren't allowed to return until eight in the morning at the earliest.

As the agent took away the samples and the reports, I comforted myself with the fact that we'd at least get to open the new samples and learn our directive. It meant we could start tomorrow morning on the front foot, which increased our chances of success.

"It's your turn," I offered to Violet, pushing the case towards her. She opened it up eagerly and then her face fell.

She slid the paperwork towards me and moved to place two test tubes into our computer so everything would be uploaded by the morning.

It was another game of spot the difference. No sample of the virus. Just two more human samples to study. I couldn't help myself as I kicked my foot against the desk in frustration. It was immature but it did make me feel better.

Now we were to study two samples from the same human. One from before infection with the virus and one from after. We were to locate the ways; if any, that the virus had affected the patient on a cellular level.

It wasn't even a sample from a current sufferer. At least with that we could have extracted some information about the virus to file away. No, it was from someone who had fully recovered.

"But how did they recover so quickly? The virus was only discovered days ago?" I couldn't help my mouth as it spilled out the words my brain had been considering since the first samples arrived. How were any of these examples able to exist given the maturity of the virus? It was theoretically impossible.

"I guess it wasn't really discovered until people started to die?" she offered in response, not turning to look at me as she fiddled with the keyboard.

"Something about this isn't right," I thought out loud. "It doesn't make sense." My brain craved logic, and it was crying out at the ridiculousness of the situation. "It's impossible."

"It's improbable. Nothing is impossible. You taught me that." Finally, she turned to look at me. Her brows were pinched and her throat was constricted. Clearly, she was as annoyed as me but she had the good sense to remember we were being monitored. "You promised you would do whatever it took, and this is what it's going to take."

"Well, whatever we need to do to help, eh?" I offered up for the benefit of the hidden microphones in the room. "Are you okay to oversee the upload alone? I'd like to get back in time to give Franklin his dinner if possible."

I'd used the excuse of Franklin knowing she wouldn't be able to refuse me. What kind of a person would refuse a mother some time with her child? I also knew that, on the surface, as my words were noted and recorded somewhere, they were a natural request. Something that couldn't be questioned in any court of law.

She nodded, absent from the conversation as I turned to leave. I gave thought to popping downstairs to visit Rus. But I knew that would just bring trouble to both our doors, so I decided against it.

If Laura was surprised to see me home early, she hid it well. Even though I knew she couldn't go anywhere, I told her she could have the rest of the day off.

Finally, I was alone with my son. I pulled him in close to me, he seemed so much heavier than before. My phone rang twice as I felt his chest rise and fall gently against mine, so I let it go to voicemail. Holding Franklin was more important to me in this moment than anything the outside world had to offer. I wasn't known for my maternal instinct, to be honest, mothering my son didn't come naturally to me. But loving him did. I forgave myself for a lot of failures because I knew the true extent of my feelings for him. No matter what anybody, even Leo, ever thought.

He was such a hands-on dad. Talking and laughing with Franklin since the day we brought him home. I'd never forget the excitement in his voice as he carried him upstairs and showed him his bedroom for the first time. I sat downstairs, slightly detached from the situation, but still, listening to the love in his voice had brought a smile to my shell-shocked face.

I sat peacefully for at least an hour as he fell asleep in my arms. My phone started ringing again, determined to interrupt my afternoon. Laura appeared at the foot of the stairs. In another life that girl could have been a ninja, I never heard her appear.

My skin bristled as she reached down to take my baby out of my arms. I must have let my feelings seep onto my face as she took a step back empty-handed. Having proved my point about who the mother in our living situation was, I stood up and handed my son to her. She nodded at me slightly, aware of my silent reprimand, and took Franklin upstairs to place him in his cot.

With a sigh, I picked up my phone and dialled into my messages. All my calls were from Jack, but he only left one note.

"Paige, I'm aware of your current work situation. Which, by the way, I wish you'd consulted with me about before signing. But because of current circumstances both in the world and your professional life, I've been advised to let you know that Leo's case has been put on hold whilst everyone deals with, and this is a direct quote, 'more' pressing matters. I'm sorry."

I couldn't bring myself to hang up. Eventually, the phone line did it automatically for me. I was in shock. More pressing matters? More. Pressing. Matters.

The three words rattled around in my brain, replacing the ones that had taken up home in there after my dream last night.

I tried to click on the social media icon on my phone but my account had been disabled. Credit where credit was due, the government were thorough when it came to their non-disclosure agreements. All I wanted to do was talk to my mum. It was a strange sensation to long for someone so absent from my life, but what I craved in that moment was her company. Her chaos. She'd make this right somehow.

As if scripted Violet walked through the door and before she could greet me, I was sobbing in her arms. It was cathartic. She held me weakly at first, but soon, her grip on me was tight and I felt the dampness of her silent tears on my shoulder.

"He's. Not. Important," I gasped between sobs. "They. Don't. Care."

"I don't understand," she replied as she peeled me off of her. "What's happened?"

"They've paused his case. They have more pressing matters." I felt like those three words were bile, regurgitated and swallowed again.

"They've stopped looking for him?" she asked, looking shocked.

"He isn't their most pressing matter." Those words again. They burned my throat.

She pulled me in again for another hug. There was less passion and grief in our embrace this time.

"But he's my most pressing matter." My voice was fragile. I would fall to pieces if she didn't respond correctly.

"Are you hungry?" she asked gently. I shook my head. Ready to scream at the pointlessness of her question. She kissed me on the forehead, took me by the hand, and led me to my bed.

She laid down next to me, wrapped her arms around my waist as I lay on my side and sobbed. She stayed silent, stroking my hair and shushing my tears where necessary.

But she didn't move. She didn't speak. She just held me. Exactly what I needed.

Friends like that don't come along every day.

# Chapter Twenty

I woke up in the middle of the night, Violet sleeping soundly beside me, to find something hard pressing against my cheek. Groggily, I pulled my fist down from under my face and opened my palm.

The note Leo left on the picture frame.

I couldn't remember leaving my bed let alone making my way to the bathroom, standing on the toilet and retrieving the shard from inside the derelict extractor fan where it had lay hidden. I really was losing the plot.

Honestly, I meant to get up out of bed and return it to its hiding place. I really did. Instead, the physical comfort I felt from holding a memory of him close lulled me back to sleep all too easily.

When my eyes opened again, the sun was peeking through the gaps in my misaligned curtains. Every morning, I added adjusting them to my to-do list, and every day without fail, I realised the unimportance of such a task. My life was a never-ending to-do list of jobs that didn't really need doing. Violet was already moving around the bedroom, trying to be quiet. A cup of coffee was waiting for me on my bedside table. The aroma stirred my rested brain.

"Hey." Softly, she sat down next to me on the bed and stroked my hair. Usually, such a show of affection would cause nausea to rumble through my stomach but until faced with such a display of tenderness, I hadn't realised how much I'd missed physical contact.

"Hey," I replied, pulling myself into a sitting position against my pillows. "I'm sorry about last night." My defence mechanisms were beginning to creep back in as I was all too aware that Leo's handwriting was hidden beneath my back. No matter how good a friend she had been last night, I wasn't about to share this secret with her. This was one part of Leo I never intended to share with anyone.

"Don't be a dick," she scolded me softly. "It's okay to cry. It was nice to actually be there for you. I was beginning to worry."

"Worry about what?"

"Well, you. You've barely reacted since it happened."

"You can say his name."

"I'm just saying. Since Leo went missing, you haven't been -"

"Reacting correctly?" How quickly words of concern could hurt. I hadn't realised my friend had been monitoring my emotional output and found it lacking. Why did people feel so entitled to my tears?

"That's not what I meant."

"Am I supposed to mourn? What if he isn't dead? Am I supposed to hope? What if he isn't alive?" I couldn't stop the words as I vomited them across the bed and onto the carpet around her bare feet. "Why don't you tell me what everyone is expecting of me because at least then I will have some idea of how I'm supposed to feel. For once in my life, I'm completely clueless. I can barely even remember what happened." I snapped my mouth shut. The words were desperate to come out. They wrapped themselves around my vocal cords and tightened across my throat until they were choked free. "Every time I get close, it's taken away."

"Taken away?"

Pausing for a breath, I took control of my voice. The mistrust in my gut roared with disappointment and I felt heartburn begin to settle across my chest. "Every time I think I might remember something, I can't. I thought being back home would trigger something, it didn't. I thought standing in his office would open the flood gates, but it didn't. I thought staring at the few remaining photos of him would stir up some kind of epiphany, but guess what? It didn't. My mind is as empty of memories now as it was the day I woke up." I was back in the safe sanctuary of my lies. My voice had ebbed and flowed around the sentiments and frustration I described, Violet wasn't to know they were words I'd borrowed from a truth I wish I held. To be truly clueless would be as welcome as to have the full memory. This life of faded nightmares was beginning to weigh on me.

These memories that come in pieces don't help me. They don't help Leo. They're nothing more than an emotionally exhausting blank jigsaw. How I longed for the true amnesia I claimed.

*"They're going to kill us Paige. They're going to kill us after what I've done." I've never heard this tone come out of his mouth in all the years I've known him. I know in my very bones that he is telling the truth. That I have no choice but to flee with him.*

*"Who, Leo? Who's coming to kill us? Why would anyone want to kill us?" I can't help but question him. I know he's telling the truth but he's withholding information and I can't stand it. If I'm about to give up everything for this man, I deserve to know the full story. Franklin stirs and I pick him up, holding him close to my chest. Holding back tears as I gently kiss his head. I never wanted this life for you kid.*

*"I'll explain on the drive." He takes Franklin from my arms and moves to the front door. "We have five minutes. Please, just pack the bag and join me in the car."*

*"You will not take my son from me." My voice begins to prickle with anger. How dare he take my son!*

*"I will if it means he gets to live." With that he's gone, walking down the path towards an empty car that's parked haphazardly at the end of our front garden. I watch as he gently buckles our son into a car seat and quietly closes the car door. He's so prepared for this moment, he's got it all planned out. Then he moves to the boot, and with heavy shoulders, opens it and checks inside. I watch the emotions flit across his face, guilt, anger and hope.*

*"Leo..." I call after him pathetically but he can't hear me, my words are lost in the noise of the car boot being closed and locked.*

*I'm ten years old again. Watching my mother walk out of the house. Leaving me behind. That was the last time I saw her outside of a courtroom.*

Softly, Violet smiled at me and squeezed my hand. "I'm sorry if I've upset you," she offered. Two apologies in such a short span of time was unheard of. She really must be feeling guilty.

"Would you mind popping me some toast in? I could do with a cold shower." Grateful to be helpful, she left the room and I listened as she walked down the stairs flat-footed. She knew my home so well, I could hear as she skipped the one creaking step.

Before I could get up and hide the frame in its previous spot, I heard the bathroom door click closed. Laura must be taking a shower. I sat in my bed and listened to the boiler as it whirled and whistled, creating the hot water we all craved in the morning. The sound of the shower blast hitting the ceramic bathtub was therapeutic.

I thumbed Leo's words and looked around my room, searching for somewhere secure to store it. I couldn't make my way downstairs to the garden, remove the loose slab and place it in there for safe keeping. There were too many eyes in my house.

Hedging my bets, I stuffed the frame deep inside my pillowcase, shoving it all the way into the bottom corner, which I then tucked underneath the headboard. I tidied the rest of the sheets so everything looked neat and felt a sense of comfort that Leo would be waiting in bed for me when night came around again.

Violet reappeared with a plate of toast and another coffee. It felt nice to have somebody take care of me. She disappeared into the en-suite and I listened as she brushed her teeth and swore at her hair. She'd always complained about how thin and lifeless it was and I'd always retort that I'd prefer simply being able to brush my hair in the morning than having to tame my curls with an assortment of oils, butters and ointments.

Finally she re-emerged ready for the day. I mumbled through a full mouth that I'd be ten minutes. Which we both knew was an over-exaggeration. It was a good job she knew me so well as I had time to shower, dress, cuddle Franklin and do my make up before our car arrived.

Another day of overpriced spot-the-difference lay ahead of us.

# Chapter Twenty-One

It was easier than expected to locate what had changed between the two samples. It was glaringly obvious in every millimetre of the post-infection sample. The subject's entire biological makeup had shifted, it was unlike anything I'd ever seen before.

Which made sense given I wasn't familiar with the scientific practices of the Dwellers. But it was clear from the ramifications of their disease that they were advanced in ways we hadn't realised. The adrenal readings were off the chart in the post-disease sample. I hadn't seen readings like it even in the most advanced stages of Cushing's syndrome I'd ever come across.

Despite our early success, I couldn't shake the question from my mind that had been dismissed by Violet yesterday. How could someone have already caught the disease and recovered from it given it was only unleased upon us a few days ago?

An agent came around lunchtime to collect our findings and release us from our NDAs. Violet asked if she could go home but the only response she received was a steely gaze. Apparently, there were still those amongst the government agents who held a distaste for those from Nomad's Land. You'd think by now the prejudice would have been eradicated.

Before he left, he handed us four identity tags. One for each member of my household, including Franklin. I couldn't help but laugh, how ridiculous a request to ask a five-month-old to wear an identity necklace. Not only was it a choking hazard but what information did they hope to gain from him? It's not exactly like he was going to wander the neighbourhood breaking lockdown.

I left his tag in my desk drawer. If anyone ever asked, I'd state that I misplaced it. I was happy to comply with a lot of things but I wouldn't put my son at risk for anyone.

Violet disappeared from the lab for about half an hour after the agent departed. When she returned, the tip of her nose was red. She'd been crying. I went to put my arms around her but she nudged me away. The barriers we'd broken down between us last night were restored.

I sent her back to my house, telling her to call her mum and have a long chat and she readily accepted. The charges she'd incur on my phone bill were worth it for the brief smile she shot me as she left.

Finally alone in my workspace, I sat at the computer and logged onto my emails. It was so refreshing to hear from people I didn't live or work with that I didn't mind half the marketing emails or requests for work experience that normally caused my eyes to roll backwards.

Obviously the world wasn't happy giving me a moment of solitude and I heard the clip of Regina's heels approaching my peace. She peered around the corner before entering, she hadn't got the memo that the NDA was lifted. I gave thought to pretending it was still in place but even my formidable mother-in-law was considered good company at the moment.

"Regina," I greeted her, speaking first to let her know it was safe. As she cautiously took steps towards my desk, I noted a run in her tights. First the wrinkled shirt and now this. She really was letting her standards slip.

"Paige, how are you?" I was disarmed by the question. I'd expected her to ask after Franklin first. My surprise quickly disappeared as she removed my chance to respond. "How did your meeting go?"

Of course that's what she wanted to discuss. I'd only focused on my feelings since the day in the interview room. I'd completely forgotten that it was her son who was missing and not just my husband. My heart contracted as I put myself in her position, imagining not knowing where Franklin was and if he was dead or alive.

"They haven't found, you know, him though. There's still hope." Compassion made me stumble over my words as I tried to find the right thing to say. In any situation, there was always the right thing to say. The words to appease someone. Finally, the words came to me. "He's still out there, Regina, I know it."

"I know he is," she seemed so certain of her statement that it broke me a little. Her hope was stronger than mine by miles. She hadn't even begun to give up on him, whereas, with every day that passed, my resolve chipped away. Soon there would be nothing left. "I have to tell you something," she began, taking a deep breath in preparation for the unburdening she was about to undertake.

She was interrupted by another set of heels clipping up the corridor towards us. Agent Cherry appeared in the doorway like the grim reaper, ready to take the companionship we'd experienced out of the air and into the grave.

"Paige Hanson." The way she spoke my name turned the air in my lungs to ice. "You're under arrest for the murder of Leo Hanson."

Regina gasped, her hand flew to her mouth and in shock I studied her fingernails. Her usual French manicure was chipped and her thumbnail had been chewed into oblivion. The pandemic and Leo were weighing heavy upon her.

Agent Cherry's words hadn't sunk in completely but I knew she was serious when Jack came hurtling into the room, panting for breath.

"Paige, don't say anything," he urged, moving to stand by my side.

"You do not have to say anything. But anything you do say can and will be used against you in the government's court."

The government's court? That was the top court in our country, reserved only for the most severe of crimes. Known for dealing out the harshest punishments possible without needing a jury of peers.

"Drop the intimidation, Agent Cherry. My client will comply." I nodded at her in agreement with his statement. Like a child, I couldn't find the words to describe how I felt. My emotions were too big and too scary to name.

"Murder?" asked Regina. Everyone had forgotten she was there. "You've found Leo?"

Agent Cherry considered her question for a moment, looking into the eyes of a frantic mother missing her son. "An agent will be by to brief you on the case after Mrs Hanson is in custody." Regina nodded and I noticed the fire of hope return to her eyes. I was glad I wouldn't be around to see it extinguished.

"Franklin," I spoke to Jack. "Franklin needs to stay with Violet."

If my mother-in-law had any arguments against my wishes, she did not voice them. She had enough respect in the moment, but I knew without a doubt she'd take Violet to court anyway to contest parental rights once my fate was decided. I knew that however temporarily; his Auntie Violet would provide him a safe and stable home full of love and laughter. There was no one more suited to take my place.

"Mrs Hanson." Agent Cherry placed a pair of electronic cuffs across my wrist. They burnt ever so slightly and I knew from my mother's experience that they would leave a permanent scar. Just another way our society shamed those who hadn't yet been proven guilty.

"I am placing you under arrest for the murder of Leo Hanson and for perjury in an ongoing investigation."

# Chapter Twenty-Two

If I thought being marched in for questioning was tough, it had nothing on arriving at the station as an alleged murderer.

Masked members of the press snapped my photo outside and got into a verbal dispute with Jack. He was at my side like a comforting shadow with every step. Holding my arm ready for when my legs would eventually give way in shock at what was occurring around me.

I was a murderer.

Or at the very least, I was suspected of being a murderer.

What happened, Leo? What happened?

The officers booking me in no longer hid their disgust behind concerned smiles.

"Nomad's never respect the law," I heard a venomous whisper behind me as Agent Cherry guided me into a waiting room.

"I'll have your badge for comments like that," she hissed behind us as she closed the door. She still had at least an ounce of respect for me, or if not that, a zero-tolerance policy on discrimination.

Once again, the three of us sat around a table but this time there was no friendly offering of a drink. The intensity of the cuffs began to grow, somebody out in the control room was playing with the settings. I refused to wince even as I felt blisters form. There was no way I'd give them any pleasure in seeing my pain. I'd learnt very young to never allow bullies to see the damage their hatred caused.

"Mrs Hanson," she began the recording. Jack's hand was openly on mine on top of the table. If she thought anything of it, she didn't let on. "We've found a body in the lake. It matches your husband's description."

A sob escaped from my throat. She looked at me with interest and made a note.

"A single gunshot wound was found in his back."

"Has it been confirmed that it's Mr Hanson?" Asked Jack, always the defender.

"We have no other missing people in the area, Mr Wright." Barely a response. Rus's formal identification report clearly hadn't been undertaken yet.

"Why is my client under suspicion?"

"How do you know Rus, Mrs Hanson?" She ignored Jack's response and it became clear to me just what had happened.

A classic trope - the gold-digging wife kills husband to make way for new lover. I didn't need Jack to ask the next question. I'd already guessed the answer.

"To whom are you referring?" Jack asked.

"Her work colleague, Honorius."

This whole situation could be cleared up so easily. So quickly. Just one confession and all suspicion would disappear. But it would mean the end of normality for Rus. For Theo. For Claire. For Rebecca.

Their entire lives would implode and I would be the sole finger on the trigger. For some of them, it could be worse than a disruption to their equilibrium, it could be the death penalty should there be evidence of my accusations. There was no doubt that the State would find the evidence should it not be given willingly.

I couldn't do it. Despite the charges currently against me, I wasn't a murderer. I wouldn't sentence my friends to death and a lifetime of shame simply for being who they were. I wasn't raised to behave like that. Besides, there was no evidence of this so-called affair. All they really had was a body and a motive. I trusted Jack enough to know he could pull one of those two pillars apart.

"I would never cheat on my husband," I spoke for the first time. "Rus wouldn't cheat on his wife either."

"I assume you have evidence of this motive?" They carried on their back and forth as though I'd never spoken.

"We have the gentleman in custody for questioning."

"So, that's a no?" His voice raised with passion. "Just to be clear, you have no identity on the body and no evidence of this motive?" She didn't reply. "What exactly are we doing here, Agent Cherry? As far as I can see, this entire arrest has been unlawful."

"We'll now transport you to your cell." She ignored Jack, instead speaking directly to me. He slammed his hands on the table, I watched and waited as it steadied itself.

"This is an outrage. She's leaving with me."

The door clicked open and four officers were waiting in the corridor.

"If you don't agree with my decision, Jack, you are more than welcome to appeal to a judge. In fact, I suggest you leave now to get a head start. Mrs Hanson will remain with me here at the station."

He was lost for words as two officers placed their hands on his arms and guided him towards the door.

"This is illegal!" he shouted, unable to break free from their grasp. "Paige, I'll get you out. I promise!"

With that, he was gone and I was alone with Agent Cherry. Left to her mercy. She stood and motioned for me to follow. There was no manhandling of me. We were followed to the cell by the remaining two officers but everyone was quiet. Keeping their distance, as if the idea of existing in the same vicinity as me was disgusting.

As she closed the metal door behind me, she paused at the bars. "When we get confirmation of the body, I will come back and let you know." She thought she was doing me a kindness. Returning to tell me in person that my husband was dead. How empathetic of her. She clipped away out of the corridor flanked by the two burly officers, her obedient little shadows.

One of the officers turned the radio on as he left, specifically so I could hear the precinct talking about me.

"Black widow."

"Murderer."

"Who did she think she was kidding?"

And so on.

Looking at the seat on offer in my cell, I chose to sit on the floor instead, it seemed cleaner somehow.

Leo is dead.

My Leo.

Dead.

I knew Jack would already be doing whatever he could to help and yet I couldn't get my head around the fact that I needed a lawyer to prove that I didn't murder my husband. It was either that or throw my friend to the wolves simply for loving someone.

By now, Violet would have had to answer a hundred calls on my mobile as the news spread. Would she accept responsibility for Franklin? Would she be strong enough to hold onto him despite Regina's lawyers?

If I could just remember. If I could just remember that night I could prove my innocence. But everything was so fragmented. Nothing made sense.

What worked, Leo?

I still don't understand what worked.

You could have been clearer. You could have left me more detail to work with. How hard would it have been to write me a letter that contained more than two words? Two words that meant nothing to me but everything to you, apparently.

Anger and resentment flew around me like birds before a storm. It was easier to be angry than to accept the truth of the situation. Leo was gone. I'd never be able to ask him what worked, or what happened to us that night. I'd never be able to rely on him to help raise Franklin. I'd never get to kiss him again. He was gone.

This was the end of our story.

# Chapter Twenty-Three

Despite my lacking memories, I was certain that I had nothing to do with Leo's death. To begin with, I'd never touched a gun in my life let alone owned one. That at least they wouldn't be able to fabricate.

"Do you have the licence?" a female voice asked on the radio.

"Yes, we have the firearm records," answered a strong male voice. They were torturing me. I wouldn't be surprised to learn that the two voices were sat together in the same room, having the conversation over the radio purely for my ears.

What firearm licence? What records? They couldn't possibly be talking about me.

"It's a match, sir," the female voice crackled over the airwaves again. The volume on the radio rose as someone turned it up.

"Hello! Who's there?" I called out to the emptiness. There was no response and no further chat on the radio to give me any further inkling of the fate I'd been dealt.

Exhaustion began to swim over me as the adrenaline from the last few hours left my body. Resting my head on the wall, my eyes fluttered closed and open for a good few minutes. What I wouldn't give for a cup of coffee to sharpen my mind and spirits. I'd even take a brew of the worst waiting room mix right now. I gazed out of the tiny window in my cell with glazed eyes, trying to focus on anything to keep myself awake. Shock was setting in and I couldn't let it snatch me away from this moment. It was important that I stayed sharp, that I said and did the right things in order to prove my innocence.

"Visitor approaching the precinct, sir," the radio sprung to life again.

Jack. Jack was finally back and would make everything okay. He always did.

I pulled myself up to stand, using the basin as leverage. My back and knees cracked and groaned under the stress. I couldn't wait to collapse into my own bed. Feeling like a small child, I pressed my face up against the window, desperate to catch sight of his silhouette, knowing that everything would be okay once I caught sight of him.

"It's L - " the radio crackled with interference, I paid it no real attention as I tried to press the wrinkles from my trousers with my hand. It was no use; they were deeply set.

"Hanson. Sir," the radio continued. So, they were talking about me again. No matter, soon I would be back home where their hateful words couldn't hurt me.

"It's Leo Hanson, sir," came the voice on the radio again.

My blood began to heat and my legs gave way from beneath me. Leo. He was here. I began to gasp for air as anxiety took hold of my lungs and months of grief washed out of my system. He'd come back to me. Finally. He was here.

I could see him. I could see him walking up the stairs towards the precinct's entrance.

"Leo!" I screamed, banging with renewed strength against the tiny reinforced glass. "Leo!" Hysteria took me over, I just needed him to look at me, I needed him to know that I was alright. That I was waiting.

I held my eyes open for as long as possible as I screamed and pounded against the wall. If I blinked, I could miss him and he was so close to walking out of my view line.

"Leo!" I called one last time. The universe was finally on my side as he paused and looked around as though somehow my voice had made its way through the concrete to his ears. He wasn't close enough for me to make out any of his features but I could tell from his stance, the way his shoulders were pulled back that he was furious. Furious at the way I had been treated. Maybe furious at himself for taking so long to come back to me. It didn't matter. We could talk about it all when we got home.

He lifted a hand to his face, shielding his eyes from the sun. Like a miracle, he looked in my direction.

I hopped up and down on the spot, waving at him through the murky window, grinning from ear to ear, hoping he could sense my joy despite the distance between us. Like a schoolgirl fan in front of her rock star crush, when he waved at me, I thought I might faint with excitement.

Then he moved out of view, coming into the building, coming to make everything right. I knew that we'd have a lot to talk through tonight. He would have to explain his disappearance and I would finally explain my past. I would finally let him see the parts of me I'd kept locked away for so long, the parts that since his disappearance had started to rear their ugly head.

There was a sharp whistle from outside my window followed by a loud thud.

"Active shooter," came the warning.

"Active shooter, get down."

"Back-up needed."

"From the roof."

"Get down!"

"Paramedics, we need paramedics."

"We have eyes on them."

Two more sharp whistles followed by thuds. Silence on the radio.

"Do you copy?"

"Do you copy?" the same voice said over and over.

"Come in. Come in."

The voice grew more desperate until, finally, I heard a scream from above me.

Sirens approached from all around, it was deafening to listen to their chorus. I could see bright lights in the night sky, the army were here.

Nobody came to talk to me. To explain what had happened. I waited and waited. I called out to them.

But nobody cared. Exhaustion eventually won its war with my anxiety and I passed out into a nightmare-filled sleep.

I awoke in a heap on the floor to the sound of my cell door being opened. Jack stood in front of me, his face grey.

"Paige..." he began, offering me a hand to stand up.

"Leo's here, Jack. They have him here somewhere. We have to help him." My words come out all at once, frantic and hopeful in equal measures.

"Leo's dead, Paige."

I shook my head. He didn't understand. He wasn't aware of what I had seen.

"No, I saw him. He's come here for me."

His shoulders sagged as he comprehended our misunderstanding.

"He did come here for you." I shook my head at him, not wanting him to continue. "Somebody shot him on the stairs before he could make it inside. He's gone, Paige."

He held me as I screamed.

# Chapter Twenty-Four

I never wanted to wear colour more than I did the morning of Leo's funeral.

He would have hated the sea of black that waited for him at the church. All he ever wanted was for life to be colourful and bright. It had been the focus of so many of our disagreements and now, more than ever, I wish I had given in on more than just the odd occasion.

Regina had pulled some strings and allowed me to view the body before he was locked inside the coffin. Agent Cherry had tried to put as many roadblocks in the way as possible but my mother-in-law was back to her roaring best and I was granted ten minutes alone with him.

Surprisingly no tears came from my eyes during those ten minutes. Maybe I was finally cried out or maybe my scientific brain kicked in but either way, all I could do with that time was study him. Commit him to memory in so many different small details.

I counted every early wrinkle around his lips. Noted the number of laughter lines around his eyes. Wondering how many I'd helped place there. Took a mental photo of each and every freckle upon his skin. I thought I knew his face but now I was sure of it.

I held his hand in mine, examining his fingernails which had been tidied and trimmed. It would have been the first manicure he ever had, preferring instead to gnaw the nails down to the beds whilst we watched the latest instalment of whatever show we were bingeing. I used to scold him for it. Tell him the noise turned my stomach. Now I'd give anything to hear it again.

I stroked the callouses that grew from his knuckles. A sign he had spent a lifetime making notes. I turned his hand over in mine and gazed at the palm. These palms had saved so many lives. Had given back so many lives. And now they were empty of their own. I traced the lines on his palm, drawing the pattern in my mind so I could always conjure them to memory.

There was a light drizzling of stubble upon his face and chin, it added to his features. Why had he never tried growing a beard? Had I told him not to? I couldn't remember us ever discussing it. Maybe it didn't interest him. But he would have looked good with a beard. I wished I could tell him that now. I wished I could tell him how handsome he was, how kind he was, how clever he was and how much I loved him. I wished I could apologise for every fight, every cross word or rolled eyes. I wished until my chest ached from the pressure of a thousand memories never to be.

Somebody had dressed him in a black turtle neck. His least favourite item of clothing. He'd had several drunken rants about how much he hated turtlenecks. They were too constricting. Made his head look like it was floating. Itchy. I'd laughed so hard each and every time as he grew more and more passionate. Then we'd stumble upstairs to our room, lie together in the dark and try to invent clothing that was more ridiculous than a turtle neck.

Nobody else would ever understand those stories or that joy. It wouldn't make sense if shared with somebody who wasn't present. They wouldn't get the humour, wouldn't grasp the jokes. Sharing moments like that removed some of the shine from them.

I apologised to him for his attire. Had I known I would have brought a shirt with me. Maybe I could ask Regina if she could sort one out before he was sealed away? People seemed to be listening to her once again.

Leo had a small birthmark on the left-hand side of his neck. It was shaped like the ace of spades but was so minuscule that even his hairdresser had never noticed it. It was my favourite part of him because it was all mine.

That was the last thing I needed to see. The last thing I needed to remind myself of. Peering around myself just to confirm I was alone, I slowly peeled the neck of the turtle neck down an inch. I just wanted to kiss that mark one last time.

There on his neck was a laceration. Just like in my dreams. I slipped my fingers further into his turtleneck and counted. Three on his left-hand side. I repeated the process on the right-hand side and, sure enough, there were three there.

My nose pressed against his flesh as I peered as closely as I could into the exposed mark. It was healed and there appeared to be layers of flesh inside of it. Vomit rose in my stomach as I snapped back to reality. I was probing my dead husband's body like he was just another cadaver in my lab.

I'm sorry Leo. That was disrespectful. I rolled the neck back to its rightful place and leaned over him, gently placing a kiss on his forehead. "I'll never forget you," I whispered. "Franklin will never forget you, I promise."

*My lungs begin to burn and I gasp for breath.*
*There is water everywhere.*
*I'm trapped back in the seatbelt.*
*Leo moves towards me, gently placing his hands either side of my head as he breathes oxygen into my mouth.*
*My fingers reach up towards his neck as I watch the lacerations open and close.*
*Impossible.*
*Gills.*

Regina was at my side.

"It's time to leave." She looked down sadly at her only son lying cold in the coffin.

As we walked out of the room, we heard the bang of the lid closing followed by the drill as they sealed it for eternity. It was too late to change his shirt. It was too late to make it right.

We held each other's hands all the way back to the car.

Now it was the day of the funeral. I looked at myself in the mirror, there was a deodorant stain on the hip of my black dress. Absentmindedly, I rubbed at it. I hadn't heard Regina let herself into my bedroom but she had a damp cloth and rubbed it against the stain, removing it from existence.

She turned me around to face her, I noticed a loose hair on her head and tucked it back into place for her. We looked at each other, words inadequate.

We held each other tight, drawing strength from our mutual devastation, and then left the house for the waiting car.

# Chapter Twenty-Five

"Nothing lasts forever," that's what my mother used to tell me when I cried.

The pain in my chest. Nothing lasts forever.

The loss in the air. Nothing lasts forever.

My marriage. Nothing lasts forever.

I repeated the mantra to myself throughout the entire funeral.

Imagining it in my mother's voice, wishing she was sat beside me holding my other hand. Regina linked her fingers between mine as soon as we sat in the front seats. As though we could share and draw strength from each other through physical connection. As the service reached its crescendo, she let go of me to openly weep into a hanky. Nothing lasts forever.

The thing that struck me most when we walked in was the emptiness. Only hospital staff were permitted to attend as we were the only ones legally able to leave our houses. It wasn't right. He deserved more than this. This room should be full of broken hearts. There was anger in my stomach at the unfairness of it all. Nothing lasts forever.

As his coffin got vaporised in the chamber and we watched his ashes be shot up into the atmosphere, I imagined him visiting again the next time a storm rolled in. We were headed into our warm spell so it could be months until we were reunited. Nothing lasts forever.

Returning home, Franklin greeted me with a gummy smile and giggle. He was six months old and despite my increasing absence from his life, I was still the centre of his world.

Nothing lasts forever.

# Chapter Twenty-Six

I called Rus for the fifth time after the funeral once Regina had left. I knew being arrested for our supposed affair must have been tough for him, but it was no excuse to miss my husband's funeral. He hadn't even sent the customary flowers when the news broke.

Every evening I waited, expecting him to turn up with a bottle of something strong and a few leaves from his tobacco plant. But the door never knocked. He didn't care. To think I had been willing to be a suspect in Leo's murder to protect his secret and he couldn't even muster up the energy to check in on me.

I was angry and I let his voicemail have the full extent of my rage. After all, I had no other outlet for it. The Dweller who'd murdered Leo had been arrested and hung without trial. Justice was served. All there was left to do was adjust to the new normal. To accept it and move on. I had to accept my new role in society, I had to behave like the widow they expected me to be, I had to comply to acceptable behaviour if I wanted to keep the life I'd fought so hard for.

I found Violet sat on the edge of my bed, staring out of the window quietly sobbing. Today must have been hard for her. She loved Leo too.

"Violet?" She turned to look at me. Her skin was ashen, there were dark bags under her eyes and her lips were trembling. She handed me her phone. An e-mail was open from the hospital containing an update on our research.

We'd both been granted a bonus for our quick response to the national crisis and our work was to be used to help protect those whom we had highlighted as vulnerable. They were to take part in a State shielding program in three of the biggest hotels that the State had available.

Just like the rest of us, they would be supplied with their weekly care packages of essentials, but other than that choreographed delivery no outside contact would be permitted until a vaccine was in place. It was a brilliant plan and would save hundreds of lives. They'd become their own little communities, taking care of each other and, in turn, when we emerged from this, perhaps the tolerance they'd learnt would seep out into the general public.

Thanks to the identity chips we'd all been given, the government had been quickly able to call on the DNA samples collected in them to locate those who were most vulnerable and get them to safety.

Violet was obviously feeling overwhelmed at going from such a low at the funeral to such a high at our work being so successful. The last few weeks had been particularly draining.

"It's good news." I sat down next to her and put her phone down at my side. She stared at me blankly, tears still running down her face. "We've saved so many lives." I felt a warmth around me. "Leo would be proud of us."

She swallowed deeply and straightened her spine.

"My mum was on that list." Her sentence lingered in the air between us. "She wasn't supposed to be on that list," she added, this time sounding angry. Which I could understand. Life was cruel and unfair, a lesson it seemed determined to drill into my soul.

"She'll be safer there than anywhere else." The State's words felt foreign on my tongue. It wasn't what I wanted to say. I wanted to rage alongside her, I wanted to question once again where the samples had come from, I wanted somebody to blame for the virus. Someone to blame for Leo. It wasn't possible, however. Not yet anyway. All we could do was hope that our President really did have our best interests at heart this time.

She took a deep breath before she revealed more. "They want to put Ada into care." She was worried about her mum of course, but mostly, she was worried about the implications for her sister who was now all alone in Nomad's Land.

"Can't you apply for temporary guardianship?" Feebly I tried to offer a solution that, deep down, I knew wasn't feasible.

Her voice was hollow now, with just a hint at building internal rage. "It's not my civic duty to go home and look after her. I'm needed here near the lab. And they won't let her travel across the border in case she's infected. I can't let the State find her."

"State care isn't all bad -" I went to reveal a little of my past to her, to bring her some comfort that spending even a month in a State-approved home wouldn't permanently damage Ada. It had barely damaged me after all.

"She's half-Dweller," she spat the truth across the room as though it were acid. Ready to erode the relationship between us. So, that was her big secret. This was what she had been protecting for all of these years. The reason why she kept herself off the radar and out of public interest. Her sister was, what the hateful would call, a half breed.

I couldn't hide the shock from my face, and she looked crushed as she mistook it for judgement. I knew I had to fix this moment before it defined our friendship forever. I knew I had to be brave.

"My step-father was a Dweller," I offered up a nugget of truth from my long-buried past. It was the only way I could let her know how much I understood. "Well, an unofficial step-father."

My mother had decided after my dad left that she would never make the mistake of marriage again. It didn't matter that it would actually be illegal for her to marry a Dweller, she'd made up her mind and no matter how kind Kyan was to us, she wouldn't entertain even the fantasy of a white dress. Or at least that had been the case until she met Jack.

Kyan was in my life for a solid three years before, one day, he simply disappeared. My mum didn't like to speak of him after that. Whenever I tried to broach the subject, she'd simply walk away from me to another room. Once, when I'd been particularly incessant with my queries, she walked out of the house and didn't come back for half an hour. That was the last time I asked after him. I had an inkling as to where he had gone, I knew he would never leave us voluntarily.

My suspicions were proved right when two months after Kyan left, my mum orchestrated the attack that would eventually land her in prison. The raid on the medical centre in Nomad's Land. From the outside, it looked like any other treatment centre, albeit a very heavily guarded one. I'd heard whispers at school of the nightmares that lived within those walls.

One girl swore blind that she'd witnessed a Dweller being dragged through the doors, blood gushing from a head wound. In the dead of night, sometimes I couldn't get that image out of my head.

I couldn't get my imagination to switch off from the horrors that I knew were being inflicted upon the prisoners inside. Because that's what it was after all, a prison dressed up as a treatment centre. Dwellers went in but they never came out.

To this day, I didn't believe that she never meant for anyone to get hurt. She could paint whatever picture she liked for the press but I was the only true witness to the fury that had built around her over those eight weeks. She knew exactly what she was doing.

My confession had done the trick. Violet now looked relieved instead of defensive. As though she'd finally found someone who could understand how her mother had fallen for a Dweller.

"What was his name?" she asked me.

"Kyan." I was enjoying my walk down memory lane. It was so difficult keeping all these secrets. Do you have any idea how hard it is to have a memory full of everything that has ever happened to you? Every argument or ill-timed comment. Every vile word that had left your lips. Every insult you'd received in return, verbatim. If I let myself focus on everything I could remember from my years on this planet, my mind would surely break. It was a constant struggle to keep elements of it locked away for my own sanity.

"Helsa?" she enquired.

Of course she knew him. Or at least knew of his ancestors. The Helsa family had become one of the national villains of the war. We were never told why they hated us so viciously but they themselves had made it very clear that their passion for our blood had never waned over the years. Consistently at the forefront of every daily battle they seemed invincible. I was surprised they hadn't been blamed for the virus yet.

But Kyan hadn't been like that. Not in the slightest.

Sure, he was abnormally tall. All Dwellers were. Yes, his overall stature and resting facial expression was on immediate impact intimidating. And yes, the colour of his eyes had scared me the first time we met. What child wouldn't be scared of meeting the nearest thing possible to a giant, with black slitted irises sat in eyes that turned up at an unnatural angle around his nose surrounded by a face adorned in stark white scars?

Even someone who had been brought up to be as open-minded as me still quivered when he appeared in the house for the first time. To be honest with you, it took a few regular visits before his presence no longer caused a weight in my stomach. I'd been taught so many violent stories in school about his kind and it was hard to shake the suspicion and hatred.

But he was patient with me. Waited for me to approach him.

Laughed softly when I asked if I could touch his long black hair. I'd been fascinated by the way it seemed to glow in certain lights. He held his arms out towards me, offering to lift me up for an inspection. My mother's smile was hopeful and I couldn't resist.

I could tell how gentle he was being with me as he lifted me up above his head. I had to duck down to make sure I didn't bang myself on the ceiling. He held me like that for twenty minutes as I slowly combed my fingers through his hair. That was the first time I'd studied something and it sparked off an interest in the world around me that, to this day, hadn't been quelled.

His arms didn't shake once as he held me safely and securely. I remembered realising just how strong he must be for his muscles to withstand that repetitive position. My mum's muscles started to shake and weaken after about two minutes of holding me above her head when we played. She wasn't a weak woman either.

"Yes. Kyan Helsa." I waited for the judgement or questions. We'd all studied the family at school but there were still many gaps in our overall knowledge of them.

"Ada's dad was a Helsa." We stared at each other in shock and then laughed as was often the way when the world handed you an impossible coincidence. "Kyan was his uncle."

"Looks like the world always wanted us to be family." For a moment, we'd forgotten all the sadness around us. Forgotten about her mum. Forgotten about the virus. Forgotten about Leo. We were always destined to be family.

As it always does, reality returned, hitting us both at the same time. It felt like we were pinned to the bed. A shared connection from our past couldn't erase anything from our present.

"Will Ada be okay?" I spoke first, desperate to concentrate on her sadness rather than my own.

Trying to be hopeful, she smiled out of the window. "Her dad will fetch her when he's able."

"Is her dad still in the picture?" I pressed her further, devouring every nugget of information I could. Violet was somebody I'd never been able to really study, never been able to really get to know. I was going to make the most of this opportunity.

"Very much so. He usually comes to see us once a week." I don't know why I was shocked that Dwellers were able to move so freely in parts of Nomad's Land. I guess I thought things might have changed since I was a child out there. "Why do you think we live on the absolute outskirts? It's hardly prime real estate."

"I didn't know where you lived, Vi." My mistake. I reminded her that she kept her real life hidden from me. I thought if I appealed to her in this moment of mutual sharing, she might stay with me. Might stay open and honest. After all, she now had one of my secrets in return for hers.

Although it hadn't been her secret to share. It had been her mum's secret that she had guarded so fiercely for most of her adult life. Things were starting to make more sense about her now. She wanted to stay hidden from the public to avoid being scrutinized. To avoid being really seen.

"No." Her voice was cold, emotionless. "I guess you didn't." She stood and pushed down her skirt. "Let's change into something comfy and watch a film."

She didn't wait for me to respond, disappearing into the en-suite with her pyjamas in hand. I could hardly judge her for keeping secrets given she only knew the me I'd curated since I changed my name and moved to the inner city. It was a friendship built on falsities on both parts.

So we sat, each with a bowl of snacks, in front of the moving screen and pretended to watch the latest blockbuster.

When Laura walked into the room to join us, neither of us could catch her up on the plot so we restarted the disc and pretended harder than before to be interested in the fiction in front of us.

But both too distracted by the web of secrets we found ourselves in.

# Chapter Twenty-Seven

There were no new samples for us at the lab, so we were instructed to stay at home just like everybody else. I tried asking the computerised voice when we might expect to be needed again but it just kept repeating the same pre-recorded message in our President's voice: "Stay alert. Stay home. We will protect you."

I'm sure it was supposed to be comforting, make us believe it was all handled and that everything would be alright, but my skin prickled at his sentiment. How could we trust a government who had shut down an entire section of the city, leaving people to possibly die? Over the years, I'd come to accept that he sent new forces every day to the frontline to die in a war for territory, I could excuse that as it served a purpose. They protected us and they lay down their lives consistently for us in the face of a never-ending foe. But this? This abandonment of Nomad's Land felt nothing short of murder.

Hanging up the phone, I listened to the whir of a drone overhead. Our groceries were here. God, I hope they've sent coffee.

Violet brought the box inside the house and lay it on the kitchen table. Peering inside, disappointment weighed in my stomach. So, this was a State care package. Every household in the inner zones would have received theirs this morning, a pre-determined set of rations based on the needs set by our identity chips. Clearly, the combined alcoholic content of the household's bloodstream had highlighted us for some sort of tee-total programme as every item in our box promoted clean living.

"Where's the wine?" She lifted the same items over and over, searching underneath them with no success.

"Where's the coffee?"

She held up a bag and pulled a face. "Decaf."

"Diet pills?" Offended, I turned the bottle over in my hands and began absentmindedly picking at the label. It was true that I was curvier than the day I got married, but who didn't end up that way? I was pretty comfortable that they couldn't class me as morbidly obese.

"It is our civic duty as a nation to lose five pounds each," she read out loud from the enclosed note stamped with the President's signature. "Weight above average has been shown to increase the effects of the virus."

"Bullshit." I snatched the letter from her hands. She had to be joking, the government couldn't mandate us all to lose weight. "Those amongst us who are seen to be at their peak will have received additional luxury items as a reward for their compliance." I scanned down the list of things given as examples of luxury. Bubble bath, alcohol, real coffee. Items I considered a necessity.

"I'm going to the store," she sounded defiant as she slipped on a pair of shoes, picked up her purse and marched out the front door. I didn't have the heart to tell her that the store probably wasn't open.

Two minutes later, she was roughly shoved back through our door by an armed guard. "That's strike one, miss." She rubbed her arm; his grip had left a red mark that would definitely bruise. Nodding silently, she walked upstairs and he disappeared down my path, slamming the door behind him.

Life in the real world without the privilege attached to our work in the lab was shocking. Sure, we'd kept up with the news and had heard about the lockdown and the care packages. But nowhere had mentioned armed police enforcing the government's bidding. Nowhere had mentioned a State-wide diet programme. So far, nobody, not even the bloggers were talking about the lockdown in Nomad's Land – the boat shouldn't be rocked lest it capsizes. It was the easier choice to make.

Just how it was easier to focus on Violet's problems in that moment than it was my own grief. I could barely fight the weight of it anymore. Leo was gone. He couldn't stay with me any longer no matter how hard I wished it so. I was glued to my seat as I let my emotions in. Barely able to breathe, such was the weight of grief on my chest. It was over. He was gone. He was never coming home. Franklin would never remember his dad. No matter how many memories I shared.

No. I couldn't think about that. I had to check on Violet. I had to keep pushing forward.

Yet I was unable to move up the stairs towards her. My hands on the bannister he'd spent hours sanding.

My feet in the carpet we'd laid together.

The air around me full of the life we'd built.

It was gone.

It was all gone.

I stood at the bottom of the stairs. Listening to Violet quietly sobbing on the bed at the cruelty of life. Franklin was calling out from his cot for attention. Laura padded to his room quietly. Even the sounds of my son in need couldn't motivate me to move. It was over. My marriage was over. My husband was dead. My best friend was dead. My hand went numb as I held it in front of me on the bannister. Unable to let go of the physical reminder of Leo. Unable to let go of the life we'd built.

It wasn't supposed to be this way. It couldn't be this way. Any minute now, he would walk through the door, kiss my forehead and put the kettle on. I knew he would if I just believed it hard enough. If I visualised it, he would come back to me. Tell me it had all been a big mistake. That he'd found his way home to us. I would give every part of me to make that the truth of my world.

"Take me instead," I offered to the great unknown. "Take whatever you want. Just bring him back."

My feet were able to move again.

Instead of moving up the stairs towards those who needed me, they walked me out of the front door. Feeling the bare paving slabs beneath my feet. The grass he'd mowed between my toes. Who'd mow it now? Where did he keep the mower? All these tiny insignificant questions sprang upon me and broke my heart all over again. Why had I never asked him where he kept the mower?

I ducked down beneath the headlights of a vehicle. The world was still and silent. As though it wasn't aware of the complete destruction of my happiness and future.

How could it be that thunder wasn't clapping above us, rain wasn't pouring down blood-red and the wind wasn't howling? How could nature ignore such a wrong? He mattered. He mattered and the world wasn't acknowledging that.

I walked aimlessly down back alleyways. Taking in the age of the trees that grew over them. Wondering if they would outlive me like they had Leo. The pavement was hot beneath my bare feet and I knew I would have blisters come the morning but I didn't care. The physical pain of them would give me something the world could recognise. That everyone could sympathise with.

The moon was cold and red in the sky. The world

was empty of dreams. There should be no dreams tonight. Sounds of a world lost came from every corner I walked to, driving my ears insane until they turned it to nothing but white noise. The sound of my heartbeat was the only thing I could hear as I picked through forgotten pathways, areas that were free of guards, and moved instinctively in a direction I wasn't aware of.

There it was in front of me.

The bench where Leo had proposed.

Just a short walk from Regina's house. The home where he'd taken his first steps. Spoke his first words. Where we'd first fallen deeply in love at a hospital dinner she'd hosted.

No clichés here. No resentment that turned to lust. No cutting retorts as we tried to deny our attraction. No lovers that were cast aside for the bigger picture.

He was mine and I was his from the moment we started talking about a movie we both loved. We spent three hours talking about everything and nothing in her living room as the other guests milled around us and then eventually disappeared. It was meant to be. Eyes for no one else. That was it. It was so simple and now it was finished.

I sat on the bench until the sun began to rise. My mouth fuzzy with thirst and my stomach grumbling with hunger. A short tap on the shoulder from an angry looking guard stirred me from my thoughts. I followed him with no resistance back to my house.

Just come home, Leo. Please. Just come home.

# Chapter Twenty-Eight

If my absence from home had been noticed, it wasn't addressed. I guess grief gives you free rein on your behaviour. I'd never been more grateful to my past self than I was when I opened our pantry to discover my stockpile of coffee and alcohol. No government could keep me sober.

We'd only just cleared away the breakfast plates when Laura insisted on taking Franklin up for his nap. Perhaps she could sense my fragile mental state but I could have done without her interference. If she'd just let me care for my son, maybe I wouldn't have added four shots of vodka to my morning orange juice. No longer caring what anyone thought of me, I pulled my nicotine inhaler from its hiding place and padded out barefoot into my garden.

The sky was beginning to gleam with shades of purple. It was highly unusual for rain to fall at this time of year, so I didn't bother to move inside to get a coat. Instead, I made my way down to Leo's shed and I sat by myself on its floor until I'd run out of orange juice. My only motivation for moving back into my house was to retrieve the vodka bottle. With nothing else in my life, not even caregiving to my son available to distract me, I may as well indulge in my ingrained vice. My selfish need to mourn, rage and grieve overshadowing my maternal instincts.

The vodka had been Leo's. Hidden away behind a box of flour we never touched. I'd never been very good at controlling myself when it came to spirits. The hit was too instant, too addictive. The warmth as it burnt my throat, the gurgle of my stomach as it greeted its long-lost friend, it was all so comforting.

Violet found me a few hours later lying on the floor of the shed, my legs up against its wall, passing in and out of consciousness. It felt good to be drunk. Easy. All I had to concentrate on was stopping the room from spinning. I didn't have the capacity to focus on anything else. The ultimate distraction. Plus, the hangover I knew was coming was a physical pain I deserved. I deserved it because I couldn't save Leo. I'd promised on our wedding day to always stand by him, always protect him, just as he had done for me. But only one of us had lived by that rule. If he'd just stayed away and left me in prison, he would still be out there somewhere. He could still find his way back to me.

"This isn't you Paige," she scolded me softly as she pushed me to a sitting position. Gently, I banged my head against the wooden wall. Slowly, I focused my eyes on her and giggled.

"You have no idea," I slurred.

Thunder clapped over us, and far too quickly rain began to pour down. You could feel the heat of it through the wood and we both moved to the centre of the shed, trying to avoid any sizzling leaks.

"Leo," I softly called out to the weather. He'd come back to me. He'd defied nature and come back to me months before he was due to. Rain was unheard of at this time of year.

Violet grabbed my arm to stop me from stepping out into the rain as I pushed the shed door open. "I promise I'll do better," I cried out to him, trying to fight her hold on me. But she was firm and I was drunk. It was a battle I had no chance of winning. "I'll do better," I repeated as tears streamed down my face.

Then the strangest thing happened. The puddles on

the ground began to sizzle. We watched with fascination as the new drops of rain tickled the surface, dancing on the top of it before disappearing in a puff of steam.

Violet was distracted by the sounds around us and I took my opportunity to step outside of the shed.

"Paige!" she called my name and reached out for me. Pulling her arm back inside automatically as a droplet hit her skin.

I stood smiling at her. Rain pouring down my face, dripping from my hair and soaking into my skin. It was cold. So cold it would be uncomfortable if I didn't have a coat of alcohol upon me.

She looked at me and laughed.

I held out my hand and she joined me in the pouring cold rain. We danced around, singing and laughing until we were both shivering. Never in our lifetimes had we known the rain to be anything other than a fearful beast that caused many childhood burns.

Turning my head up to the sky, I opened my mouth in a wide smile. The rain stroked my face. Sobering me up. Running across my eyelids. Clearing my tears. Weaving itself through my hair. Bringing me comfort.

Leo.

Leo had come back to us in the most magical way.

# Chapter Twenty-Nine

I woke up with a fresh outlook on the day and a desperate need to put kindness out into the world. It was with this drive I picked up my phone and dialled Theo's number. If Rus wouldn't talk to me, then I knew that Theo would.

He was far too polite to ignore someone, manners had been thrust upon him from birth and repeated every day thereafter, so when he left the family home, he left it as a polite young man with a side dose of social anxiety. No matter what you do as a parent, you end up screwing your kids up. You just get to choose at what level that screw up is.

I knew that we would mirror that upbringing with Franklin. He would be polite and kind to everyone from the cleaner to the CEO. We'd make sure of it. And if he ended up being a man in his thirties whose main problem was being a people-pleaser, then in the grand scheme of things, that was the best gift we could grant him.

We.
We.
There wasn't a we anymore.

Me.
Me.
It's just me now.

I buried the grief down behind a false smile. It was always useful to smile when making a phone call, the caller could hear it in your voice. Another trick I'd learned from a childhood of watching my mother. So I dialled his number. I waited as it rang and rang. Then his voicemail clicked in. I paused for too long and left a two-second silent message. I wasn't expecting that.

Taking a big inhale and a slow exhale, trying to hold onto the kindness I'd started the day with, I redialled Theo's number. I was sure he was just lost in his own world, trying to finish his latest novel. I knew I was interrupting but I had to clear the air with Rus and he was my only viable link.

"Paige," I'd never heard him sound anything other than pleasant, but the way he spat my name down the phone I could feel the saliva on my face.

"Hi, Theo." Stay pleasant. Stay positive. Stay kind. You catch more bees with honey. "Can I speak to Rus, please?"

He scoffed dryly and I heard him cover the receiver as he whispered to someone in the room with him. I couldn't make out his words but his tone was pure fury.

"Is this a joke?" he asked, his voice now high-pitched and tense. "Is this your idea of a pissing joke, Paige?" I mean, it wasn't the worst curse word he could use but I was still taken aback by his use of it.

"Look, I'm sorry Rus got dragged into all of this." He went to interrupt me but I steamrolled on, desperately trying to hold onto my kindness instead of playing the victim. Instead of manipulating my way into victory. "I have to say, I was surprised not to see you both at the funeral." Bang. There it is. My constant need to be a martyr.

"I was sorry to hear about Leo." Momentarily, he was kind. The Theo I knew was back. I had hope I could still salvage my friendship with them all. "But there is no amount of money on this earth that would have made me stand there by your side." Dial tone. He was gone.

I needed Rus. It was like an animal instinct, my gut was raging to talk to him. I wanted to shout, scream and confide. I was so sick of keeping secrets and I knew they would be safe with him. I couldn't explain it, I just knew they would. I had so many words bubbling up inside of me, if I didn't get them out then they'd end up in the wrong hands.

Who shouldn't I trust, Leo?

What worked?

Where were we going?

How did we crash?

When did you grow gills? Gills! I think I'm going crazy.

Grief does strange things to people.

In my case, it causes hallucinations.

It was impossible. It was all so impossible.

I hadn't thought about that moment in the morgue until now. Buried down inside my bones as an impossible nightmare. It was an aching reminder with every creaking step I'd taken since. Forever unable to leave it behind. What happened? What could possibly have happened to Leo to cause such a mutation? Was it the murky water we found ourselves in? Had that caused some kind of chemical malfunction within him?

It was impossible.

Entirely impossible.

Much more logical that grief has driven me mad.

I locked the memory away again, deep down inside my skin, past my muscles and through to the centre of my bones where it would remain. I didn't have the energy to deal with the impossible right now.

I had more pressing issues to consider. Why had Theo been so hateful? I had never heard him speak to anybody like that. I didn't think him capable of such cruelty. And it was cruel. No matter how much the allegations of our affair had affected them, there was no excuse to speak to me like that. Besides, surely being accused of an affair would only add weight to the lie they were all forced to live under?

My phone beeped. Expecting an apology or explanation from Theo, I was surprised to see an e-mail from Bailey. She'd finally responded to my request for help, she was too late. Before her message had even loaded, I was composing a scathing reply in my head, conjuring up words to make sure she knew exactly how much she let me down. How much her delay cost me. There were five words on my screen that caused an itch in my throat.

I know who you are.

Heading downstairs, I passed Violet on the landing.

"Has Rus come by at all?" I asked her again, knowing the answer. I couldn't think about the message from Bailey. I couldn't.

She went to respond automatically, to tell me once again in so few words that he had abandoned me, but she paused before she spoke.

"There's something you need to know. But Regina doesn't think I should tell you." Regina? When had she spoken to Regina? I wasn't even aware that they were on terms even close to speaking. "She's worried about you. We all are."

"What is it?" I didn't have time for other people's worries. They meant very little to me these days.

"It's Rus." She paused, taking a deep breath, ready for the messenger to be shot. "He's been arrested."

"I know that. We both got arrested at the same time." I shook my head at her lack of memory and took two steps downstairs.

"He's been arrested for being a homosexual."

She blurted the truth out as though keeping it in any longer was burning her mouth and causing welts on her tongue. I reached out for the bannister to steady myself. Reaching out for that reminder of Leo to fill me with strength. I went to speak but I couldn't find words, she watched me open and close my mouth repeatedly before she carried on with her explanation.

"He's been in custody since the day you were free to go." So, there it was. The price for my freedom.

I couldn't help the anger as I turned to look at her. "You should have told me."

"I'm so sorry. He's due for trial at the government's court next week. You know what sentence they'll pass. Paige, I'm s-"

She moved to comfort me, but I pushed her away. She winced as her arm hit the wall, but I didn't apologise. Her physical pain was nothing compared to what Rus was going through. I had to fix it.

"I'm sorry," she finishes. I knew she meant it. I knew she meant well. I knew she just wanted to protect me. I knew all of this and yet I didn't care.

"I'll confess to the affair."

"It won't do any good."

"I'll give them details they won't be able to disbelieve."

"You'll be seen as a sympathiser."

"There are worse things to be." I could feel my mother's blood begin to seep through my veins, the anger at the injustice of the world we lived in. The wrath was boiling just beneath my skin. They would not get away with this. I would not let them.

"Think about Franklin. He'll be taken into care." Violet was trying to reason with me, she could see the anger in my eyes, and though she didn't know about my past, she could sense a danger beginning to emit from me.

They stole the children of those they deemed sympathisers under the guise of protecting the younger generation from being poisoned against the State that cared for them. My grandad had to fight every day for nearly a year to win full custody of me back from them. Denouncing his own daughter as evil just to save me. His vicious testimonial was cited in the press as being the main reason for her long-term imprisonment. He loved her though. No matter what he said in court or to journalists, he did love her. Families are complicated.

Violet had made the winning point. I couldn't lose Franklin. I couldn't choose my ideals over him. At the end of it all, despite the passion against injustice I felt, I wasn't my mother.

Mum.

She's the answer.

Without saying another word to Violet, I moved into my bedroom, shut the door, and pulled out my phone.

"Jack," I greeted him before he could even say hello. "I need you to defend Rus."

"I can't -"

I cut him off. "I don't care what your personal views are, Jack, I need you to do this for me."

"He hasn't been granted a defence." So, he'd already looked into it. Jack really was one of the good guys.

But without a defence, there was only one outcome available to Rus. Guilty.

"Have you called -" His turn to cut me off.

"Already taken care of." Without saying goodbye, we mutually hung up.

I sent a wish out to Leo, asking him to protect Rus.

If anybody was able to save him, it would be my mother. I knew that by asking Jack to call her, she would know that I supported her. That perhaps I'd always supported her. She'd see the glimmer of hope for a real relationship between the two of us.

A glimmer of hope I'd exploit by whatever means to save Rus. Oddly enough, I knew she'd be proud of the levels I'd sink to in order to do what was right.

# Chapter Thirty

Unbeknownst to me, Laura had taken Franklin out for a walk. State-sanctioned caregivers were allowed to go on one accompanied walk per day, provided the infant in their care was under five years old. It struck me as a very specific rule but perhaps one introduced to give the parents that happened to be hospital workers a little peace and quiet on their days off. Whatever the reasoning behind the legislation, I was grateful this morning to be able to lock myself in the bathroom without my returning parent guilt pushing me to rush.

I sat on the edge of the bath as I ran it, enjoying the feel of the cold tiles beneath my aching feet. I flexed my toes and curled the arch, relishing in the familiar sting as I did so. Since having Franklin, I'd had a near consistent pain on the top of my foot, something I'd put down to rocking his bouncer to get him to sleep. My colleague had advised pain killers and rest, neither of which were practical given my love of wine and the fact I was a parent to a small child who would only sleep during the day if in motion. It was fine. I could rest when he grew up.

The water was trickling through at a slower than usual pace. A sign of the times. Without the manpower in the water towers, we were down to the bare essentials.

With time on my hands, I picked up my tablet from the counter. Taking a breath, I turned it on, time for a deep dive into the Internet. Social media. News outlets. Blogs. I was going to look at it all and learn everything

I'd missed since the news broke and a wall of silence had been forced upon me. I prepared myself for the inevitable headache and started reading. I'd allow myself to search for anything except Bailey. Her message was clearly a warning, one I was determined to heed.

Every home in the State was on lockdown. That much was obvious. But still, I hovered in the comments section of the official updates to see if there was any show of discontent from other citizens. Of course, there wasn't. Everyone praised our President for putting lives before livelihood. He was a true hero in these times of a new and cruel war.

There were many 'think pieces' from journalists about the Dwellers and the assumed reasoning behind their attack. All of which focused on their dwindling troops, which was a direct juxtaposition to the one our President had taken just weeks ago. Back then, we'd needed more people to enlist. More bodies for the inevitable bags. They were an almighty force that could never be quenched. But now? Now they were weak and on the edge of defeat. Now we needed a reason to justify their attack and that reason was that they were on their last legs.

If we could just buckle up and do what needed to be done for the sake of our survival, then we would emerge victorious. The history books would praise us as the generation who hunkered down without complaint, who accepted that needs must and who trusted in our President to steer us through this nightmare. After all, history books are always written by the victor.

There were a minority of blogs that had yet to be removed that told a different story. That alluded to the virus being a hoax to add another level of control to our lives. I dismissed these instantly as nonsense. Having seen the scientific evidence first-hand, I wasn't about to waste my energy on simpletons who thought they knew better than cold hard facts. Bloody sheeple.

Social media was awash with people who had lost someone. Or individuals who thought they were suffering the symptoms that they had self-diagnosed as having 'the disease', as they named it, in hushed whispers accompanied by sepia-toned photographs of them looking peaky. I guess one's mortality was as big a social draw as ever judging from the amount of responses these posts garnered. "Get well soon babe", "praying for you", "I am SO sorry you've caught it." All mindless sentiments serving nothing more than ego. Both of the poster and the commenter.

One of the major problems of the virus you see was its symptoms. They went hand in hand with the common cold. We may have upgraded to a new Earth, but even that couldn't free us from the inevitable runny nose two times a year.

A slightly raised temperature. A tickle in your throat. A headache. Aches and pains. A cough. A sneeze. It could all be 'the disease' sent to wipe us out. Or it could be a cold. Or allergies. Or a brain tumour. Or throat cancer. It could be anything. The symptom list on the government website meant that 99% of the population were classed as suffering from the attack and, therefore, were not allowed to seek medical care in person lest they become a 'super spreader' and rob somebody of their life. The message was simple – stay home.

So many people would needlessly suffer and die of the usual maladies just because they had a raised temperature. It was frustrating.

There was only one article I could find anywhere that was written by a survivor. They'd even had a positive test confirmed. Though God knows where that test came from.

I took in their every word multiple times as they

described the agony they'd suffered. As they waxed lyrically about the care they'd been provided by the team at my hospital. Their survivor's guilt at having witnessed other patients overcome with the illness, wheeled away downstairs to Rus. My empathy was full after the sixth reading, and I was exhausted. The bath was finally full, and switching off from the world, I peeled off my clothes and sank into the warm water.

Our world was grieving collectively. Grieving for those we'd lost and grieving for the life we'd lost. Things would never go back to the way they were after this. If the human race survived this and went on to win the war against the Dwellers, then we'd be an entirely different race. One tainted with grief and loss and anger. I took comfort in the fact that the work we had undertaken, that had at the time seemed pointless, might help save lives now the vulnerable in our society were being protected. We'd done that. Me and Violet had helped save countless lives in the face of such a relentless enemy.

Our government was doing all that it could to support and protect us. Whilst we were on lockdown, all of our outgoings were taken care of. The State provided all the energy that ran our homes. As well as 99% of the roofs over our heads. Therefore, it was thankfully within their power to waver any charges during this time period and they'd done so without question or hesitation. If you took that alongside the care packages they were delivering weekly, it was hard to see a problem with their action plan. All of our needs were met. We were being asked to take paid vacation in our homes. That's not so hard.

I closed my eyes. Taking in the silence in my home. Letting the water and soft lavender-scented oil I'd poured in overwhelm me and take my troubles away. For a few minutes, I forgot everything.

I forgot about the virus. I forgot about lockdown. I forgot about Leo. I forgot about the accident. I forgot about Bailey's e-mail. There was nothing but peace around me.

"Don't trust -" the words whispered in my ears. I tried to keep my eyes closed. Tried to ignore the pressure building in my ears as Leo's voice flowed through them. "Don't trust -" he said again. There it was. My bubbles burst. Who shouldn't I trust, Leo? What happened that night? Why couldn't you leave me with answers?

Something inside my mind clicked and I was sat in my mother's kitchen again. A child.

*"I refuse to get a State job," she screams down the phone at my father. "I refuse to work for them." I stare up at her in awe as I always did when she spoke with such passion. Her words were always so honest and true, they were impossible to ignore.*

*"They're all State jobs you idiot!" I'm fully aware that she's holding in rude words because I'm present. "Fine! We don't need anything from you anyway!" With that, she slams the phone on the table.*

*"Promise me." She grabs my hands in hers, a look of desperation on her face, "Promise me you won't fall into the trap."*

*"What trap?" I ask. She smiles at me. Always happiest when I ask questions because she knows that means I'm engaged. I learnt that about her as soon as I could talk. Give her your attention and she'll give you her love.*

*"It's all a trap, my darling. State jobs pay State money which pays State bills. It's an illusion of freedom." She smiles down at me, her face full of warmth and concern.*

*I've never felt safer than when my mother's focus was on me. I nod my head happily and she pulls me into a tight bear hug. "I love you," she whispers into my hair. "I love you so much."*

The front door slamming startled me back to the present day. I listened as Laura chatted mindlessly to Franklin and Violet. Sitting up in the bath, I moved to pick up my towel and hesitated. She was right, of course. I'd dismissed so much of her from my mind that I'd lost the few flecks of wisdom she passed down. It was all well and good being grateful to the State for waving our bills whilst we weren't working.

But whilst we weren't working, whilst we were unable to seek medical assistance, whilst we weren't using their vehicles or roads for transport, whilst we weren't dining out in their establishments, they weren't paying any wages. Every job in the inner zones were for the State.

The State paid your wages. You paid the State for your expenses. The supermarkets were owned by them. Our homes were full of their carefully curated lab-grown food and drink. They even owned the power and water plants. The only thing they didn't seem to own were the sparse fields in Nomad's Land that grew native produce, the only kind that could survive naturally through the weather, but even the most rebellious amongst us in the inner zones hadn't dared to seek out their taste yet.

Whether we worked or not meant no difference to their budget. Keeping us all home and rationing our supplies was probably saving them money. Paying a salary was just an illusion of freedom that they granted us. My mum had hit the nail on the head all those years ago and I'd been stupid enough not to believe her.

My skin prickled with irritation as I thought more

about the subject, but before I could delve too deeply, somebody knocked at the bathroom door.

"Mrs Hanson. Paige." It was Laura. She sounded distraught. My only thought was something was wrong with Franklin. Why else would she disturb me?

Pulling my towel around me, I threw the door open and moved past her down the stairs. I could hear sobbing from the living room. My baby. What has happened to my baby?

He was sat in his pushchair, happy as anything. But there on the floor was Violet. Crumpled. Broken.

"My mum," was all she could utter.

# Chapter Thirty-One

It had been a week since Violet received the call about her mother. She hung around the house like a ghost. Not eating and forever lurking in the shadows, peering in at a normality that had been robbed from her.

It turned out that when the government sent the orders to round up all those at risk of dying from the disease, they failed to test any of them for it before locking them in the hotels for their own safety.

It had ripped through the inhabitants like wildfire.

Ravaging the life from them, leaving them husks gasping for mercy from some divine being. But no one came. No one intervened. They were left to care for each other, which only sped up the transfer rate. They thought they were doing their civic duty checking on their neighbour, but they were just inviting the grim reaper to their own door.

Violet's mum had been the third person to die, and by the time the news of the 'oversight' as it was deemed broke in the press, it was too late. They were all dead within days of each other.

You'd think the surviving population would be incised at the malpractice behind the President's orders. But they weren't. They were cowering in fear at their own mortality, mourning the life they'd once known and following orders in the hopes that being good citizens would save them and their families. All of which I could empathise with. Besides, I felt enough rage at the situation to make up for their apathy in the face of out-and-out murder.

Murder that me and my work had been complicit in. If we'd never invented the 'death test', those people would never have been ripped from their homes and placed into protection with each other. They'd have never been sitting targets for the virus. They could have died in their own homes surrounded by loved ones. They may even have avoided infection long enough for a cure. But no. They'd been sent to the firing squad on the back of our work.

I knew the guilt was eating away at Violet too. In her sleep, she kept apologising over and over. When she thought I was asleep, she'd quietly sob, muttering words I couldn't make out. She would barely communicate in the daylight hours, so I'd hold her frantic whispers close in the night, wanting the universe to know that somebody had heard her words. Had heard her apologies.

One day, out of the blue, she sought me out as I put away laundry.

"When does it stop?" she inquired, lost as a lamb without its flock. I didn't need her to give me any more details, I knew exactly what she meant. It was a question I'd asked myself numerous times. When is grief done with you?

I don't think grief ever leaves you.

It's never fully done with you. It embeds itself deep down in your cells. Your skin grows thicker, more resilient. Your heart beats with new edges as the sorrow drags itself through your veins and arteries. The synapses in your brain rewire so slightly, it could never be seen. But they are fundamentally altered forever, unable to return to what they once were. And when all of those changes have occurred, you feel better. Lighter somehow. You've come out the other side.

But you haven't. Not really. Grief forever amends you and what you now believe to be happiness is permanently a fraction less happy than you were prior to your loss. The only reason you think you've completed the grieving process is because, silently, grief has changed your entire make-up.

It explains how grief can strike again however it pleases.

You could be walking around a supermarket, minding your own business when you see a pack of confectionary that reminds you of the person wiped out of existence. And bam. Like that, the lump of grief in your throat is back and you try to hold back tears in the grocery store as you place the sweets in your basket and head for the checkout.

Grief can reappear in an instant because it's always with you. Because it infected you the day you heard the news. And there is no cure.

It sounds bleak, but there was no other way to explain it. When you lose someone you truly love, you lose a part of yourself. Some of your innocence, naivety and joy disappears into the universe with them.

If you're a lucky person, you are born blessed with enough joy to survive grief.

You'll never outlive it, but you can learn to live alongside it. Like depression, you become aware of its constant presence. Some of the greatest creative minds humanity has ever known were powered by grief.

In the right hands, it could be an infinite well of strength to draw from. It could encourage a person to seek out and grow kindness to mask over the damage they've been left to live with. Grief could, in some ways, be the greatest change a person could suffer.

On the other side of the argument, grief could make you cold. Harsh. Mean. It could grow bitterness on your tongue and violence in your breath. Those newly altered synapses could leave you with a permanent sense of life being unfair. Grief could ruin a person.

Me? I fell somewhere between the two camps. I was all too familiar with grief.

I'd felt it take occupancy in my bones and watched as it changed the way my eyes viewed the world. Leo. Grandpa Joseph. My absent father. My imprisoned mother. The so-called 'dark year' at college where we lost three friends in close succession. The missed call from a suicidal confidant. Grief weaved its way into my body with each of those losses. Sometimes I thought I was more grief than Paige.

But I couldn't explain any of this to her. I couldn't tell her these truths. She wanted to know when and how she would get better.

"It just takes time," I offered. One of those empty condolences we all needed to hear.

She'd learn. Over the next few weeks and months, she'd learn the truth. I'd be there for her then just as I was now.

Whether for good or bad, grief brings people together.

She left my room as though she'd never been there, and I went back to the task at hand. Folding up the household clothes and finding homes for them. It was mundane, repetitive and exactly what I needed to keep my head clear.

Before I knew what was happening, my phone was in my hand, Bailey's message opened upon it and the response window ready for me. What could I possibly have to say to this woman? This woman who'd let me down at two of the most important moments of my life? This woman who'd tried to scare me into silence by mentioning my truths. I couldn't let her win. I wouldn't let her manipulate her way out of this. She may have thought she knew me but, in truth, she knew nothing about me. If she did, she never would have taunted me.

November 3rd.

I typed, clicking send before I could second-guess myself. Before logic took my brain back over. To anybody else, it was a random date. It didn't allude to anything in the history books. But to Bailey, it would mean everything. It would mean that she understood just how much I knew. It would mean I now had the upper hand. After all, it was a date that would only mean anything to three people. My mum, Bailey and me. It was the date she gave my mother the location of the treatment centre.

The date the massacre was set in motion.

# Chapter Thirty-Two

Rus was scheduled to stand trial in three weeks' time. They'd delayed the original date, clearly, they wanted to keep him locked in a cell for as long as possible. I couldn't imagine the kind of torture they were enjoying inflicting on him. The news headlines were taking great delight in using as many homophobic slurs and puns as they could. After all, it had been a while since somebody hadn't complied with the Repopulation Act, and it made a change from writing about the virus. A bit of light entertainment in the drudgery of the daily death toll.

I hadn't heard anything from my mum. Every night I took one last look out of my window, expecting to see a blackout, which could signal her arrival. I knew from my childhood that she always preferred to work in darkness, away from any potential CCTV sightings. But the lights stayed on. The sounds of a city still echoed through the speakers all night. Something must be wrong.

It was impossible to reach Jack on the phone and it was hardly something I could leave a voicemail regarding. "Hi, Jack. Could you call me back about my criminal mastermind mother and her plan to break my homosexual friend out of prison before he gets executed?" No. It would not be wise to leave such a message. Besides, now that Leo was officially dead, there was very little logical reason for me to contact him. He was, after all, just my lawyer. It wouldn't do my reputation any good to be linked to the brainwashed husband of a cult leader for too long. That's what they used to call her. A cult leader. The mother of rebellion. A criminal mastermind. A freedom fighter. Depending on who you spoke to, she had a different nickname, but they all agreed she was dangerous. They all agreed that she was a force to be reckoned with. They weren't wrong.

With sick fascination, I watched the news reports hounding Theo, Rebecca and Claire. They were accused of being sympathisers, of being accomplices, and rumours were beginning to do the rounds that perhaps Rus wasn't the only 'queer' living in their house.

I listened as, with pain only I could hear, they washed their hands of Rus. Using the same disgusting slurs as everyone else. Denouncing his sexuality as selfish. The cameras seemed to linger in particular on Theo as Claire played the part of the wronged wife. She spoke with malice and anger. I knew her true feelings were aimed at those questioning her, but she disguised it with the words of her answers. It was then that I saw him.

Jack.

Stood in the background to their left. Barely a shadow on camera. He was the driving force behind this press conference. Theo cleared his throat and the room fell silent.

"Rus has been a part of our family since it was first formed. In fact, he introduced me to my wife, so in a lot of ways, I will always be grateful to him." A small cough from Jack broke the tension in the room. A clear reminder to Theo to stay on brand. "But had I known then what I know now, I would never have welcomed him into my life. To think I've spent years with this man, this…" a pause as he strengthened himself, "abomination makes me sick to my stomach. We spent so much time together over the years as our wives worked tirelessly on the front lines as the heroes they are, time spent eating together. Talking together. Laughing together." A tear threatened to spill from his unblinking eyes. I couldn't imagine how much this was hurting him. He loved Rus with everything he had. And now he had to play a part in his sentencing to save Claire and Rebecca's lives. I had no doubt in my mind that was the only reason he was standing here today. If it had just been his life on the line, he'd be sat in a cell with Rus waiting to die alongside him.

"And it was all a lie. A great big perverted lie."

Rebecca moved to his side and took his hand in a show of solidarity.

"Whilst we have hearts full of sympathy for our dear friend, Claire." She paused for effect, turning to smile at Claire who was openly crying. An acceptable break in the charade considering, in the eyes of the world, she had been betrayed the deepest. "We cannot continue to let this crime overshadow our lives. Especially when it's no longer just the lives of the three of us we have to consider." A tender hand on her stomach.

The room lit up with camera flashes and loud shouts of congratulations. It was as if the original reason for the conference had been forgotten. Now there was just positivity surrounding the three of them. Pity. Respect. Support. I watched as a small smile twitched at the corner of Jack's mouth. That clever bastard. Even if there were still suspicions about the trio, the government would never dare to follow through on them now. Not now another child was coming into the world. The child of a war hero no less. It was perfect.

Rebecca waited with a happy smile for the room to calm down.

"As you can imagine, this situation has been incredibly upsetting for us, even though we completely understand the intrusion upon our lives in the name of justice. However, we wanted to bring you all together today to make our feelings clear on the matter one final time and to explain the reason behind our decision to take leave from the front line and recuperate in privacy. We have been given permission to temporarily move home to reduce stress levels, mine in particular, and from here on out, will be complying along with the rest of the nation with the lockdown. Thank you for your time and your kind words."

With that, the three of them left the podium. Jack's hand in the small of Claire's back guiding her through the doors. Another smart move that would be played over in courtrooms. He was, after, always rumoured to be sleeping with his clients. His affair and marriage to my mother had started that reputation and he never seemed keen to remove it. Now I understood why. It was yet another thing he could use to protect those who needed defending.

Well played, Jack. Well played.

You saved three lives at the cost of one.

It was either that or lose four.

I understood why he'd taken such necessary actions. But it didn't help the stone in my stomach that knew Rus would soon be publicly executed. The trial was just a formality after all. They wouldn't settle for anything less than the death penalty. Especially considering the emotional damage his lie had caused. Emotional damage that Jack had conjured up to save the day.

I only hoped my mum hadn't agreed with his plan of action. That she had a miracle in mind. Surely she wouldn't have agreed with it? It was, after all, my grandfather's testimony that had led to her lifetime incarceration. A heavy decision he had made to save me from State care. But one she had screamed in the courtroom that she would never forgive. There was no way she would have agreed for the same thing to happen to Rus. Impossible.

I just hoped that whatever state he was currently in, he hadn't been subjected to a viewing of the press conference. That would have been a cruelty I hoped they hadn't thought of.

# Chapter Thirty-Three

Have you ever been so anxious that you hold your breath in your lungs until it burns? Until you feel lightheaded? Because you know that once you take your next breath, everything will change. Everything will be forever broken?

Your whole body fights you to release the air. The roof of your mouth tingles uncomfortably. As the pressure inside you builds, you feel your brain begin to panic. It fills your bloodstream with signals to breathe, floods your nervous system with adrenaline as it tries to get you to understand that you need to let the air out.

Eventually, you give yourself a mild panic attack after you release the carbon dioxide from your body. Then your brain punishes you further by making you think about every breath you take. The process. The meaning. You're exhausted from fully comprehending every breath your body automatically takes. Tears build behind your eyes, it's so tiring just thinking about how to live.

You did all of this to yourself because you tried to control the impossible. You tried to stop time from crashing down upon you. It's a pointless battle. Time will always win. It's what I always did when I could no longer control the world around me. I tried to control the world within me.

This was the routine I started every day with at the moment. If I could just keep my eyes closed and my breath inside me, then I could stop the madness that was all around me.

The virus would disappear. Rus would be back with Theo. Leo would walk through the door. Everything would be okay if I could just break the pattern.

But every morning, my body fought to live, reality fought to exist and I lay defeated in bed until I heard somebody turn the kettle on.

This morning was different. This morning, as I held my breath, I remembered. I remembered what had happened in the car. The lack of oxygen in my brain had unlocked a memory I'd scratched at since I woke up in the hospital bed.

*"How could you be so stupid?" I hiss at Leo as we speed past Laura's house. Franklin is grumbling in his car seat as our speed creeps up. "Why would you ever agree to do that in the first place?"*

*Leo doesn't answer me. His jaw is tense and his eyes narrow as he adds pressure to the accelerator. The engine purrs, happy to be put to the test once again.*

*"Leo!" I snap his name, wanting a response so I have an excuse to lose myself in the anger that vibrates through me. "Leo, you can't ignore me."*

*He looks in the rear-view mirror. Headlights are flashing behind us.*

*"We need to pull over." I ask, still he ignores me. "Stop. We need to pull over."*

*"I can't do that." The first response I've had since we left our home. The frantically packed backpack is pressing up against my foot uncomfortably. Have I packed enough formula for Franklin? Enough bottles? Did I remember to put his favourite blanket in there?*

*"Please slow down." He ignores me again. His hands white on the steering wheel as he weaves around the road.*

*The glass in our back window shatters. Franklin screams.*

*"Oh my God!" Without hesitation, I unbuckle my seatbelt and climb over the clutch, squeezing myself between the two seats to get to him.*

*"Paige!" Leo shouts at me in anger as I nudge him on my way to our son. I shoot him a look that would turn his blood to ice.*

*Brushing broken glass from the seat, I check Franklin over for cuts. Thankfully, he is safe. Leo glances back at us in the mirror and briefly nods in my direction, a non-verbal check on our son. One that in my mind is not enough. Franklin's face is red from screams, his little eyes screw up as he stares at the ceiling, arms and legs flailing. I move to undo his child seat, to hold him close to my body and bring him comfort.*

*"Paige. You need to take the wheel." His tone is authoritative, demanding.*

*"Don't be so ridiculous." He rummages in the glove box, never taking his eyes off the road as I dismiss his request.*

*"It's that or be in charge of the gun." I can't believe the words I am hearing but there it is in his hands as clear as day. A handgun.*

*Another bang comes from behind us as the headlights close in, I duck and feel the wind move around my ear. The bullet pierces through the headrest of the passenger seat.*

*"Paige, now!" We've hit a straight in the road and he's scooting over to the passenger seat. Yanking me forward by my arm so hard I know it will have already bruised.*

*I move into the driver's seat and place my hands on the wheel. It feels so foreign under my skin.*

*"Just keep your foot on the peddle and follow the road," he instructs as he fires a shot backwards through our missing window. I scream nearly as loud as Franklin at the noise. "I'm sorry," he apologises to us both. "Fuck. I'm so sorry."*

*The road begins to bend and I no longer have time to panic. I have to concentrate. My foot is gentle on the accelerator and I can tell the car behind us is catching up. They return fire but I've already cleared the corner and I hear the bullet embed itself in the side of the car.*

*"Why did you do this to us?" I mutter through clenched teeth. "Why?"*

*"I had no choice. If I didn't agree, they would have come after you and Franklin," he responds, climbing into the backseat. With one hand resting on Franklin's chest, he shushes to him, trying to reassure him that everything is okay. Just as the baby's screams have softened, he fires another bullet at our pursuers and the fear in Franklin starts all over again.*

*"You're going to deafen him!"*

*Suddenly, the road in front of us is full of light. I can see shapes behind it. A blockade. Whoever is in the car behind us has managed to direct us exactly to where they wanted. Like everything has been planned out this way all along.*

*"Shit." Leo stares out of the front window then looks back at the car pursuing us. "Go through it," he orders. Jaw tense again. Eyes devoid of compassion. "Don't stop."*

*I nod silently. There is no other option.*

*But the decision is not mine to make. A shot rings out around us. Louder than any other I've heard. It hasn't come from the car chasing us. It hit the side of the front wheel and I lose control of the steering.*

*"Steer!"*

*"I'm trying!"*

*"Brake!"*

*I apply desperate pressure to the brake pad but nothing happens. They've taken out our brakes too. I hadn't heard a second shot because of the overwhelming dread that descended on me.*

*The car begins to drag itself to the left. Towards the wrong side of the road.*

*"Leo!" I call, turning back to look at him. "Franklin." He is already holding our son in his arms, and he passes him to me through the gap in the chairs. It takes a split second, but it feels like eternity. I hold him as close as I can, trying to pass onto him all the love I can muster as I watch our headlights light up the landscape in front of us.*

*A lake.*

*We are going to crash into a lake.*

"I'm so sorry," are the last words Leo speaks to me as we leave the ground.

I hear a woman scream.

# Chapter Thirty-Four

The oxygen sped out of my body at a record pace as I panted with adrenaline. I grasped at the side of my bed to ground myself. To remind myself that I was no longer hurtling through the air. I was no longer in the car. I was home. I was safe.

So, now I had two clear memories of the night that was missing. One of being saved by Leo and his subsequent warning to mistrust. And one of how we ended up in the lake. But I still didn't know what worked. I still didn't know why somebody would be trying to kill us. The scream I couldn't pinpoint, I just knew it hadn't stemmed from my lungs.

It was easier when I couldn't remember anything. I had less questions that way.

Violet seemed a little more herself this morning, as though she had really bought into my line about time healing all. She was still closely followed by the shadow of grief but there was definitely the re-emergence of the flame in her belly that would eventually bring her back to me. All we needed was a project to get our teeth into and we'd both begin the healing process. I kept my phone near my side at all times, waiting for our next call to action, but so far just radio silence.

One thing in my house that wasn't silent was the television. It felt like it automatically turned on with a new update every half an hour. A new announcement to keep us fearful, to stop us from seeing the injustice that had been served against those who had died in the hotels. After all, who had time for empathy when the whole world had gone to shit?

"I know many of you are questioning why lockdown measures are still in place," a familiar voice pipped my interest. It was my old professor. The only person at the centre of it all that I actually trusted. A man of science, not of politics. He'd aged dramatically under the spotlight, never having signed up for a life of press conferences and his words being dissected and pasted across the world. "Although it is true that the imminent danger has now passed, those who we sadly lost were more dispositioned to dying from the virus. However, what we have yet to establish is the danger of the viral load on those who aren't marked as being vulnerable."

"To be frank with you, we don't know the long-term effects of this virus that has been unleashed upon us. We don't know how it damages those it doesn't kill. Therefore, lockdown measures will remain in place as per the President's address." I heard Violet groan beside me. She would be apart from Ada even longer. "However, I have consulted today with the President and his advisors and put forward what I feel is a fairer way to handle this situation. We face an epidemic of mental health issues once this is all over with and that's where my focus is today. My focus is on the future that I know we will reach."

"The human race is more resilient than the Dwellers give us credit for. We've survived so much already. We've survived wars, poverty, viruses…" He paused to make his next point. The sorrow in his voice clear.

"We survived the destruction of Earth One and we arrived here on Earth Two and proved that we could survive on a planet alien to us. There is no doubt in my mind that we will survive this too. Not all of us, sadly. But the human race will survive. There is nothing they can throw at us that we can't survive."

Rapturous applause in the conference room and indeed in my living room. I'd forgotten how engaging and passionate he was when he spoke. He'd united the nation in minutes at a time where our President seemed incapable of doing anything more than scaring us into submission. And he was right. We as a race would survive this. We could survive anything.

"Which is why I've put forward that all citizens of Earth Two shall be allowed to go on daily State-approved walks."

Walks?

The passion in my stomach turned to lead. That was his great plan? His great way to protect our mental health? State-approved walks? I couldn't help myself as I scoffed out loud. Violet raised her eyebrow at me, a simple sign between us that she agreed with my sentiment.

"Each household will be escorted for a fifteen-minute walk around their local block in an effort to relieve the pressure of being stuck inside. I am confident that this change, however small it may seem, will bring positivity to those who are suffering mentally. Thank you."

And with that, the television turned itself off. They were done with us for now at least. Silence returned to my home as we absorbed the latest update.

"So," I started, not intending my sentence to go anywhere.

"So," she responded. We were both too flabbergasted by the professor's marvellous plan.

"Coffee?" I offered. She nodded, after all, it was too early for wine. As I waited for the kettle to boil, I checked my e-mails, re-reading the one-word response from Bailey she'd sent last night.

Sorry.

That was it. Just a simple word that was supposed to un-write a lifetime of wrongs. If she'd never given my mum the location, I'd never have been separated from her. Never had to give up my family name. Never turned my back on all that I was. On the flip side, if she'd never given my mum the location, I'd never have had a reason to change my identity and run away. I'd never have met Leo. Never have had Franklin.

That one word brought on such a complex array of emotions within me that my head ached every time I considered it. What did she want me to say in response? That it was okay? That she did me a favour? Did she want me to absolve her?

Because I wouldn't. Her guilt was something I could hold over her, that I could use to sway her if needed. I'd spent last night tossing and turning, scenarios running through my head, words I'd never speak hurtling through my dreams. What did I need from Bailey?

There it was again. My mother's voice in my head. Her example overshadowing the personality I'd rebuilt for myself. Whilst I couldn't deny the success of her teachings, I'd told myself I'd never sink to her levels. Never treat people as pawns in my plan, exploit their respect for me or their fears. I was better than her.

Sure, I enjoyed studying human nature. I always knew the right thing to say or the correct way to behave to result in the most pleasing outcome, but that didn't mean I was like her. That didn't mean I'd rise to her levels of control. I didn't have it in me.

The voices in my dreams knew better though, they knew of the thoughts I kept locked so far down that I wasn't even aware of them. They knew of the thrill it brought me to weave sentences that would bring people to me. They knew of the butterflies in my stomach that would take residence the second a lie formed itself on my lips. They knew of the murderous rage that sometimes took hold of my fingers that itched to right wrongs.

It was with these voices racing through my head that I allowed myself to type a response to Bailey's apology. A response that I knew she wouldn't be able to resist. A secret I knew would make her salivate and a question that had been at the back of my mind since the first day we received samples in the lab. A question I'd tried desperately to stop myself from conceiving:

Find the source of the disease. I'll find a cure.

A simple demand. A precise one. I'd passed the thread to somebody I knew could unravel it. With a sense of dread, I wondered how many knots she'd have to unpick before she had the answer.

# Chapter Thirty-Five

Someone was in my shed.

I noticed their shadow moving around inside as I washed the dinner plates. Franklin was asleep. Laura was up in her room watching television in bed and Violet was taking a much-deserved nap. So, I didn't have to make any excuses as I slid the kitchen door open and stepped barefoot onto my patio.

The floor was still warm from the sun despite it having set hours ago. The heat even managed to penetrate deep through the dead skin and callouses on the soles of my feet, a remaining scar from a previous carefree life. 'Cheeky feet,' my mum used to call it when we went without shoes. We'd dance around hot puddles, avoiding the splatters, or take long walks through the grass on a nearby field, sometimes we'd even climb trees and sit in their branches barefoot and happy. She always told me it was important to have a physical connection with the Earth. But I'd never explained any of that to Leo when I'd once asked him to kick off his shoes and walk down the street with me.

His mother had drilled into him the importance of other people's expectations, and no matter how hard he tried to be free, her warnings had embedded themselves in his bones. I never asked him again. I knew it was a battle I could never win.

So, I padded towards the shed, unaffected by the gravel underfoot. My body instinctively knowing how to balance to avoid any sharp edges. A tiny part of my heart hoped it was Leo hiding out in the shed. That, somehow, he'd fake the whole thing just to safely return to me. We could move out to Nomad's Land when the restrictions were lifted, he could change his hair, put on a little weight. The three of us could be a family again without anybody bothering us.

But as I heard a woman cough, any hope I had faded. It had just been a childish wish after all. As a woman in my mid-thirties, you'd think I'd have grown out of that by now. But no. The dreams and wishes were still there. Just now as an adult I knew to keep them to myself.

A painful groan drew me out of my self-centred pity. Whoever was in the shed was in trouble. Was it my mum?

I opened the door with a new sense of fear. No child wanted to see their parent in trouble. Despite all the time we'd lost, she would always be my mother, and I never wanted to lose her.

There on the floor was a figure I wasn't expecting.

Masquerading in the shards of light leaking through the gaps in the wood panels was Agent Cherry. Her face covered in a mask but there was no mistaking her sense of style. Her usual black attire made only the more fashionable by the trickle of blood from underneath her ribs.

"Paige," my name sounded like a curse as she panted it out between staggered breaths. "Help me."

I moved to her side, my medical training kicking in as I shrugged off my jacket and pressed it into the wound. A stab wound. Deep but not terminal. From the looks of the bleeding, nothing major had been ruptured. There was nothing in the shed that could help me care for her.

"Wait here," I ordered pointlessly, watching as she slipped in and out of consciousness. The gravel struck in the arch of my foot as I ran back to my kitchen, praying everybody was still upstairs. My body too tense to instinctively balance as I moved.

I threw the pantry door open and pulled out a bottle of vodka, clean cloths, a blanket and Leo's spare medical bag. It would have to do.

Taking a swig of vodka, I returned to the shed, making sure to lock the door to the garden behind me, leaving the key in the lock to prevent anyone from following me. Laura or Violet couldn't know about the patient in my shed. They wouldn't understand.

Opening the shed doors, I was greeted by silence. The emptiness inside of it was overwhelming. There wasn't even a droplet of blood to prove that she'd been here. She had though. Hadn't she? I'd heard her panicked breathing. My name on her lips causing goosebumps. The red of her blood seeping across the black of her skirt. It had happened. Hadn't it? She'd been here. She'd existed.

I'd been drinking too much recently.

Grieving too much recently.

It was clearly taking its toll. First the gills and now this. It was time to reach out to my old therapist. Get the help I needed. Stop myself from becoming my mother.

Travelling further down this road of self-destruction wasn't an option. Not when I had Franklin. It wasn't like the good old days where I could comfortably try to lose months of my life in a haze of good times and bad decisions. No. I had responsibilities now. I had to keep my sanity this time.

I heard a knocking at the kitchen door behind me. Violet was stood gesturing at the lock. I shook my head as though I was absentminded and moved towards her. The air was unusually chilly for this time of year and I wished I was wearing a jacket.

# Chapter Thirty-Six

The days were endless and repetitive. The same faces, the same conversations, the same government updates. Even on our accompanied daily walks, we never saw sight of another soul. It was a beautiful ballet of control and we were all the prima ballerinas of our own show.

As pleasant as they were, I longed for conversation with anyone other than the women I lived with. And yet I couldn't bring myself to pick up the phone to call anyone outside of my household. Prematurely weary of having the same conversations with new voices. Yes, we were all well. No, we didn't know anything different. Yes, it was terrifying. No, we didn't have any spare toilet roll.

A never-ending cycle of drudgery was upon us, put in place to keep us safe, but it was clear from social media I wasn't the only person beginning to grow twitchy at how little we were being told. The evidence was slim at best as to the viral load argument. Plus, the government had recalculated the death and infection toll so many times, it was difficult to know what to trust anymore.

At the centre of all my frustration was Rus. The reports on his impending trial were slim and always biased. No one was talking about how he was, just what he'd been accused of. There weren't any grainy images released of his arrest nor of his mugshot. It was as if he were nothing more than a name. I'd had no contact from my mum or Jack. No inkling of whether they would pull through and do the right thing. All I had was silence. Punctuated by worthless conversations. Yes, I was well. No, I didn't know anything new. Yes, I was terrified. No, we don't have any toilet roll. Yes, I was planning to do something stupid. No, I wouldn't be caught.

My fingers shook as I typed out a new status on my social media:

"People shouldn't die because of who they love."

It was as simple as it was true. And it was as dangerous as it was simple. Posting this would bring countless questions to my door. In all honesty, the State would delete it after a few minutes but I had to put my feelings out into the world. I had to stem the tide of bile drowning my friend. They could call me a sympathiser all they liked; I was prepared for their hatred. Their distrust. I'd first experienced society turning against me at such a young age that it had hardened me to any threat of it in the future.

Franklin.

The one thread holding me to the straight and narrow. To obeying the party line.

I hit the backspace button furiously. Annoyed in some irrational way at my child for existing. For causing me to be a more rational person. For giving me a reason to live a better life. I wondered in this moment how many times my mother had felt like that towards me? An overwhelming sense of love but the resentment that went alongside the responsibility of that. For the first time in many years, I wondered what it had been in the end that had caused her to dive off into the deep end of anarchy? To have turned her back on motherhood and the undeniable love she had for me.

All I had were questions. Questions upon questions with no hope of an answer. What was the turning point for my mother when her values became more important than her child?

Would I ever reach that line?

What was Rus suffering through?

Who was chasing us in the car?

How did Leo grow gills?

Why can't I trust anyone?

What worked?

What worked?

It always came back to those last words from Leo no matter the route I took. Everything came back to those three words left inside a photo frame to guide me. If I could just solve that first riddle, everything else would fall into place. I was sure of it.

My phone message tone beeped. Perhaps Bailey had finally started to unpick the puzzle I was too busy to solve.

A number I didn't have saved.

"Your mother-in-law really didn't want you going to prison."

I texted back a question mark and received a note to say my message was undeliverable. I rang the number and received a dial tone.

Moving back to my message inbox, I tried to find the message again, I needed to sit and ponder the words. Let them seep into my brain so I could unpick them.

But the message was gone.

I finished my vodka cocktail in one heavy swallow, left my phone on the sofa and wandered into the kitchen to refill my glass.

The monotony of life was really starting to claw at my sanity.

# Chapter Thirty-Seven

They announced the news at lunchtime. By the time the full report was over, I'd sunk two glasses of wine.

Rus was to be executed publicly in four days. With lockdown in place, his death would be a forced broadcast that would be pumped to all our screens so we could watch the moment the life was choked from his body from the comfort of our own homes. They didn't want the virus to rob us of our entertainment after all.

I knew deep down that execution would be his sentence, there would have been no other possible outcome, but it didn't stop the tears from spilling down my face at the announcement. Then things took an unexpected turn. It was my face on the television screen. My stupid, idiotic face taken from the hospital's 'meet the team' page. It was so out of date; my hair wasn't even that length anymore.

They held me up as the saviour of the Repopulation Act, claimed it had been my testimony in the interview room that had led to the unpicking of his lies. A testimony I never gave. I would forever be remembered in history as a bigot. As the woman who sentenced her friend to death.

They would have told him these lies too. He would have spent his last few days believing I had betrayed him. That I had broken my promise. That I didn't care.

How was it possible to tell such a lie? How could the people behind this farce live with themselves?

My social media icon began to ping as messages

flooded in, a stream of patriotism congratulating me for my hard work, for doing the right thing, for putting the human race at the forefront of my decisions. I was selfless. I was honest. I was a saint. Before I could reply and start to set the tidal wave of awe straight, my doorbell rang.

Laura was standing on the doorstep crying. A cloud of grey that appeared to be human stood behind her, his hand lingering on her shoulder. She couldn't look me in the eye, instead, keeping her gaze fixed on the empty stroller.

My blood pressure rose as panic took me over. "Franklin?" I asked to nobody in particular. The Man in Grey directed her up the stairs, watching her walk with a leery eye as she did so.

"What's happened?" I asked, my voice a lot calmer than I expected.

"Your son has been taken into care," he replied, finally taking his eyes off Laura's retreating form.

I didn't mean for the next sound out of my mouth to be quite so animalistic, but to describe it as a growl would have been kind. My heartbeat echoed in my ears as my blood pressure rose to heights it had never reached before.

As I reached out to hurt the stranger in my home, I felt four strong arms reach out to me from behind and force me down onto the sofa. My face was pressed into the pillows as strange hands patted me down. Lingering in places they weren't welcome.

"Violet!" I called out, but my words were muffled. I needed her to hear me. I needed her to save me.

"Dr Joseph." He paused. "Mrs Hanson, please just stay calm." A needle pierced the back of my neck. I knew the sensation of the mild sedative as it wept through my veins a memory from my brief time in State care. It removed any trace of fight I had left in me. I could see why they thought it necessary, I would tear each of them limb from limb to get my son back.

Roughly, I was pulled into a sitting position, the masked guards who had manhandled me left the house. They were lingering just outside my front door no doubt and I was left helpless with the Man in Grey.

"It has come to our attention that this home may no longer be the safest place for Franklin. The State has decided to take temporary care of him for a week. Just a week." He was trying to soothe me, noticing the way my body vibrated with tears I couldn't bring to the surface.

"We have reason to believe you may be a sympathiser. Of course, all the evidence on the surface points to the contrary you are, after all, now a national hero after turning in your friend for his perverted choices, and yet there's an inkling of doubt about you, Paige. Just an inkling but it is there nonetheless." He licked his cracked lips, and I watched the way the corner of his left eye twitched. His blood pressure was spiking, he was enjoying himself.

"On the day of his execution, you will give a speech to the nation. You will speak out about his crimes, about the selfishness he has displayed with his choice, emphasise the word choice, please. You will tell everyone how rewarding you find motherhood; how much the Repopulation Act means to you. You will remind everyone of your scientific achievements and how the State supported you in these. You will give us the credit we are due. Once that is done, we will review your case."

He placed his hand on my thigh and slowly moved it up an inch as he looked me squarely in the eye. "You're still in your fertile years, you know." I was frozen in shock, unable to react, unable to move. "As such a supporter of the Repopulation Act, we assume you'll be looking to remarry next year?"

"Next year?" I managed to stutter as the sedative began to wear off, all too aware of the heat from his skin seeping through my jeans down to my bones. Move your hand. Move your hand.

His fingers crept up millimetres but it felt like he was reaching deep down into the core of me. "You're a very useful woman to the State, it would be a shame to lose you."

"Get your hand off of her." Her voice was fierce and it was like a charge through my system. I forcibly pushed his hand from the top of my thigh into his own lap.

Violet loomed over us in all her defensive glory. Hair wild and un-brushed. Dressed in mismatched pyjamas. But it didn't matter how she looked because the energy pulsating around her told us everything we needed to know. She was a woman protecting her family.

"Well then," he composed himself, closed his notepad and brushed imaginary crumbs from his lap. "The State will, of course, allow you to visit Franklin whilst your case is under review." We both gasped but before we could protest, he continued, "All I will say to you, Ms Joseph," invoking my maiden name to remind me of my new status, "is compliance is always counted as a positive in these kinds of things."

Violet pulled him to his feet by the collar on his shirt. Her face pressed up so close to his that he could probably taste her coffee-scented breath from deep within her stomach. "If you ever lay foot in this house again, then trust me, you will no longer be relevant to the Repopulation Act."

Without another word, she left the room. Moving into the kitchen to catch her breath. Leaving on a high note. In that moment, I loved her more than I'd ever loved anyone. She was astounding.

The government drone left my house without a second glance back at me. Pausing only to pick up one of Franklin's toys on his way out. A subtle reminder that they had my son. His passive-aggressive way of telling me that he still had control despite the fear Violet had instilled in him.

I felt so stupid having wasted my power over Bailey on the origins of the disease. On a half-formed conspiracy theory at the edge of my mind. I could have asked her to look into the Man in Grey. To find Franklin. To work out just how Rus's world fell apart around him. All of these things would have been more useful to me right now than sending her on some wild goose chase that I didn't truthfully want the answer to.

Walking into the kitchen, Violet handed me a glass of wine. Over the last few months, my tolerance for alcohol had increased tenfold, with each piece of bad news, it became even stronger. If I was not careful, I'd end up falling down the rabbit hole again.

She looked mildly perplexed as I set the glass down without taking a sip. I needed to let my head clear, I needed the curtains to part and logic to return.

I needed answers.

# Chapter Thirty-Eight

I sobered up sometime around midnight.

I knew I was sober because my hands were trembling and I had a taste at the back of my throat that could only be cured by a glass of wine.

But unlike so many of the nights since lockdown, I sat it out. I didn't plod downstairs for a swift one. I stayed sat in my bed and allowed the headache to descend upon me. I sat as my mouth grew fuzzy, my brows furrowed and the room span gently. There was one name on my mind as I felt the hangover eventually set me free.

Regina.

Regina.

Regina.

Her name ravaged me, cleansing my brain of its need to self-destruct, renewing my logic and igniting my resentment of her that I thought had been extinguished with Leo's death.

Regina.

Regina.

Regina.

Like deathly poetry through my mind.

I had focus now. I had something in my crosshairs again. I had something I could pour myself into again. Something I could control. Regina. The name I had spat at Violet whilst I ranted about her latest infringement on my married life, the way she always tried to insert herself into our relationship, desperate to always be the number one woman in Leo's life. Me and Leo had wasted so much time arguing about her, talking about her, worrying about her. Time I could never get back. Time we could never make up for.

Every time we gave an inch, she then wanted to take a mile. If we invited her over for Sunday lunch, she then expected it to be a weekly occurrence. A wave of phone calls, each more emotionally manipulative than the last. Eventually, our spines became shiny and sharp, we were able to resist her crocodile tears and Leo began to stick up for himself. Began to stick up for me. But still, she was there, always there lurking at the edge of our happiness with her micro-aggressions and judgement.

She was at the centre of it all. The text message on my phone may have disappeared, but its words were just trapped in the back of my consistently tipsy mind. Of course she was responsible for this. There was nothing on this planet that she didn't have her perfectly manicured claws into. But how to get to her?

"Violet," I whispered at her sleeping form. "Violet," I repeated at a higher volume. She grunted and turned towards me. "I need to go to the lab."

"Why?" she asked sleepily.

"I left something of Leo's in my drawer." The words were so easy to say, it was so easy to lie. Always has been, I suppose.

"You won't be able to get in."

"I'll break in if I have to." I made sure to add a level of unhinged to my tone. I needed her to worry about me. To make the call I knew she would. "You have to help me get out."

She nodded in agreement, but I saw her thumb her phone into the pocket of her pyjamas when she thought she was out of my eye-line. Good. I paced back and forth in front of my door, stealing glances through the curtains and then muttering to myself. It was easy to pretend to be crazy when you'd never felt so sane.

Regina. Regina. Regina.

Her name pounding through my body every time my heart beat. She was at the centre of this all. It was all her fault. Whatever they were hunting Leo for that night was somehow her fault. It didn't have to be logical; I instinctively knew. Every decision he made in life was influenced by her, whether he was aware of it or not. He was an attentive parent because she was not. He was a caring doctor because she was not. He was an empathetic human being because she was not.

"I need you to cause a distraction."

"Paige, can't we wait until later?" she tried to pacify me without patronizing me, afraid of hitting my self-implode button.

"Easier to move before the sun comes up." Logic. She couldn't argue with logic.

"What do you want me to do?" She sighed and pulled her dressing gown tighter.

"Go and tell the guards what you think of lockdown." I chose a distraction I knew she wouldn't be able to resist, it would give her grief and anger an itch to scratch. A direction to fall in.

"Are you serious? Do you know what they'll do to me?" Her protests were only half-hearted, she was more concerned for me in this moment than she was for herself.

"Lock you back in the house?" I shrugged. We were already imprisoned, the worst they would do was make our provisions even more boring than before.

"Fine. But you owe me." I smiled at her. Letting it reach the edges of my eyes until they turned upwards in a frenzy. She had to believe that I'd snapped.

Regina. Regina. Regina. Regina. Regina. Regina.

My blood pressure rose with every blast of my synapses that brought with it resentful memories.

Holding my newborn for three hours. Ignoring me in the corridors at work. Forcing herself to be the centre of attention at my wedding. Every passive-aggressive complaint she'd aimed at me over the last few years was there at the surface of my skin, causing the hair on my arms to stand to attention. Regina. Regina. Regina. It would all end before the sun rose.

I made my way back from the cutlery drawer as I heard Violet's voice rise in passion. She truly was selling this plan to the guard positioned to the left of our door. I heard him respond, at first trying to keep his voice calm and measured, but soon matching her in decibel and pitch.

I took my chance and snuck away from the house, hiding in the shadows, avoiding the streets. Slowly, I made my way towards the hospital, making the most of shift changes between guards. As they debriefed each other or engaged in mindless gossip, I crept behind them. Onto the next street. On and on. Moving closer and closer to where I knew my target would be heading. I was a huntress just like my mother.

Always had been, no matter how much I tried to run from it. Her blood, her passion, her self-righteousness would always be a part of me. Finally, I was ready to embrace who I truly was. Finally, I was ready to be the daughter she'd always wanted.

Violet would have made the call out of concern. Regina would be heading to the hospital to try and save me from myself.

When she was the one who needed saving.

# Chapter Thirty-Nine

My pass worked at the staff entrance. She'd granted me access. Like I knew she would. The predictability of people was so often their downfall.

I padded barefoot up to my lab. Enjoying the feel of a different sensation on my soles. It felt like an eternity since I'd felt laminate flooring beneath my toes. I'm connected to the Earth, Mum. I'm drawing from its strength just like you taught me.

My lab was empty. I began rummaging aimlessly in my desk, frantically shifting the belongings of my drawers around. I needed her to believe in the chaos of my grief.

"Paige," her voice was honeyed, concerned and full of empathy.

She herself was a widow, she had first-hand experience of the pain I was living with. The pain Theo had been robbed from openly experiencing. There would be no kind hands reaching out to comfort him, no thoughtful words to soften the blow of his broken heart, he would never be able to receive the love the world showed to me and Regina in our time of need.

At least Theo knew he'd lost the love of his life because the world was full of hatred. Hatred she'd brought to the surface. Leo, on the other hand, had been murdered with no explanation, no reason or confession. I had nobody to blame. I jumped in falsity. Playing the part of the unhinged drunk.

"Regina. I, I don't know," I stammered. Letting tears fall from my eyes. It wasn't hard to cry these days.

Grief was always there, lurking close to the surface. My stammer may have been false but the mascara rivers on my cheeks were not. Everything hurt.

I'd been acting since the day I changed my name. Constantly playing the role of somebody I longed to be. Somebody without the baggage of my past. Someone who could fall in love easily and live an uncomplicated life. But it seemed that fate never wanted me to have that.

As she moved towards me to pull me into an embrace, I thumbed the device from Jack in my jeans pocket. My home may now be open to surveillance, but my lab was not. I let her hold me tightly. Returned the pressure around her chest as she held me. I sobbed into her shoulder, great big gulping sobs of regret over what was to happen next. I wasn't this person. I couldn't be this person. This was Leo's mum.

No matter what she'd been to me throughout the years, she was his mum. I tried to remember the good moments we'd shared across the years. Her pride at my professional achievements. The day she'd finally given her blessing to our engagement. It was hard to draw up positivity when my mind had become so clouded with resentment. After all, she may have given us her blessing to get married but the next day she threw an engagement meal we never wanted, sat opposite us the entire time and made sure she gave a weepy toast that kept the spotlight on her and on the son she was losing rather than the daughter she stood to gain. I could still picture Leo's smile at the end of her toast, warm and grateful. Thankful for an open display of affection from her. Oblivious to the negative undertones that had been uttered about me. It was one of the few times I hadn't picked a fight with him on the way home from his mother's. I wanted him to enjoy the feeling of being openly loved.

I couldn't do this to her. I shouldn't do this to her.

"Remember what happened," my mother's voice whispered in my ear. A memory from conversations years ago, relevant to this moment. Every infliction in her tone urged action from deep within me. I could fall under her spell like everyone else. It would be so easy to do.

I had to think about Rus. I had to do this for him. Somebody had to answer for the wrongs dealt to him. He was a good man. A good friend. He deserved better than the plate she'd served him up on.

"I can't find Leo's wedding ring," I offered by way of an explanation. She stroked my face gently in understanding, using her thumbs to wipe away my tears just as a mother would to her child. I could understand Leo's desperate need for her approval in that moment, feeling loved by her made me feel as though my soul was glowing. As though I were the only other person in the world. It's the way Franklin must already feel when she focuses her energy towards him. What a beautiful sensation.

"Where else can we look?" She wanted to help me. Longed to help me. I was the only child she had left to care for. I looked around my workplace as though I was lost. This was my last chance to take a step back. My last chance to call off this god-forsaken mission of revenge I'd talked myself into. Step back. It's not too late to stop.

"Remember what happened," came my mother's voice again. Her words whipped through my eardrums and infected my brain. Give in. It's not too late to give in.

She knows.

She knows something.

She might know everything.

Why else would she save me by sacrificing Rus?

With me out of the picture, Franklin would be hers in no time. With me in prison for life, she could finally have her chance at motherhood again. Why would she give all that up if she didn't have a reason?

"In the lab, maybe?" My voice was trembling with fear. This was it. This was the moment to turn back and leave. She nodded sweetly at me and scanned the doors open with her handprint, one of the few people in the hospital who was authorised to access my sanctuary. I watched as she took two steps inside before turning around, and with so much love and concern on her face, she smiled at me. She cared. She finally really cared.

"Don't fall for it." Echoes of memories I'd so often longed to forget came to me again. I was curled into a small ball at the top of the stairs, trying to keep myself as hidden as possible as I listened to my mother wax lyrically to a handful of faceless people. "They'll do anything to trick you. To make you turn back. Don't fall for it." She was firm in her tone. An enemy not to be crossed.

Before I could change my mind, I placed my hands on the authorisation panel and locked the door behind her. I keyed in the master code. Leo's birthday. He'd been so touched when he realised. A stupid show of kindness he lapped up in a time of drought. It disabled the alarms inside, turned off the exit panels. Still, she tried, bashing at the scanner until it broke.

"Paige?" she asked, worry finally replacing concern on her features. It aged her. For the first time since she stepped into my workstation, I looked at her. Really looked at her. She repeated my name as I took in the lipstick that was bleeding at its edges. Her eyeliner wasn't equal and her hair hadn't been pulled back within an inch of its life. She was falling apart. No longer my immaculate enemy. Just a woman. She must have tried to call my name five times by now.

"Regina," I finally returned, looking her in the eyes. "What did you do?"

"What do you mean?" So, she was going to play dumb with me. That was fine. I had time.

"What did you do to Rus?" My mother stoked the fire that was beginning to roar in my stomach. Finally, I was ready to embrace my heritage. To become the woman she always wanted me to be.

She looked momentarily relieved and then shocked. Unsure as to how I knew her secret. But that brief flicker of relief, the way her shoulders temporarily relaxed, what else was she hiding?

"Honorius is the son of a dear family friend. Trust me when I say I'm as saddened as anyone to learn of his sentence and of course, his crimes."

"Here's the thing though, Regina." I keyed a code into the panel and the lab began to spray itself down with chemicals. Disinfecting the world inside. I heard her cry out in pain as the liquid droplets touched areas of her skin that were bare. "I don't trust you." She was shielding her face. Unfortunately for me, the majority of her was covered in the thick woollen jumper and tights she chose to wear for her planned intervention, but I knew her shoulders would be scarred for at least a week. They hadn't escaped.

After a while, I grew bored of her whimpers. I would get no answers this way. I turned the chemicals off and waited for her to calm down. "Tell me the truth."

"I did what I had to do," she snapped at me. Her composure disintegrating. "Just let me out and we can move on from this. You're clearly not well. I can help. We can work through this."

"There isn't a we here, Regina." I admired her strength as she pulled herself to her feet. The welts on her exposed shoulders were bright and bubbling.

I thought about her as a mother. The way she would have comforted Leo when he cried in the night. How she would have held his small body against hers, bringing him reassurance when he was too little to make sense of the word. I saw the way she smiled at him the first time he laughed, the first time he uttered the word mama and the way she held his hand as he took his first unsteady steps. Without Regina, there would have been no Leo. No Franklin. I hoped with everything I had that Leo wasn't watching right now. His mother may have been colder than most, but she wasn't a monster. She was still his mum.

"Don't fall for it. Stay strong. Do what's right," my mother's words in my brain again. Her followers that night had allowed her strength and fury to weave itself around them, providing them the stones they needed to do what needed to be done. I was ready to do the same.

"Why did you do it? Everything would have been fine if you'd just kept your mouth shut!" My emotions were getting the better of me. My morals were seeping back into my mind. No. I couldn't let my morals win. I had to fight off the person I'd become. The person I'd worked so hard to become.

I typed another code into the panel. The incineration code. A clock started counting down inside the lab. She looked around herself frantically, knowing full well what the alarms meant. She banged on the door with all the energy she had left. Screaming my name. Begging for her life. Over and over.

"I did what I had to." She pressed her face as close to the glass door as possible, desperately trying to bore her words into my soul before it was too late.

"You didn't have to do anything!" I screamed back at her as the clock moved into single digits. "You didn't have to do anything!" I repeated, hysterical now as I battled my internal demons. "I didn't kill Leo. I said all along I didn't know what happened. You could have just believed me!" Regina as a mother. Regina as an enemy. Regina as family. Regina as a murderer by proxy.

She glanced at the clock, following my gaze until, finally, she decided to stop relying on lies and emotional manipulation and blurted out, "I didn't know Leo would come for you!"

That sentence.

That sentence changed everything.

Just as the clock reached its final countdown, I cancelled the incineration. I opened the doors. She collapsed on the floor, body-wrenching sobs escaping from her body. I laid next to her. I held her hand as she cried.

It's all over.

# Chapter Forty

Regina didn't call security on me. Nor the police. That was the point at which I realised she was mentally broken too. No sane person would let someone get away with what I had just put her through.

Instead, she reached for my hand, pulled me to my feet and guided me through the hospital corridors, avoiding the cleaners, until we were in her office. We held shaking hands the whole way as I stole glances at the welts on her shoulder. Soon to be scars on her airbrushed skin. A permanent reminder of the daughter my mother raised.

She closed the door behind us, leaned on it and took a deep breath.

"We need to get you home." She rustled through her desk drawers, placing items into her handbag. Getting ready to leave.

"What did you mean?" The question that had been stuck in my head on a loop finally made its way to my lips.

"We have to get you home before they realise you've gone." She moved to pick up her phone in order to call us a car. In order to save me from repercussions.

"What did you mean about Leo?" I ignored her deflection and saw a wildness flash through her eyes. Like a caged animal, she realised she couldn't gaslight her way out of the conversation.

"Paige, I," she gave herself one last attempt at telling me yet another lie. One last attempt to do the wrong thing. "Merde," she sighed in her thick natural accent. Gone was the plummy tone she usually masked herself with. All pretence was gone.

I'd never heard my mother-in-law swear, not really. Maybe when she'd stubbed a toe or a patient's results hadn't been what she wanted. But not like this. Not out of personal weakness.

"I told him you wouldn't have taken the hint." The wrinkles on her face began to shine through despite the layers of foundation that were in place to mask them. She was finally being honest. I was speechless. I thought my suspicion of her had been nothing more than an alcohol-induced mental breakdown. She'd left me wondering all of this time. Left me at the centre of suspicion for all this time. "I'm so sorry."

She put her hand on my arm, which I pushed away viciously. I couldn't stand her. She knew he was alive all along. She knew and she left me blind. "Do it!" roared my mother's voice in my mind, her anger matching mine. Instinctively, I strike Regina across the face. The skin on my palm stung with the impact and she stumbled backwards but made no move to leave.

"I had no idea at first. I promise you that," she offered. Still, I couldn't find any rational words for her.

"Fuck you," I whispered, over and over. At her and her son. They'd both deceived me. Left me in the dark. Left me grieving before there was a body to grieve. But he was actually gone now, my wrath only had her as a target. "Fuck you both."

Angry tears were spilling out of my eyes at a rapid pace. I didn't want to cry. I didn't want to be weak but I was so frustrated, my body had taken control of its own functions. Short wiring as my synapses clicked into realisation, trying to respond in the way it felt best in the situation.

"The coffee. The day I brought you the coffee. He said you'd know. Said you'd know straight away that I wouldn't remember how you liked it. Two and a half spoons of sugar exactly. Something he said only he knew. Quite a ridiculous thing to hide if you ask me." She'd slipped back into her former character, looking to assassinate me and my choices in life.

Shaking her head, removing the venom from herself, she continued, "He came to me the night before I brought you the coffee to see how you were doing. I couldn't quite believe my eyes when my son emerged from the stream at the back of my house." Of course, she had her own stream. Of course she bloody did. "But there he was. Alive. Different but alive. I wanted to drive him to the hospital to see you, but he said it wasn't safe. He said so long as he was alive, it wasn't safe for you or Franklin."

"Why?"

"I don't know. He told me so little, said it was for my own safety. He said he left you a message?"

The photo frame. That had been his message? I'd always hoped he'd left more and I just hadn't stumbled across it yet. What sort of message was that to leave?

"Something innocent-seeming should it be found by the wrong eyes. He said only you would understand."

I didn't, Leo. I still didn't understand. I remained silent and let her unburden herself.

"I promised him I would do everything I could to keep the two of you safe. Not just because he loved you, or because you're family. He said you were the answer. Just over and over, he kept stressing to me how important your safety was to everyone. All of us. He was manic. Confused. He was wheezing if you can believe it. It was like he'd aged years since the accident."

She sat in her chair, not meeting my line of vision. I tried staring into the depths of her soul, but without reciprocating eye contact, my intimidation tactic was failing.

"There's something else I have to tell you."

Here it was. The confession that had brought me here. The action that had blown up four lives and robbed me of my son.

"The only reason you're still alive is because we all threatened to leave should any harm come to you. We were all in agreement when it became obvious that you weren't supposed to ever leave the hospital."

"Who's we?"

"The board. You may not like us, Paige, but we've always been fond of you, and it was very clear from the State's interest in your case that something sinister was lurking at the edge of their mind. I don't know what Leo did to cause all of this, but we've done all we can to protect you."

"Do you want a thank you?" My tone was surly. Defiant. She paused, waiting patiently. Hoping her confession about saving my life would have taken away from her betrayal. "Do you want me to say cheers, Regina? Thanks for keeping me prisoner in this hospital. Thanks for letting them run every test under the sun on me. Thanks for allowing them to bug my lab. Thanks for providing them with my home address, oh yes, and a great big thank you for knowing that my husband was alive and never telling me."

"It's what he wanted." She was trying to appeal to my empathy, trying to connect to me as a mother. After all, wouldn't I stand by Franklin no matter what?

"His opinion didn't matter. I was the one being affected by the mess he left behind. You could have ended that. You could have stopped it all at any time. But you didn't. You chose not to. You chose to comply with somebody else's wishes rather than supporting the people that were being hounded."

Her shoulders sagged, her wrinkles crept into her features and the greys in her hair grew more prominent.

This was it. She knew any hope of reconciliation we would ever have would die with her next confession.

"I told the State about Rus."

I couldn't help myself as I flung the ornament from her desk across the room. It smashed into tiny pieces that dropped down the wall.

"I didn't know Leo would come for you. I couldn't let them lock you up. I couldn't let them take Franklin from you."

"Thanks to you, they've done that anyway."

She looked shocked. Finally, a piece of the puzzle she wasn't involved in.

"Oh yes, he was seized by the State today. His care to be reviewed after a week provided I comply with their demands."

"What do they want?"

"I don't think that's any of your concern anymore."

"I'm sorry. I'm so sorry." She sobbed into her hands. Her whole world crumbling before her eyes. Her carefully constructed web of a life disintegrating in the wind.

I stood to leave and paused at the door. There was a security camera on the other side. I could hear the sound of voices in the corridor, the hospital was coming to life.

"CCTV was the first item I cut from our electricity budget when lockdown happened." She handed me her coat and hat. "Paige -"

I snatched them from her and shrugged them on.

"Don't ever call us."

"But Franklin," his name was hollow on her breath as I heard her heart break. She loves him. She loves him nearly as much as I do.

"Don't ever call us," I repeated before leaving. Skulking around corridors, avoiding eye contact until I was safely on my way home.

Violet was waiting in the living room for me when I got home. I collapsed in her lap and unloaded everything I could.

She listened calmly as I explained about the speech I had to make at the execution, how I had to turn my back on my friend to save my son, how I'd started imagining things. She asked for specific examples but I wouldn't be pressed.

Something about a full confession made the hair on my neck stand up. I laid in her arms and cried about the unfairness of it all. The inevitability of it all. I wailed about losing the love of my life. I swore at her for not being him, for being unable to bring me the comfort and reassurance only he could. I accused her of stupidity for signing away our lives, for keeping her sister's heritage a secret for so long and for never really letting me know the real her.

Through it all, she spoke understanding words. Met my rage and sadness with kindness. Stroked my hair and handed me tissues to blow my nose. No matter what I threw in her direction, she would not leave. She would never leave.

That's what true friendship was all about.

# Chapter Forty-One

Regret was a familiar feeling to me these days.

I regretted Rus being brought into this cycle of madness that surrounded me. I regretted turning my back on my mother. I regretted telling Regina to never call. I regretted never letting Leo love the whole of me, secrets and all.

I loved him with everything I could, but there was always a part of me that held back. An inch of my heart that I simply couldn't give to him. I regretted every minute I hadn't told him the truth. It prevented the love I had for him from becoming all-encompassing, overwhelming, consuming. Now I had nothing but regrets and secrets that seemed less worth keeping with each day that passed.

Perhaps if he hadn't been so influenced by his mother's invisible hand, I would have had the courage to give him my everything. I was sure he would have accepted me. In time, he may even have been happy to meet my mum. I knew deep down that he was a better man than most and yet I'd never given him a chance to prove that to me. I'd never trusted him quite enough to show him my complete raw and naked past. Too afraid he would turn his back on me as so many had when I was young. I'd judged him by the failings of others, and I'd lost my chance to ever make that right.

Leo. You are where it all began and where it all ends. I always thought the day I met you would be the day my world couldn't possibly be turned any further upside down. But it was the day that I lost you, the conversations I couldn't remember, the feelings I couldn't quite bring to the surface those are the things that have shaken me to my core in a way that first love never could.

The irony being that I knew if he were here, he'd be able to put me back together again. He'd listen to my worries and find the right words to soothe my anxiety. I wasted the love of my life on mistrust, too hung up on my past and my mother's teachings to really celebrate one of the most powerful emotions in humanity.

As much as it made my skin crawl, I knew I had no choice but to comply with the State's demands, to stand there directly after my friend's murder to slander and denounce him. I had no choice because when it came to Franklin's safety, there would never be a choice. He would always come first.

I will never become like my mother. I will never choose my convictions over my kin.

The day of the execution loomed and each morning the State delivered something new to my front door as part of a sick countdown, always wrapped in a blood-red ribbon. The same colour the President always chose to wear on his pocket squares. A clear message that I belonged to the party just as he did.

To be fair to them, they had kept their word and I was allowed to interact with Franklin once a day under supervision. Something that was rarely granted to potential sympathisers. They were highlighting my worth to me whilst, at the same time, reminding me of exactly what I had to lose. All I had to do to return to my comfortable normality was demonise somebody I cared about deeply, paint myself as a patriotic bigot and rally the creaking trust of the nation into standing beside me in the fight against this virus. Easy.

The first day after they took Franklin, they delivered my speech. Full of hateful language and slurs.

Peppered with reminders of how the State has always cared about us and a nice paragraph in closing about how I stand beside our President who has enabled me to cure so many illnesses and ailments in my time at the hospital. I was the human figurehead of healthcare, I had to be the friendly relatable face everyone could still believe in. I thought I felt paraded when Regina used to send me in for all the interviews for the hospital and the board, but this was another level of advantage being taken.

The second day after they took Franklin, they delivered my outfit for the address. A pinstripe skirt and jacket that was tailored exactly to my measurements and a plain white shirt to wear tucked into the waistband. They'd even supplied me with a hairband. I wasn't cleared to pick my own accessories. Heaven forbid I show a bit of personality during this farce. My unruly mane was to be pulled back into a neat, but not too tight ponytail, with a few stray strands left hanging loose around my face. Professional but approachable.

The third day after they took Franklin, the day before the execution, they sent me a reminder to wear my wedding ring. All too aware of the power a widow's words could hold over sympathetic ears. Especially the widow who lost her husband at the hands of a Dweller.

It was all a farce, a circus of manipulation to be played out in front of an unwitting, trusting audience. But I would comply. This was just a new persona to add to my rotating list of characters. Lost child. Orphan. Star pupil. Flushed bride. Caring mother. State sacrifice.

Just another hat to add to my collection.

I sat in my living room dressed up like their toy and waited patiently for the car to arrive. My speech was memorised along with the emotional moments to punctuate it, a rise of tone here, a pause to wipe a tear there, a subtle clenching of fists to show my disdain. It would all be so easy and over so quickly.

I only hoped Rus would be granted the same small mercy at his end.

# Chapter Forty-Two

The car arrived promptly twenty minutes before the execution was due to start. Twenty minutes before Rus was walked up the platform to be publicly hung. Twenty minutes before I sold out my morals for the sake of my son.

The camera crews would have completed their sound checks and finished adjusting the white balance on their equipment. The journalists would have tested and double-tested their dictaphones, adjusted their collars and teased their hair. The President would be sitting in a makeup chair hoping that the dusty orange pallor of his skin could be brought back to a more neutral tone for such a sombre occasion.

I wondered which mistress would be sat with him. It probably wouldn't be the pregnant one. He didn't tend to stick around long after they fell pregnant. Something about the way their figures changed and adapted to carrying life clearly wasn't appealing to him. It mattered not, there was always surprisingly another one waiting in the wings to entertain him until the same fate became her.

It had always been believed that he had at least seven children by various women but he, of course, had never confirmed any of that. Preferring instead to focus attention on the legitimate children from his two previous wives and the one due from his much younger current fiancé. It was always dismissed as a coincidence that the women he would often be pictured in public with, his temporary advisor of whichever sector he decided, would retire from their position due to an unexpected pregnancy. Nothing to do with him of course, some other heartless cad had knocked them up and abandoned them. Quietly, they were paid off with public funds and the whole sorry mess would disappear from public memory.

I sat in the car as I was driven to the government's court, concentrating on the President's shortfalls to take my mind off the steps I was soon due to make. It gave me something to focus my rage on instead of feeling the waves of dread and sorrow crash upon me.

There were eighteen steps into the courtroom. Into the open arena where they would hang Rus. Eighteen steps until I turned my back on all my values to save my son.

The car came to a halt and the doors opened automatically. I hesitated. Finally beginning to understand why my mother had chosen her ideals over me on that fateful day. She'd wanted to make the world a better place for me and had taken the actions she thought would achieve that.

My grandad had acted like a parent and put my needs first. He always did. He agreed with many of her principles, but he never agreed with her abandonment of me to follow them.

But was it abandonment?

Was it really? When she did it for me? For all the other children like me destined to grow up in such a controlled society? She did it for the children who would have to hide their sexuality forever. For the children who would grow up not wanting children. For the children who didn't want to give their lives to the ongoing war. She did it for each and every one of us and I finally grasped the weight of that. She did it so we could all be free.

The car started sounding an alarm to let me know

my exit was being not so kindly requested. What would happen if I just stayed here? If I refused to get out of the car?

What if I was brave like my mother and stood up for what I believed in? What if I took a stand against the Repopulation Act? What if I told the nation that Rus had been murdered, not punished? What if I told them that people had recovered from the virus before we were made aware of it?

What if I started pulling at that particular thread? The one that had been scratching at the edges of my brain since we first received samples. Always there in the background, niggling away at my sanity, pulling me closer to madness. I wondered fleetingly as to whether Bailey had taken me up on my challenge; if she'd understood my request. It had been radio silence since I'd sent her the e-mail.

I'd be assassinated before the words had finished leaving my mouth. Franklin would be all alone in the world, destined to grow up in a State home with his brain being washed daily. They'd make him hate me. They'd fill his mind with the garbage I'd managed to fight off about my mother. He'd denounce me as I denounced her.

No, I couldn't do that.

The kitten heels on the boots they'd provided me clicked elegantly on the pavement as I made my way towards those eighteen steps. With a deep breath, I began to climb towards the entrance.

First step. Mum, please do something.

Second step. I have to do something.

Third step. I can't do anything.

Fourth step. Save me.

Fifth step. Save Franklin.

Sixth step. Save Rus.

I paused to swallow a lump in my throat. I'd been

explicitly told that crying over my friend's fate was not allowed. I would have to grieve in private. Once again, grief would come looking for me. My never-ending admirer.

Seventh step. Jack will fix it. He fixes everything.

Eighth step. Franklin, I'm so sorry. I'm so, so sorry.

Ninth step. I love you.

Tenth step. What worked? Leo, what worked?

Looking around me, I took in the sunrise, the soft clouds on the orange horizon, the sound of the native animals crying for attention on the outskirts of Nomad's Land. It was a sound you could only tune into if you were looking for it. It reminded me of my childhood. Our family home had been close to the border of the Dwellers' land. I'd sit up in my bed every morning and listen to the creatures hollering and shouting in the distance. Longing to put an image to the sounds. But I never got the chance. Kyan had promised to take me one day, but he'd disappeared before we could set a date.

Eleventh step. I won't do it.

Twelfth step. I can't do it.

Thirteenth step. Leo. Leo. Leo.

Fourteenth step. I have to save Rus.

What a ridiculous thought. My feet fought against my brain and I stood planted to the fourteenth step. It was implausible that I could take any action to change the outcome of my friend's fate. I wouldn't be anywhere near the platform they'd hang him from. I wouldn't be near him until he was cold and dead. Then they'd wheel me out and I'd have to make my speech in close proximity to his corpse.

Fifteenth step. I have to try.

Sixteenth step. Franklin will hate me.

Seventeenth step. Unless it makes a difference.

Eighteenth step. Franklin. Franklin. Franklin.

I repeated his name to myself over and over, sometimes out loud, sometimes in my head as they marched me towards my waiting room. A large TV displaying the live feed was the only object within it.

No chair.

No window.

Nothing to look at apart from the threat of death.

# Chapter Forty-Three

I stood in my room and watched as the broadcast began. They brought him out without a hood covering his face. I hadn't expected that.

It was protocol to bring those who had a death sentence out with their face covered in a bright orange hood. Orange so the colour would really 'pop' on camera, the hood so the audience wouldn't have to put up with watching the fear on the face of the condemned. So the audience didn't have to humanise them. After all, if anyone began to feel sympathy towards those with the death sentence, then they might start questioning the laws that put them there in the first place.

They may have broken his spirit; and from the looks of his limp, his body too, but they couldn't break the beauty that shone out of him. I scrunched my eyes together so tightly I could feel the wrinkles beginning to ebb into my skin, leaving a permanent reminder of the stress I was under right now. Yellow lines of lights appeared across my eyelids but I kept squeezing. Maybe if I squeezed them hard enough, I'd stop being able to see entirely.

"Ms Joseph?" His voice broke my concentration. I gave thought to refusing to look away from the screen, somehow, watching my friend being marched to his end was emotionally preferable to meeting the Man in Grey's eye-line. But avoiding a nightmare never made it disappear and so I turned to look at him. I could feel his lip curl up in appreciation as he noticed I had complied implicitly with my wardrobe orders. Orders he had no doubt issued. A man who liked control. Such a cliché. "Could you come with me?" The trumpets were beginning to sound, the President was taking to the stage.

I shook my head, closed my eyes, and covered my ears. This isn't happening. None of this is happening.

I am in a coma. Leo is by my side waiting for me to wake up. "Wake up, Paige," I can hear him whispering to me. "Come back to me, PJ."

The only person who was ever allowed to refer to me by my stolen initials. I wish I'd heard my real name on his lips. Just once. Paige Kearney. Please just say my name, Leo. Say the name I've kept locked inside for so long. Forgive my mother's crime. Realise I was innocent. Please. Just know me.

"Dr Joseph." The Man in Grey roughly pulled my hands away from my ears. If it had been any other situation, I would have given thought to striking him, the demon of my mother's spirit would have demanded no less. But not now. Not here. Not when everything was broken.

The world was burning. People were dying because of chemical warfare. My mother-in-law had sentenced my friend to death for simply loving somebody. My son had been taken into State care. My husband had been murdered. And there at the centre of it all, the strings holding the whole picture together, was me. Somehow, all of this was my fault, I just knew it. In the same way I'd known it was my fault when my mother had killed those people. It was always to do with me. I was always at the centre of chaos.

The Man in Grey took advantage of my mental breakdown and led my living corpse into the main arena.

The studio lighting blinded me, and the sound of

the national anthem was blasting all around me. Hundreds of different voices, different tones - all singing the President's praises. A song he'd written himself many, many years ago when he first won his seat. I could see dozens of red dots out in the empty seating area, cameras were positioned everywhere. Desperate to get the best angles. Salivating for the money shot.

"Remember your place," the Man in Grey whispered in my ear as he pulled the corner of Franklin's blanket out of his pocket; a small glimpse of the hold he had over me. I had to be strong for my son. I had to pull myself together and survive this to get back to him. I was the only parent he had left.

I sat gracefully next to the Man in Grey. Agents in black all around us. Crossing my legs at the ankle, I straightened my back and plastered on a small smile as I gently applauded the President's arrival.

Rus didn't glance in my direction as he stood next to the noose. Not once. I knew because I kept him in my peripheral, ready to convey all the love I had for him into one quick glance that might not be picked up by the cameras.

I was ready but he wasn't willing.

Instead, he bravely stared ahead, directly into the sea of cameras upon him. Defiantly, he sneered as the President took his seat in front of the podium Rus had been placed upon. The last piece of ground his feet would touch. He wasn't about to let the world see his fear, I loved him for that. I wish I could be that brave.

There was no public breakdown of his crimes, simply an automated voice repeating:

"You have been found guilty and sentenced to death." It was far more cut-throat than the usual public address given by the President when sending someone to their death, it was unlike him to miss an opportunity to speak publicly.

After the fifth repetition, the automated voice stopped and we were plunged into silence, the only sound punctuating the air were the footsteps of the executioner as he made a beeline for Rus. A spotlight followed his movement through the arena. They really were pulling out all the stops for this show of patriotism.

I closed my eyes as he headed up the stairs towards my friend who stood bound, gagged and bruised but proud. There must be a sense of relief at no longer having to live a lie that he felt in that moment. He would go to his grave as his most honest self, which was more than I could hope for.

A sharp elbow in my side winded me as the Man in Grey nodded towards the noose that was now being tied around Rus's neck. It was clear that was where my attention needed to be focused. This man was not about to miss another opportunity to enjoy his power over me.

Rus held eye contact with the executioner, cementing himself in his subconscious. Wanting to be the guilt that ate away at him every night, longing to be the cold sweat that would haunt the back of his neck forever. Rus wanted revenge on the man who would kill him. A reasonable thing to lust after.

Please, Mum. It's now or never. Please.

The executioner tugged harshly on the knot around Rus's neck. Checking its security. Still, my friend did not flinch. He would not die ashamed of himself. He stepped onto the drop platform before he was asked. One step. Two steps. Always keeping eye contact.

The executioner stepped away from him and the Man in Grey squeezed my upper arm to make sure my attention stayed where he wanted it.

Mum. Please.

The executioner's hand was on the switch for the platform. It was as steady as could be.

I thought my heart might explode. I was trying not to hyperventilate. Trying to comply with the State's orders. If I lost Franklin, I might as well be up on that platform with Rus, standing by my beliefs instead of down here in the audience watching it all unfold.

"Not a word," the Man in Grey slithered his voice into my ears. It was hot and sticky on my skin, I couldn't help the shudder of disgust that crawled down my spine.

The President raised his hand as though he was some ancient Roman ruler. I remembered learning about them in school, looking at the sketches and paintings of artists long gone of glorious leaders who sentenced men to death for entertainment. It seems that not much ever changes.

It has to happen now. She has to bring the chaos now.

Silence. Nothing but silence. No cavalry to save the day.

He turned his thumb down and the executioner hit the switch. Rus plummeted through the floor, kicking his legs in a natural reaction. His face turned blue as the life was choked out of him. After a few seconds, his flailing stopped, and he swung gently from the noose.

"Time for your speech." The Man in Grey's lips turned up cruelly as he passed me a microphone. How could I possibly force words from my mouth now? I could barely breathe for holding in tears. But still, I stood up. I pushed down my skirt absentmindedly and cleared my throat. The world was watching, and I had another role to play.

My hands were shaking too much to hold the microphone, so with a heavy sigh, the Man in Grey stood next to me, holding it so close to my mouth that my shaking breath echoed around the stadium.

It's now or never.

With a deep breath, I centred myself, trying to look at the situation logically. With just a few sentences, this would all be over. I could be back with my son. I could honour my friend's memory in private. I could fix everything once these words were out of my mouth.

The microphone fell to the floor and feedback rang out. I looked down at my skirt. It was covered in flesh and blood.

The Man in Grey was clawing at my leg as blood gushed out of his chest.

"Help me," he begged, air gushing out of his lungs in large hungry bites.

I kneeled down next to him, shielding us both from the view of the camera in a show of consideration. I was, after all, a doctor, I had taken an oath to heal.

I peered into his eyes, offered a kind smile and placed one of my hands on top of his on the wound on his chest.

"No," I responded as I placed my other hand over his mouth and nose. I watched as panic took over his body as he tried to fight me off and flailed in agony as he was denied oxygen. Once I was certain he was dead, I removed my hand and turned my now blood-soaked frame towards the cameras.

"Please, somebody help us!" I pleaded to the sea of nothingness that stared back at me. The show had to go on after all.

Looking back at the terror frozen permanently onto his features, I couldn't help but feel a sense of euphoria. I had slain a beast. I had become my own hero. I had righted this one wrong.

Logic fought its way through the endorphins. It reminded me of the oath I swore when I qualified.

It confirmed to me what I'd always known.

That the apple never fell far from the tree.

# Chapter Forty-Four

Before I could sink into the rational feeling of guilt over what I had just done, I felt the unmistakable barrel of a gun pressing into my back.

The world slowed in front of me, and I heard my heartbeat in my ears. So, this is what true panic feels like. I watched as the President disappeared before my eyes, nothing more than a hologram. That would explain why he didn't make his usual speech, they never quite managed to sync the hologram's movements to his impassioned manner of speaking. Were they expecting this?

Government agents swarmed the arena. I watched as they each fell to the floor, felled by unseen assassins. The red lights on the cameras blinked out one by one, accompanied by a blood-curdling scream. There was death all around me but all I could see was Rus's lifeless body, it was the only murder that mattered to me.

"Traitor," an unseen voice aimed at me, its accusation carried around the room and into multiple homes as the broadcast was cut from the airways via my discarded microphone. So, this is how it ends, those are the last words the world will hear about me. Traitor. It's apt, I suppose.

My identity chip was ripped from my neck and a bag was placed over my head and I was roughly pulled and pushed out of the arena in a cloud of displaced confusion. I was dragged away from centre stage.

Away from Rus's body.

Away from my chance to save Franklin.

I screamed and screamed. Using every expletive I could think of. Levelling threats against my unseen captor that would make any sane person's blood freeze.

I told them I had access to a wide range of diseases and would take great pleasure in using them personally as a test subject. I swore I would tear their families apart as they were doing to mine. Finally, just as I reached my peak, I invoked my mother's name. My last hope for survival.

"Di Kearney will make you pay for this," I hissed at them as I was pushed face-first into a vehicle and the doors slammed behind me.

"Don't you mean Deidamia," came a familiar voice as the hood over my eyes was pulled back over my head, tugging my hair alongside it. I blinked in the light of the car, letting the world come into focus as my pulse continued to climb.

There she was.

In her full glory.

My blood-splattered mother.

She'd gone by the name Di since she'd arrived on Earth Two at a very young age after being adopted by a kind but firm couple who wanted the picture-perfect family. A young Greek girl hadn't been their ideal pairing but so few children had won the ticket lottery for the escape from Earth One without their legal guardians, that they were left with very slim pickings.

She'd explained to me when I was very young that being ripped from her family, leaving them behind to perish in the fire of Earth One was the sole motivation behind all of her political views. It hadn't been fair. My father used to say it was a very naïve point of view but one that I could never disagree with. Life wasn't fair, it was just fairer than death, that's all.

Which was why she was so obsessed with the unfairness in the new society she was thrust into.

I knew without her ever admitting it that there would always be a part of her that wished she'd stayed behind and died with her family. Even my honest to a fault mother would never admit to her only child that she'd rather be dead than live in a world with so many injustices. I couldn't say I blamed her; life would be a lot easier if I was no longer in it. At least for me anyway.

Her broken childhood had been the main reason mine was so full of love and laughter. The driving factor behind Grandad Joseph's determination to keep me out of State care and with my family.

I hadn't actually realised that they weren't my biological family until I was old enough to realise the science behind all of our differing skin tones.

My mum had deep olive skin, with dark wild hair. Grandpa Joseph and Nana Joyce were as pale as the snow that punctuated our summer season. I took after my dad, with my curly untamed hair and dark skin.

Once I realised we were all biologically different, I loved my family even more. They loved us because they wanted to, not because they had to.

It made it hurt all the more when Grandad Joseph condemned my mum to a life in prison. I was the straw that broke the love between them. My existence tore our family apart. It was one of the many strands of guilt I'd wrapped around myself at a young age.

Now here she was. Standing before me. Five minutes too late. All the resentment I had inside of me came bubbling to the surface and I lunged at her. Longing to scratch all my feelings onto her face. With a move impressive for a woman of her age, she pinned me into the seat.

"Calm down love," she repeated at me over and over as the wails from my body matched my flailing limbs. I kicked out at her legs and felt satisfaction as I hit her knee and a shadow of pain swept across her face.

She was late. She was too late. She'd robbed Rus of his life. She'd snatched Franklin away from me.

Over and over, she shushed me as my angry shouts turned to sobs and then silent shakes until all the emotions had left my body. Only then did she release her firm grip from my chest and throat, pulling me into her arms and stroking my hair as I sat shell-shocked.

The car rocked back and forth as we sped away from the stadium and towards an unknown location. Feeling the engine rev beneath me threw me back to the night we crashed.

*"You have to cure it. I know you'll work it out." Leo tries to placate me with a compliment as I run around the house packing a bag. "Please hurry."*

*I turn to look at him, nothing but disappointment in my gaze.*

*"How could you be so stupid?" They are the first words I've uttered to him since I threw the photo frame at his head when he came back to check on my packing process.*

*What toys should I take? What's Franklin's favourite at the moment?*

*"Please, Paige. You have to understand. I couldn't say no. I couldn't do that to the two of you. They left me no choice." The sad fact is that I did understand. I know exactly why he'd made the decisions he had.*

*The decisions that led to us having to flee our home when we should be getting dressed up to celebrate our anniversary. He really didn't have any other choice. I stare helplessly at the broken photo frame on the floor. A victim of my reaction.*

*"How many of them, Leo? How many people died?"*

*"Eight." I can see the grief in his eyes, they were his team. Their blood was on his hands and yet to think he pushed past that and carried on with his work. He isn't the man I thought I knew.*

*"We have to go. Now." His voice is demanding as he peers through the curtains, looking at the streets that surround our house.*

*Checking for the impending danger that is heading our way. It is a long drive to the outskirts of Nomad's Land and he is desperate to get started.*

*How could he have been so stupid? How could he have helped them?*

*The Disease.*

*It is coming for us all.*

Leo knew about the disease. My ears rang with memories, cross words, discussions I couldn't quite bring to the surface. Our voices white noise to soothe me as the car came to a halt and my mother took my hand.

"Welcome home," she exclaimed grandly as she opened the door, expecting some kind of response no doubt. I wouldn't please her with one. I would no longer comply for anyone other than myself.

"Do you realise what you've done?" I shot at her as I left the car and stepped into a large warehouse. It was full of people, and I got jostled around at the speed by which they were moving. It had obviously been a big day for the Anarchists. Despite my resentment at my mother, I couldn't help but marvel at the world she'd managed to create around herself. The warehouse was full of life, colour and laughter.

Stalls punctuated the space, full of homemade treats and crafts. Wind chimes, stained glass, large chunks of cheese and meat smoking over charcoal. In any other circumstance, I would have taken time to walk between the people here, listen to their conversations, take in the smells and the sights and emerge myself in their lives in the hopes I could replicate it.

"Saved your life?" She was proud of herself for being a good mum. She always thought she was a good mum.

"Ended Franklin's." I waited for her face to pale in realisation at the depth of what her little stunt had done. But it didn't come.

"Franklin is on his way," she offered before marching on ahead, the sea of people parting for her. I often wondered when my mother would be able to stop enthralling everyone she met. "Gina went to fetch him."

I didn't want to look desperate and run after her, so instead, I walked as quickly as I could whilst trying to maintain an open sense of resentment. Had she really achieved what I couldn't? Had she really got Franklin out of State care?

"Gina?" I asked as I followed her into a room.

It was clearly her quarters judging by the elective mash of knickknacks and the brightly coloured walls. There was an old photograph of me on the wall, taken from newspaper coverage of her case. It had been my first school photograph, the only one the press ever had access to after the judge granted me anonymity. I could still remember the itchy feeling of the collar of my new shirt, but I felt so proud to be wearing it. A feeling that was clear from my toothy grin directly down the lens of the photographer's camera. It had been so long since I'd seen a picture of myself before everything in my life changed. Before my mother went off the deep end. I couldn't remember being that little girl. I couldn't remember the happiness on her face.

She offered me a cloth to clean the blood and flesh from my skirt as she rinsed the death from her own skin. She didn't care too much though as the blood still stained the wrinkles around her lips.

"Regina these days, I suppose."

# Chapter Forty-Five

"Regina?" I spluttered as my mum turned to grin at me. She'd been waiting to tell me this for a while, I could tell. I couldn't help but return her smile, her joy just like her chaos was infectious, and now I had her assurance that Franklin was coming back to me, the resentment in my soul had begun to melt.

"I knew Gina when I was very young. We were friends right up until she met Billy. Sorry, he always hated it when I called him that. Right up until she met William. I couldn't keep up with her social circle and she wouldn't share my ideals. So, that was the end of that." She shrugged nonchalantly. My mum had never been short of friends in life, but it was interesting to finally hear of someone who put themselves above her bullshit. Gina. Regina.

"She doesn't know about you and I, of course. She reached out to me recently quite by chance to ask me to help her grandson and daughter-in-law. Explained her reasons for doing so. Volunteered to save him herself because nobody would suspect her. It turns out she's grown into quite a surprising woman." A glint of admiration was in my mother's eyes. There was nothing she admired more in life than a strong woman.

Regina was going to give up everything she had for me and Franklin. Perhaps after this sacrifice on her behalf, I could one day forgive her for what she did to Rus. For what she did to me.

"Where is he?" I was impatient. I'd been kept apart from Franklin for too long already. All I wanted was to hold my son in my arms, close against my chest and feel his heartbeat.

"They should be here soon." She checked her watch. "Until then, I think it will be good for you to meet a few people." She knocked on the wall of her room and the front door creaked open. "Why don't you go and take a look around whilst I take care of some business?" It sounded like an offer, but I knew it was an order. And one I was happy to accept.

I left her quarters and began walking at a leisurely pace around the warehouse. I took in the sights and sounds, pausing to hear the different natural accents and languages I'd never heard history of. It was a rainbow of culture and now it was to be my home.

A woman around my age apologised as her daughter ran head-first into my legs, the little girl grinned up at me, oblivious to the entanglement she'd caused. I smiled at her and her mother and watched as they carried on with their day. The girl seemed so happy, laughing, skipping and waving at everyone she encountered. It was exactly how a child should be able to behave. It was how I hoped Franklin would grow up, so full of trust and happiness in the world around him.

As I casually thumbed through some glistening trinkets on a stall, I noticed three familiar faces in the distance. My mind was playing tricks on me once again, hope was defying logic. It had always been the way when I'd been in close proximity to my mother. Her thrall always left you with an impossible sense of hope. I blinked a few times, hoping for the phantoms to disappear and be replaced by something logical, something true. No matter how many times I opened and closed my eyes, the three familiar figures stood tall and strong in front of me.

There stood Theo, Claire and Rebecca. We all hesitated for a moment before Theo stepped forward and cleared his throat.

"I am so sorry for the way I spoke to you, Paige. I know now you had nothing to do with what happened to Rus."

"But how are you here?" Part of me wanted to scold him for even momentarily believing I would betray them all. It was better to have answers than pride though.

"Jack put us in touch with Di," he replied. So, he didn't know she was my mother. Good. That was easier than having to unravel years of storytelling. I wondered if she knew I'd killed her off in the history I had weaved for myself. If she'd ever known the truth, she'd never let it cloud our passive-aggressive relationship. I was the only person she'd ever been capable of showing forgiveness towards.

"She told us we could finally live somewhere where we didn't have to hide who we really were," he continued. It was then I noticed that Claire and Rebecca were holding hands. Their arms intertwined. So, they'd gotten a happy ending after all. They were all finally free to be who they wanted to be. Everyone other than Rus, that was.

We all felt overwhelmed in the presence of each other, words couldn't do justice to all that had passed between us, so instead, we stood in comfortable silence as they joined me in searching through the stall's products. I watched as Claire picked up a toy bunny and showed it to Rebecca.

"The baby would love this." The happiness and love shone from their skin so intensely that I began to feel warm. Their child would be so loved. So safe. They deserved nothing less.

Theo handed me a package, hastily wrapped in the red tissue paper behind the counter. I pulled the paper back; it was a wooden train. "For Franklin," he offered as a final olive branch between us. I hugged him in gratitude and placed it into my pocket. Franklin was going to love his Uncle Theo.

"Hello, love," a familiar gravelly voice interrupted my thoughts. Another impossibility. Perhaps I'd been jostled about too much after the execution, could it be a head trauma?

Rus walked towards me, a smile painted wide upon his face, though his eyes looked exhausted. There were large welts around his neck from the noose and he was wheezing slightly. But he was here. He was alive.

I took two steps towards him and threw my arms around him. He pulled away from me after returning my embrace and then laced his arms around Theo. They were together. They were finally together.

My mum was standing at his side, pride painted across her face. "You didn't think I'd really let them hang him, right?" She laughed at my naivety.

"But I was there. I saw you." My brain couldn't keep up with my racing heart.

"It's easy to play dead when you've spent your whole life working with them." He laughed, coming up for air from Theo's lips. The strain of joy on his chest turned into a hacking cough and Theo gently rubbed his back. Finally, they could be as open with each other as I'd seen in the privacy of their own home. Something good had finally come from this whole mess. I just wished desperately that Leo could be here so we could finally be truly and completely honest with each other.

A stranger came marching towards us and pulled my mother aside.

I paid their exchange no mind as I watched my friends blossom under their newfound freedom. I predicted another double wedding would be on the cards soon, but this time, the vows would be shared between the right parties.

I heard an unusual sound from my mother.

She was crying.

Oh, God. Something must have happened to Jack.

I moved to her side and hugged her, wanting to make everything better for her as it turned out she had finally done for me.

A new life for all of us, one without the constant threat of the State. Franklin and I could go wherever we chose; we could disappear together. Maybe live in a little cabin on the outskirts of the Dwellers' border. He could learn all about their culture and animals just as I had. It would be magical.

She squeezed the small of my back as though I was the one who needed comfort. "I'm sorry," she whispered into my ears. "I'm so sorry."

# Chapter Forty-Six

Regina was dead.

She'd been shot in the back of the head by agents who stopped her when she'd tried to leave with Franklin. They'd missed him by an inch.

Franklin had been seized by those agents and was currently in an as yet unknown State-sanctioned facility. He wasn't coming. We wouldn't be reunited.

My mum had tried to comfort me, but I'd pushed her away. Years of resentment and depression spilled over in that moment. She was just lucky I still had enough self-control to leave the situation rather than unleashing the full extent of my feelings in that moment.

I sometimes wondered if I'd always been an angry person. Looking back at my childhood, I didn't remember ever really feeling rage. I got frustrated and stroppy, of course, but never really angry. Not until my mum's arrest. Not until I had to watch the world tear her apart and their words began to cloud my judgement and memories of her. That's when I really began to understand how angry I could be. I channelled that anger into achievements. It was what pushed me to succeed in every challenge. And now without anything left to excel at, I had no outlet. I just had rage.

I hid down an alley next to the warehouse, hyperventilating, beyond tears. The smell of tobacco called to me.

"I'm so sorry, Paige," Rus spoke as he handed me a

cigarette, not smoking one himself. I held it between shaking fingers and took a drag. I didn't have words to offer in return. Words were as pointless as action in this moment.

He stood silently next to me as I smoked. Not touching me. Not pushing me for conversation. Giving me the space I needed to process the wave of emotions I currently felt. I smoked my way through three cigarettes before I felt like speaking.

"I need to go home." From the moment my mum told me about the bullet hitting Regina, I knew what my decision had to be.

"They won't let you have him back." Rus was trying to play the logical cop.

"I have more chance there than I do here." An indisputable fact.

"You don't know what hoops they'll make you jump through." He tried invoking a sense of fear, he wanted me to know exactly what I was walking back into.

"Doesn't matter. I have to go home." My love for Franklin overwhelmed my love for myself. The love that I could grow for this new community, for the freedom it promised. It all meant nothing without my son. I am not my mother.

He couldn't argue with my logic. It stemmed from a natural instinct to want to be there for your young. Something I didn't really understand after his birth but was coming to realise more and more as each day passed.

He followed me back into the warehouse, matching me step for step. It felt so good to know he was alive and that the four of them could now live all together as they pleased. It would be so easy to stay here with them. To join my mother's resistance, stand by her side, rebuild our relationship. So much simpler than the alternative.

But I had no choice.

"Mum?" I offered as a way of an apology, addressing her by the title I knew meant so much to her in front of everybody. Now I had calmed down, I knew Regina's death had nothing to do with my mother. Regina had contacted her. Regina had taken the risk herself knowing full well the consequences she faced should she fail. My mum had not put her into any position she wasn't more than willing to take up. Rus and Theo shot each other surprised glances and I shrugged at them by way of a nonchalant answer. "Mum, I need to go home."

"You can't," she spoke harshly, as though I was one of her mindless followers. "If you go home, they'll punish you. You don't understand what we're dealing with -"

"Enough. Please. That's enough. I'm not a child anymore. You can't tell me what to do. I can't choose myself over my son." My words stung. She knew the unspoken truth behind them. I won't choose myself over my child because I'm not like that. Because I'm not like you.

"Then the less you know, the better I suppose." She sighed, openly disappointed in my decision. "We can always try to get him another time?" she offered, a last-ditch attempt to bring me on side.

"When would that be though, Mum? Tomorrow? Next week? A month from now? What if you fail again?" She couldn't answer any of my questions, she couldn't give me an estimate as to when I'd hold my son again. Truth be told, I didn't think I'd have accepted any answer other than immediately.

"I'll go myself," emotion was beginning to make her desperate. "I'll go tomorrow and do whatever I have to do."

"Going home is the right thing to do. For him. For me."

"You don't know what they've got planned, you don't understand -"

I cut her off. "The less I know, the better, right?" She nodded, finally accepting my decision.

"Then I guess you'll need someone to accompany you back to the border." She turned and walked away from me, another dramatic unspoken goodbye. I stood and watched her retreating back. The child inside me longing to call out to her. Mummy, please come back. Please come back to me.

The familiar sound of a clip-clop pair of high heels approached me from behind.

The third impossibility of my day walked up behind me.

Agent Cherry. Georgia.

"Paige." She offered her hand for me to shake. "Pleased to see you again."

# Chapter Forty-Seven

She could clearly see the shock painted across my face as my mouth gaped open and closed, at a loss for words. "I believe this is yours." She held out my jacket in the space between us. It had been real; she had been in my shed. "Thank you for helping me. I didn't expect it." With a nod of her head, she gestured for me to follow her out of the warehouse. "I'll take you home."

I took one last look at my mother's retreating back; at the world I was leaving behind. Full of possibility and happiness. Choose me, Mum. Come with me. Please just choose me. But she never turned around, never took a second glance in my direction, so instead, I chose to blindly follow Agent Cherry. She was the only path back to my son.

She clearly wasn't comfortable with silence as I dropped into step alongside her and so she decided to fill the void between us with what I at first thought was inane chatter.

"I didn't know what to make of you when we first met, y'know? Obviously, my colleagues all assumed you were guilty but there was something about the situation I just couldn't quite push a pin in. Something about you that just didn't add up. I mean, it all makes sense now, of course, but back then, I didn't know what you were hiding. I just presumed it was something awful.

Then I got the call about the shooting at the precinct. I knew you were being held there and I was only around the corner grabbing a coffee so decided to make my way down despite it being a local issue, not traditionally my jurisdiction. I don't know why I cared so much but something inside my head told me to check on you.

Whilst everyone else was flapping about outside like headless chickens, I made my way up to the roof. Honestly, even now, I can't believe that nobody else thought to do that. We knew there was an active shooter and the only vantage point that would have allowed them to kill Leo was the roof of the building. And yet I found myself climbing up there alone. God, it was a stupid decision. I've been told that over and over again. But I couldn't help it. Something was calling out to me. Like it was controlling my movements.

You know the Dweller they executed for Leo's murder? He attacked me too. I found him unconscious on the roof. As I stepped near him, he came to and lashed out at me in panic. Apparently, he struck me so hard that I was out cold for twenty-four hours. I'm lucky to be alive. But how could he have made the shot if he was unconscious? That's all I could think about when I woke up in the hospital bed. It didn't work. Something about the story didn't work.

They put me on leave after that. Said it was so I could recover. Yet they'd call me on the regular into the office to answer questions about the shooting, always probing me about what I'd witnessed. I guess that must have been how you felt sometimes?

Anyway, I don't know why but I always kept my mouth shut. Something told me I'd have to keep the truth to myself. That's when Di made contact. They got a message to me in the hospital. Gave me your address as a meeting point if I ever needed them. I dismissed it as crackpot conspiracy, any sane person would. Figured she was a relative of someone I'd arrested previously out to get revenge.

Everything was relatively settled until my partner,

Saff, came over to visit one day. It was awkward enough given our personal history, but she turned up with coffee and my favourite chocolates. I really thought she wanted to make amends, so I welcomed her into my home as I had many times previously.

Our conversation turned sour when we started speaking about your friend Rus. Despite the fact we'd been a couple for two years before breaking up last summer, she stood by the State's decision to execute him. It was like she'd forgotten we'd spent two years of our lives committing the same crimes he had. But I suppose it made sense, since she got engaged to one of our senior officers, she'd changed. Like she'd forgotten herself.

It turns out that she hadn't come over to check on me. She'd come over to recruit me. Wanted me to take part in the testing they were undertaking in some departments. They were intentionally infecting staff, and she wanted me to take part. To prove my loyalty to the State.

It didn't make sense. She'd heard the same rumours I had. Sure, some people seemed to be completely unaffected but they were the lucky ones. It changed people. Made them stronger, more resilient. But some of them had already died. Just days after manifesting new capabilities. It's like this virus just picks and chooses how long it takes to kill you.

Why would she want me to do that? I knew she'd loved me in the past, so why would she want to cause me harm?

It turns out I wasn't really supposed to have a choice. She threatened to tell her fiancé about my dabblings with women, forgetting entirely that she had been one of them. She spat insults and homophobia across my face as her tone took a violent turn. She grabbed my arm in an attempt to force me out of the house. Things escalated pretty quickly from there. I wasn't about to put myself at risk and I couldn't let her open up the Pandora's box that was my love life. So, I hit her. I struck her across the face as hard as I could, trying to knock some sense into her. Trying to get the Saff back that I'd known and loved.

But that person didn't exist anymore. My Saff would never have moved towards the knife block and pulled out the largest blade she could lay her hands on. My Saff hated violence, used to turn off the television at the President's death card, wanting to shield herself from the ugliness of our world. She was a pretty terrible agent in that respect. It wasn't the woman I loved who lunged at me with force, who cut into my flesh and applied pressure to the blade as it sliced through muscle.

Better that I die on my living room floor than live as a State traitor, she said. I truly believe she would have killed me. I didn't mean to push her so hard. I really didn't mean to. You have to believe that. She may not have been the woman I loved, but I would never have wished her harm.

That's when I found Di's note again. I had no choice but to flee. They found me in your garden. Saved my life. Covered my tracks. Disposed of Saff."

She looked at me as though I was supposed to say something to absolve her. To forgive her for killing her ex-lover in self-defence. It was too much information. She'd given me too much information to process.

"Are we nearly there?" I asked her as we picked through thorny bushes heading towards the border. The mud smeared on my clothes along with the scratches left by the vines would only add to the story that we'd escaped a kidnapping.

She looked at me sadly. She'd been desperate to connect. "Probably another hundred yards," she replied, fixing her gaze on the faded lights in the distance. Back to business. It was easier that way.

# Chapter Forty-Eight

She stopped walking when we were about twenty yards from the border check. "Are you sure about this?" Her voice was full of concern. "You know what waits for us across that line?"

"You're coming too?" I'd sort of assumed she'd go back to the life I'd left behind. That she'd choose freedom.

"Someone has to look out for you." She smiled at me, a level of friendship I couldn't yet return. My head was spinning with the last twenty-four hours. Rus was alive. Regina was dead. Franklin was lost. I killed a man. Oh my God, I killed a man.

"A forced marriage?" I answered her original question. "Forced infection?" It was a small nod to her offloading from earlier and at least let her know she was heard. Plus, it was a distraction from the cyclone of guilt that was threatening to eat me alive.

"Among things. They won't trust us."

"I haven't been trusted for a while." She had the grace to look apologetic for her role in that.

"Whatever happens, just remember that if something seems too straightforward, it probably is."

"Leo?" She's caught my interest.

"I think there's more to it. I promise you I will get to the bottom of what happened to him." She meant every word. I could see the honesty glittering in her eyes. She was a good agent. A good person. She wanted to find me justice.

Unfortunately for her, justice wasn't something that

really existed in our world.

There was a crack of a tree branch behind us, a foot stepping down on it. This was it. We'd run out of luck. We both turned around, hands in the air, ready to meet our maker. The figure standing before us was cloaked from head to toe in beige material, wrapped around them like a mummy. The only part of them visible were their eyes. Women's eyes.

"Paige Kearney," she said. If Agent Cherry had noted my surname, she made no show of it. "I got your message." Slowly, the woman pulled the material away from her face and standing before us was a woman just a few years younger than my mother. Though, clearly, she'd taken better care of her skin as the laughter lines around her eyes were less defined.

"Bailey?" I offered the only name that came to my mind. Who else had I sent a message to?

"I've been looking for the disease." Clearly, Bailey wasn't a big believer in small talk. "We don't have time right now." We could all hear the approaching sound of voices. "Do everything they ask of you. I will do everything I can to get you out."

"Out?" Agent Cherry queried.

"I'm so sorry." Bailey ignored Agent Cherry in her entirety and kept her eyes locked on mine. We both knew she was apologizing for a lifetime of fuckups. "I really am."

"Where do we need to get out of Bailey?" I asked her, my voice beginning to rise in panic.

"Play the part. Both of you. Make them love you." Finally, she looked at my companion. "You have to play the part."

Agent Cherry and I turned to look behind us as we heard approaching gunshots and just like that, Bailey had disappeared. We stood facing each other in shock and confusion.

"We have to play the part," I repeated Bailey's last words as I shrugged at Agent Cherry. "We have to carry on."

"One question," she began as we emerged from the bushes and started our dramatic stumble to the finish line. As she spoke, she summoned tears to her eyes, and I began to hyperventilate. We clung to each other, our clothes ripped, our hair torn and blood flowing from a hundred cuts and grazes left as markers of our journey. "What worked?"

I was floored. How long had she known about Leo's message? When did she find it? How? This was the woman I was entrusting my life to. The woman who had shared her deepest darkest secrets with me. The woman who would do everything she could to reunite me with my son, simply because it was the right thing to do.

And yet Leo's voice was there inside of me. "Don't trust," he repeated. His tone soothing my nerves as I myself began to sob as border police moved towards us, their guns pointed in our direction. "Don't trust -" he repeated.

"The wood glue. I told him it wouldn't hold," I replied as we were forced onto the ground, bodies holding us down, guns nuzzled into the back of our heads by masked strangers. Camera lightbulbs flashed all around us, somebody had alerted the press to our arrival. Bailey. She was giving us the chance to play the part of rescued damsels the public could fall in love with. Figureheads for the State to manipulate. A way to prevent bullets being placed in the back of our skulls.

I held my breath until I heard their radios crackle in response.

"Bring them in alive," came the order.

And just like that, my world changed all over again.

# To Be Continued

Please consider leaving a review or a rating for The Diseased - it helps independent authors like me in so many ways and I always love hearing from Readers.

## ABOUT THE AUTHOR

Steph is currently working on "Body Count", which is book two of the 'Paige Hanson' series.

**"Widowed sounded better than divorced.
Or at least it did the first time."**

Body Count.
Coming 2023.

Updates and pre-orders available at:

Printed in Great Britain
by Amazon